SPEED DEMON

Also by Jim Bosworth

The Long Way North

SPEED DEMON

JIM BOSWORTH

CUTTING EDGE

The author wishes to express thanks to the Royal Automobile Club of England, to Briggs Cunningham, George Brown and to the other members of the sports car fraternity who with technical contribution and enthusiasm have made this task easier.

ISBN-13: 978-1-952138-67-6

Published by
Cutting Edge Books
PO Box 8212
Calabasas, CA 91372
www.cuttingedgebooks.com

To my father,
who bought one first.

To my mother,
who is tolerant about it.

To my wife,
who has stood forgotten at the
edge of so many road races.

To my second daughter,
whose first word was car.

To my first daughter,
who is more interested in bears.

A NOTE FROM
THE AUTHOR:

Foreign sports cars have become common on our roads in recent years, but not common in themselves. They never will be. It would be hard to gather all the feelings one can acquire with the purchase of a car of great character, hard to put on record the emotions of driving it and knowing it in its lifetime, the pain of turning away from it when the last mile has been driven.

The important thing is owning a sports car, knowing the thrill of real driving, and belonging to the wonderful fraternity that binds together all who drive them. This book is for all of those people and those who are with them in spirit, with the hope that it lives up to all that the subject deserves.

This is not an attempt to picture the entire scene. To do so would be, by comparison, to drive like Tazio Nuvolari, to build automobiles as Ettore Bugatti built them, and perhaps to win over the thousand miles of the Mille Miglia a half dozen times in one's short life.

This, rather, is perhaps but one turn in the roads of racing.

—J.B.

PROLOGUE ...

What kind of man? Where does the craving begin ... what kind of chemistry to set this man apart with his particular kind of brilliance?

The machine exists. Metal, rubber, fuel and electricity, all the elements of power and motion rendered by formula into the supreme instrument ... a jewel, a brightness in the sun. A superb machine, a racer ....

Something to touch, to see, to hear and know ... a tangible.

But what kind of man?

CHAPTER ONE

THE TURN comes swiftly. Grip the shift lever, but let the Corsatti sing and rush an instant longer and watch for the one particular tree chosen to mark the cut-off point. It blurs past. Stab the brake pedal ... knock the clutch out, rev the engine high and shift down to third ... smoothly, again to second ... the turn is there. Swing close to the inside ... toe and heel the brake and throttle to keep the rpm up ... drift a little, hold it out of a skid with a cautious wheel, and then burn the tires on the pavement to accelerate violently into the next straight. Automatically, the mind leading up the road in advance of the car, knowing the next turn. Preparing for it ... Watch that Jaguar ... the tach swinging up toward the red line ... this straight good for one twenty-five miles an hour ... a glance at the board held up by pit Number Three.

Still second place, Canfield leading, Ericson ten seconds behind at third. Last lap coming, pour it on. A jumble of activity at the start-finish line ... the man with the blue-and-white last-lap flag holding it stretched, close to the plummeting cars ... then lost in a blur. All out as never before ... whittle at the lap time with every trick, but there is a limit and beyond the limit is like driving on ice. The pattern is set and there is no changing it now—not in a two-point, seven-mile lap.

Tired ... fingers feel welded to the wheel, legs aching, and a kind of electricity charging through the body after a hundred miles of the turning, drifting, booming, with the high shrieking whine of the Corsatti tearing at the ears ... passing and repassing the slower cars, trying to catch the black, British Hammond Mark II a few seconds ahead ... and at last, the final straight again to the checkered flag, the ballet-like salute of it to the last hell-sprint of the cars coming over the finish. The end of the Torrey Pines Road Race, and second place. A safety lap around, and slowing for congratulations from the award boys at the finish line, and in to the pits ... then sit for the minute in the sudden silence before walking over to the winning car, after the wind and howl of engines, silence in a cheering crowd.

"Good race, Eric." Martin Janis slapped him on the back.

Eric Canfield tossed his helmet into the Mark II, next to the silver cup he had just won, and smoothed back his ruffled, graying hair. He grinned easily, looking relaxed and not really tired, and looking very much the sportsman. Indeed, wrap a silk scarf around his neck below the deep tan and the toothbrush mustache and hand him a glass, and there it was. The sportsman condescending to pose for a magazine ad with a glass of The Brew in his hand.

"Thanks, Mart. Or should I say, no thanks to you? That damn Italian seems to get a little hotter every time you take it out. I suppose you will be plaguing me with it at Pebble Beach in April?"

"My turn to win, isn't?"

Eric laughed and nudged the girl who had come to stand by him.

"I told you about Mart, honey. We're each other's chief competition. The magazines of the trade are very kind to us. The top two sports car drivers in the nation. Actually, it's a matter of arrangement. I let him win now and then—just to keep the sport alive. Isn't that right, Mart?"

"I'll humor you, Eric ..." Mart looked at the girl, the tall, slim but full-figured girl with the short-clipped copper hair and the child's face ... the wide and honest brown eyes that regarded him.

"Now look, Janis," Canfield began to frown in a stage manner. "I know you. Don't get any ideas about introductions. My solemn duty to protect the treasures of the world from the heathen hordes. Run along like a good heathen and check your carburetors."

"You rich boys are so polite."

"Will you be at the race dinner tonight, Mr. Janis?" A friendly smile touched her face.

"Yes, if this dirty old man can spare you for one dance."

"I'm sure he can, Mr. Janis. It would be a pleasure."

"Fine. So long, Canfield."

"Peasant!"

Martin laughed and went to reclaim his car from the admirers who always gathered in the pits after a race. Slowly he drove out of there, out of the course area and up the highway to the inn a short distance away. Mart parked it at the side and went up to his room. He found Anna Barkdale sitting by the window. He sent his helmet rolling across the floor and lit a cigarette.

"You weren't waiting in the car," he said.

Anna primped at her long black hair and smiled, the olive of her skin making her teeth brilliant. She was Italian, and all her ancestry and inheritance of classic line and color made her one of the most beautiful creatures alive.

"I know. It was growing cold, Martin. The fog was coming in. It was coming in as I have seen it drift inland from the Adriatic, at a place called San Dona Piave. Beautiful—but I'm afraid I was not dressed for it. It was cold. And besides—"

"But the fog came in when I only had four or five laps left. Look, I know you better than that. What's the matter?"

"Ah, you worry for me. This is very flattering."

"No, I'm not worried. But what the hell, you're always so concerned about how I'm driving my race." He grinned a little at the thought. "All through last season, hanging around the turns, analyzing them and me like a coach, or practically sitting on top of the flagman to watch me come in. So today you leave early, at the most crucial time of the race. Are you sick? What goes?"

"I was about to tell you. You were not winning the race and I do not like to see that."

"Oh? Maybe that explains your behavior after I lost that one at Reno, and the one at Golden Gate Park. These crumby second places put me in the doghouse.' He raised an eyebrow at her. "I get the picture Just like the gals who used to run around with the emperors in your home town. Shacking up with the emperor on one hand and some promising young Christian-killer on the other. And boy, look out! First time that guy doesn't knock off enough Christians to amuse her, he's a sandwich for the lions."

"Martin! You are being perfectly ridiculous. Stop teasing."

"I don't know, look at the facts. Fact number one. Ramsey Barkdale, old and worth millions, goes to Rome and buys a Corsatti and a wife and brings both back here. A hot sports car, and an equally warm female. He's too old to get any use out of the car, and you're nothing more than a walking version of those marble statues he brought back. Just to look at. That's what was going on that day I dropped in, wasn't it? Had you standing nude between a couple of statues with a bunch of grapes in your hand."

Anna laughed explosively and collapsed on the bed beside him. Mart had a hard time stopping from laughing himself.

"Fact number two. He wants to see the car get a little glory. It's kind of funny, and yet kind of nice. A few victories really add something to the beauty of a car. So he looks around for a likely looking driver. At your advice he picks me. I'm hired, on a salary of seventy-five a week. What more could a young car nut ask? I get rid of the heap I was trying to put together for one more race. I quit my job at the box factory. I'm in with the fast gang with a car that would've cost me six or seven years' worth of salary if I gave up eating—fifteen thousand clams!"

"Martin, stop it." She laughed and put her hand to his mouth. He took her hand away and kept from grinning.

"Now what happens to the gal who's been living like a statue? It's a dull life, being an ornament. She needs a toy. Like the one who drives the old man's car. It's glamorous, exciting, the sound of motors, speed, the heroic young men in the gleaming helmets—it's very nice of the old man to let her pick one out for him so that she might share in the glory, let it rub off on her rich hide. And what happens after the races? Ah, yes! What the old man doesn't know won't hurt him. Right?"

He pulled her rich young body against him and kissed her, pulling on her long, black hair until it was tight across her head. She nestled down on his shoulder.

"I like to see you win your races—all of them. You placed second today, and second is good in any race. But I know how you like to win and how you need to win, and it hurts when you cannot."

"Sure, but it isn't that important. Don't take it so damned seriously."

"I have told you my father was of nobility in his short life. His name was mentioned in the same breath as the king," she went on, almost whispering. "As a child I knew wealth, the grandeur of a fine house in Rome, parties, fine cars, clothes. I attended royal functions, circulated with most of the greats of Europe and Italy. Little Anna Pavanne.... I was fifteen when all of that dissolved in the war. The money went. My parents were killed in Naples—"

"So you cadged cigarettes with the other war orphans."

"Please do not make fun of it. I did the best I could, and I promised myself that someday I would be wealthy again."

"Well, you're rich now."

"Yes, but Ramsey does not move with great people. He is like a recluse. It is his big house and this sickening obsession with beauty. This is his world. I need more than that. I need you."

Mart laughed at her.

"You expect to find nobility at the race courses? Through me? Now look, there's a lot of money in and around road races. But not me. I'm the son of a prune rancher, remember? I worked in a box factory. I don't even own my own car."

"You don't understand. Now listen to me. I expect to find greatness in you. You will be a great driver someday—perhaps even in Europe—and as such, you will move in the best circles."

"Me? Europe? This is how you expect to get back among your greats of Europe? On my driving? I see ..."

"Martin, if what you are thinking now were true—your being only a means to an end—would I not be attaching myself to a driver who is already established among the great? You do not see. It is for *you*. I know how it is to be rich and among great people. I know the wonderful life a great driver can know in Europe. I want you to know these things too. This is why I want to buy you good cars when the time comes that I leave Ramsey. I have to leave him—I love you so much. It hurts to see you with so little, unable to do the things you are really capable of. I want to see you climb—I want to help you as much as I can. This will take time. I need more money. But this is what I must do."

"What ever happened to the idea of a man doing it on his own hook instead of using a woman's money?"

"Pride is silly when there is so much love." She took his hands and held them to her breasts. She kissed him for a long time.

He began unbuttoning her blouse, but she shook her head.

"You must sleep now, Martin. Rest. I will see you at the victory dinner tonight. And afterwards ... but sleep now."

Anna left and he stared happily at the ceiling for a moment. A car of his own and racing all over the country, and being with Anna all the time. That was fine. But a great driver? In Europe? That was wild. And it was ridiculous. But he loved her and if it made her happy to dream these things, let her dream.

He closed his eyes and went through the ritual of trying to relax, to escape the tension of a hundred fast miles that knotted his mind and body. It was always this way after a race—the agitation of mind and muscles, a noisy, out-of-focus picture pressing on him until he gave in and let it all come back, the things he had done when there was no time to think about it. No time to really think about it during the race, but now there was time, and almost a fear—seeing the things that could have happened, the chances and possibilities that become giants with speed—it always came … the road beginning to unravel before his closed eyes in startling clarity, the rushing panorama of crowd and cars and trees, the pavement rushing beneath his wheels in an ever-increasing velocity until it was a thrashing black ribbon and the roar of the engines was more than an echo coming up from his mind. Speed … always like a sensation of falling, hurtling head-long through space and no controlling it, the car taking over and leaving him only to steer with the tach stuck in the red line and the speedometer touching one forty-five. There was never any finish line, no stopping—always this way, a nightmare awake, gradually fading, diminishing…. He was sweating as he fell asleep.

At eight thirty, Martin Janis walked downstairs and went outside to stand in the chilled fog that was sifting in from the Pacific. The race was still with him—tired, sore-muscled, the skin of his face burning a little, still a little tense. It was hard to slow down. But it was better now, breathing the cool, moist air and standing in the darkness.

Tonight the air was full of rasping engines. The sports car crowd working off their enthusiasms on the quiet roads bordering the Pacific. Here and there, the crackling, popping roar of a race casualty towed this far for the better lights and the accumulated know-how of the bunch, being coaxed back into running for the long trip home. Tired, angry, their faces and hands smeared with the grease of a temperamental car, but like him, already itching for the next one. Whatever the fortune or misadventure, the fears and apprehensions, it was worth it just to try, to be part of the picture.

"Mr. Janis, is that you?"

He turned and saw Canfield's redhead standing there.

"Hi. Where's the dirty old man?"

"Inside. I've been kind of waiting for you."

"Well, let's join the party. I've got a dance coming, remember?"

"I'd rather not. I don't really care for parties."

"I don't either. But if you're going to let me down—" "I'm sorry. It's just that Eric has had too much to drink. He's kind of…"

Mart grinned at the expression on her face—impatience, a touch of anger, and possibly a pinch around the eyes as if she were worried about something.

"At these shindigs, he's always kind of. You know, if I thought Eric wouldn't mind, I'd suggest that we go somewhere else."

"I was hoping you would." She smiled at him nervously. Nervously… some women looked bad with it. This one seemed to wear it like a charm, like modesty. It was deceptive, and disturbing. Eric always picked the right ones.

"Let's go then."

"Wait—I'm sorry. I forgot you came with someone."

"Anna? You know about Anna?"

"Eric told me about her. On the way over here."

Mart hesitated. Anna was expecting him, as always. But he really didn't want to get involved in a party. It was crowded and noisy and hot in there. And Anna was on her fourth Manhattan by now and surrounded by a half dozen handsome young drivers. He could see her later and it would be all right. He wanted quiet and cool air, and for a little while, the company of this strangely disturbing young lady.

"Anna won't mind. We can be unfaithful together."

"Are you sure?" She tried to smile at the way he put it.

"Where shall we go?"

"Oh, any place where it isn't crowded. Have a couple of drinks and talk—anything you like." She smiled openly now and something tugged at him inside.

"Fine. Suits me." He took her arm and they walked to the car. "You're going to have to put up with a lot of wind. Small wind-screens."

"That's all right. I don't mind. Just don't try it on a girl with a permanent wave sometime!"

"All right, Miss So-and-so, we're off."

"Charlotte Greyne."

He nodded and started up the Corsatti and they rolled up to the highway and pointed in the direction of Del Mar. The fog left them, and held in great rolling blankets to their left. Above, the stars had come out, and the wind was cool. She sat stiffly.

"Too breezy."

"No. Don't worry about it. I'm fine." But she didn't relax.

With the two of them shoulder-tight in the narrow seats and a full array of dancing needles on the *facia* before them, Mart bore heavily down on the throttle and the roadster leaped into the darkness, trying to devour the bright beams of light stabbing ahead. His mind wandered away from the girl a minute, feeling the firm suspension on the road, the quick, flexible power of the motor. He drifted through a turn and accelerated out and stretched smoothly into high speed that carried them through the night air as if it were the bottom of a black bowl. When a cluster of colored lights grew rapidly in front of them, he shifted down, touched the brake and pulled to the side of a small roadside tavern.

"You drivers are all alike, showing how good you are with a car. Like a little boy doing cartwheels for his girl." She was smiling at him, like a woman might smile at a wayward child, only it didn't work out too well with her child's face.

"Don't flatter yourself," he said. "When I'm driving, the passenger is only so much excess weight."

"Even Anna?"

"Even Anna."

"You drivers, that's all you can ever think about. Cars."

"Not quite." He made an elaborate business of looking at the line of her throat and the swelling of her blouse where the coat parted.

"You mean something else could actually interest you? My, I couldn't guess what that could be, not watching you around the car and hearing you talk. Really."

"Really?"

He watched her profile a moment and then he leaned over and kissed her. She resisted gently.

"Is that interesting?" Her voice trembled a little.

He kissed her again. Impulsively, his fingers dipped under her skirt and slid into the warmth of her thighs. Her breath cut short and her nails dug into his wrist. She struggled free and sat there gasping, redness and surprise blustering into her face, and quickly, the wetness of fear in her eyes.

He watched her for a moment, surprised, a little angry, and then feeling like a fool, he sat back fumbling for a cigarette.

"Charlotte—look, I'm sorry. Hell, I'm really sorry! I thought that was what you expected."

"What do you mean?"

"The way you look at a guy, and the way you talk—I guess I read them wrong. Any of the girls that go with Eric—but you're just a kid!"

"I'm nineteen." A sob had crept into her throat.

"Obviously. I think I'd better take you back to the inn."

She stared out into the darkness, trembling a little. She wiped her eyes and blew her nose.

"Really, I'm sorry. What more can I say? You're very attractive, and I had the wrong idea—funny how a man's imagination can run wild over the slightest suggestion of something, even if the suggestion didn't mean anything at all. I guess we flatter ourselves."

"It's all right, Mart. I'm all right now..."

"I'll take you back."

"No! Please—let's go inside."

"After what I did?" His voice showed surprise. "What's with you?"

"Nothing. And you don't have to shout."

He got out and went around, watched her sitting there looking scared and too young.

"Just for a little while then," he said gently.

Inside they found a booth in the back and ordered martinis and sat for a long time saying nothing. Then, in embarrassed tones, she finally broke the silence.

"This must be a big laugh to you, with someone so young …"

"I was just opening my big mouth after the surprise of getting caught off base. Never did have much tact. Maybe you are a kid in some ways. But hell, I'm not so old and wise myself!"

"You're about thirty-five. That makes a difference."

"Guess again. Knock ten years off."

"Twenty-five? I thought—but you seem older!"

"Maybe it's the crowd I run with. That would put wrinkles on anybody."

"No, seriously. I think you're older than your age. Everyone thinks I'm still a child. Even dad. Dad most of all."

"All right, so what if you are. Keep it. It looks good on you. Beautiful figure, pretty face, and no complications to ruin it."

"I'm sorry I gave you the wrong impression." She stared at her glass, frowning.

"Forget it. I just don't know why—say, what's between you and Eric anyway?"

"Nothing. Should there be?"

"Look, no girl is just a friend of Eric Canfield."

"I just met him this morning."

"I see. Well, Eric's a good friend of mine, I like to race against him and I like to drink with him—but like I said."

"You're different?"

"No," he said, and then: "I asked for that, didn't I?"

"I'm sorry. I shouldn't have said it."

"That's all right. We're all great moralists until our blood gets too warm." He swallowed the rest of his drink. "Where do you live?"

"My father runs a garage and gas station a little ways up the road from Torrey Pines. We have a cottage in back." She paused, and then went on as if she wanted to talk about it. "Eric came in to borrow our grease rack. We got to talking about the car and—well, he invited me out to see the races and to the dinner afterwards. I thought he was nice and the races were exciting, but ..."

"I gather Eric made a swipe at you. I should've guessed."

"He had a few drinks before he picked me up this evening," She was calmer now. "We went for a drive to get some air before the party began. When we got back and parked, he tried to—well, I jumped out and ran. He was real mad. I thought he was going to come after me, but he went inside instead. A few minutes later you came along. I wanted to ask you to take me away from there, but I knew if I did I'd bust down, especially if I asked to be taken home. So I tried to act like a ..."

"Like a calm, experienced woman of the world?"

"You seemed so nice—I'm sorry, you *are* nice, and I mean that—and I thought if we went somewhere else for a little while, it'd all go away and be all right and I'd be myself again, and I could ask to be taken home in a graceful, normal way."

"Along I come, the prospective hero, and pull the same stunt."

"You're different than Eric."

"The only difference is that he's rich—the gentleman sportster with his own car and every minute for his own pleasure. Until recently I worked as a clerk in the stock room of a box factory in South San Francisco. Now I drive for a multimillionaire fossile named Ramsey Barkdale who gives me a small weekly check to go out with his fifteen-thousand-dollar car and win races for him. It's a nice setup. But I'm not rich and independent."

"There's still a difference."

"Maybe you can see it, but I can't."

"You felt bad about it and apologized. Eric wouldn't have done that in a hundred years. And apologizing like that has made it—well, like it didn't happen. That makes the difference."

"Well, thanks for the difference. How about another drink and then I'll take you home."

"What about Anna? I mean, this dumb stunt of mine, it's made you keep her waiting."

"Do her good. I've spoiled her."

"But isn't she ..." Charlotte stammered.

"Isn't she what? Barkdale's wife? Yes, but what's so embarrassing about that?"

"Forget I asked, Mart. Oh, I'm putting my foot in it again."

"You're not putting your foot in anything. Look, she's young and she's married to a man forty-five years older than she is. There's a lot of money there, and all the comforts. But she likes fun, and that big mausoleum she lives in gets boring after a while. She likes auto racing. She's been going to races ever since she was a kid back in Italy. All right, so I drive her husband's car. She comes and watches the races I drive in, and we have a few drinks afterwards. It's all for laughs. I suppose Eric gave you a different picture."

"He hinted at it."

"That's because Eric is a dirty old man. Some women collect authors for their teas, or painters or famous musicians to bring to their hen clubs. Anna collects drivers. It's harmless."

He thought of Anna, tall and full-breasted and with long, shapely legs—his after the races, and his any other time she could get away from the old man. In love with her? Yes ....

Anna was rich now. Her own fortune, given to her by the old man. And she often talked of leaving him soon. As soon as she could wangle a little more out of him.

"We'll travel all over and even catch that race in Mexico— enter all the races. I'll buy you another car, just like this one or better. You won't have to go back to work. Perhaps Europe … drive and win races and be famous and we'll be terribly happy. You'll find my world and it will be your world too." That's what he's been hearing from Anna.

He couldn't get it out of his mind. Dream stuff. *Own* a Corsatti? Or something better? It was wild, and living with Anna all the time. Sure, he went along with it, no matter how hard to believe it seemed. It seemed so far away. A few months, maybe a year, Anna had told him.

At first he had felt pangs of conscience about it, going up to the mansion at Atherton and talking to Barkdale, taking the Corsatti out of the big garage and heading off to some race with it as if that were all there was to it, pretending in Ramsey's presence that Anna was merely a race enthusiast to be transported there and back and nothing more. But that soon vanished from his feelings. Anna wasn't Ramsey's wife, but merely a decoration, an object of art, something to place among the great paintings and statues and the acres of gardens. His marriage had merely been a purchase, and more than likely when Anna left him, there would be another purchase, and perhaps another, until death turned the place into a museum.

He couldn't explain it to Charlotte. What would be the use of it? She was young and sweet, and perhaps wouldn't understand.

The second round of drinks came, and Charlotte Greyne seemed almost to relax in his company. She chatted about her father and how she helped him with the station, where she had gone to school, how quiet and lonely that kind of life was and how she would like to see the world sometime, a little about sports cars, and then the question out of the blue.

"Why do you race?"

He snapped out of space, realizing she was repeating the question.

"Race? Because I like to. What other reason is there? We aren't professionals. No prize money to break our necks for."

"Isn't it a little scary sometimes?"

"Sure. All of us have been scared white one time or another."

"And yet you *like* it. Even with the risk? I never could see why men did things like that."

"Well, my reasons are somewhat the same as anyone else's. But to tell you would take too long, and you've got to get home."

"Tell me anyway. How did you get started?"

He had gotten that summer job between school terms. Down at Gus Brodie's garage and service station. It sat at the edge of U.S. 101, about a mile and a half north of Morgan. Gus's place was old, having done business on that spot with its round sign swinging in the wind for many years. It still had the glass tanks on top of the hand-operated pumps so that you could watch the strawberry-colored gasoline rising in them until it reached the top marker. Gus had two pumps, and a rack, dirty tools and a back yard full of dead tires, and a brand new, red soft drink dispenser that clashed with the place as badly as bright lipstick on an aging prostitute.

And Gus himself—a thick, bent, short man with dirty gray hair and a greasy skullcap of quilted silk. Gray was the word for him—gray all over, gray skin that looked and probably was dirty, gray eyes and the gray in his mind. That, and a perpetual beer breath. You could place him at about sixty-three, but he was neither that nor any age. He was merely part of a station, and a memory that could recall every car that had ever been made.

They came into the station often. The kids with their Model A frames and the full-race Mercury engines, or whatever suited their own private theories and wants. The real ones—you didn't pay any attention to the others—with their beautiful body work and their snarling exhausts, the immaculate engines chromed down to the last bolt...

"You like those, eh, boy?" Gus asked.

"Yes, sir."

"I dunno what's the matter with you kids, wantin' all that noise and bright paint and those narrow little windshields you have to squint through to see. Now maybe these rods look better than the original, and there ain't no doubt some of the motors have been improved over the original. But it don't stop there. You got to have suspension. Not one in ten of them buzz buggies has a decent suspension. And if you ain't got that, there ain't no point in drivin' fast, unless you got a mind toward suicide. No, sir. One of these days, when I got time, I'll tell you about the real cars."

"But they're still fun, Mr. Brodie."

Gus looked down at him with patient lights in his eyes.

"I'll allow they'd be more fun than a family sedan."

"Yes, sir. And there's no other choice, is there?"

That remembering came into Gus's face again, and he patted Mart on the shoulder and shook his head.

"Yes, but not for you and me anyway. Not for you and me."

Mart found Charlotte waving a hand in front of his eyes.

"Where did you go?"

"I was just remembering something."

He heard a rumbling out by the pumps, a different kind of rumbling. Not the jazzy burbling of a hot rod or the kind that came from a gutted muffler, but a deep-throated sound that came from power and purpose.

The car was low and stark-looking. The paint was immaculate bone-white, and the wheels with the small cycle fenders were tall and black-spoked, the front ones almost completely in front of a nearly square radiator, the rears almost directly under the cockpit. A simple windshield. Right-hand drive. That was the silhouette. Low, three-fourths hood, one-fourth seats and spare, and that hood was longer than imagination on a second look. Three pipes ran out on either side of the hood and extended down underneath to the rear. Looked nice. He touched one and drew his hand back in painful surprise. They were real, and they were hot! Not just for show ....

"I don't know. I guess it started there, as far as getting the bug for sports cars goes, in Gus Brodie's garage, up in Morgan. This fire-spitting monster came in and I saw it up close and when it left, old Brodie told me what it was. He told me it was a Mercedes Benz. Nineteen twenty-nine model. An SSK Mercedes. And he told me that Europe always was ahead of us with cars, and that the SSK could hit well over a hundred miles an hour—even in 1929. Well, the monster shot out on the highway and I could hear it leaving for a mile. And Brodie told me something then, and I can remember his exact words, for some reason ..."

"What did he say?"

He had a funny tone to his voice. He said, 'Remember what you saw, son. That was a real car. Made for a man, and made for the fun of driving. Somehow we forgot all those things when we stopped making the Stutz and the Duesenberg, the Mercer—that was before your time, boy. You got to go to Europe now to see the good ones. But you remember ...'"

"That's how it began, then?"

"Yeah, I guess so. I went on and had my hotrods, but they never were the same for me after that. I suppose I'd still be trying to make my own if it wasn't for a few smart cookies in Europe taking note of what the American housewife had done to the auto industry in this country."

"Come now. What's she got to do with it?"

"I'm serious. Take a look at the cars on the road. A real look. Hell, they stopped looking and acting like cars years ago. More and more women were driving or influencing their husbands to buy cars. And what woman wants to be jarred around like she's riding in a coal cart? Detroit saw that. Now we have cars that ride like marshmallows in a cup of cocoa, and a couple of tons of chrome and unnecessary gadgets, and fenders you could hide in. The women like them, and I'm sorry to say, most of the men. Brass-band advertising did it. But to me they look like something you'd bury an Egyptian in."

"I've heard there are a lot of imported cars in Hollywood. I mean even before the war. Years before."

"Sure. Rolls Royces, a couple of Delages and Isottas, things like that. Fine cars. But what the hell, those people didn't know what they were riding around in. Not really. They bought them for the same reason they bought swimming pools and fancy houses. Prestige."

Charlotte smiled.

"Don't you get a little prestige in that expensive Corsatti?"

"Oh, sure. I suppose so ... but look, Charlotte. Look at the foreign sports car. Small, clean, free of chrome and excess weight and silly gadgets. Most of them will accelerate from a dead stop to a hundred and come back to a stop well within sixty seconds. They go around corners safely at speeds that would stand our domestic brands on their door handles. So not everyone wants to race. Think of the safety factor in performance like that. An imported sports car, and even the sedans, can cruise as safely at ninety as our domestics can at forty-five."

"There's a speed limit," Charlotte said.

"Sure, I know that! You aren't getting the point."

Charlotte smiled again. "Yes I am. If a car is safe at high speed, it's that much safer at normal speeds. I was just prodding. I like to hear a man talk about something he believes in."

"I'm glad," he said quietly, and with a trace of bitterness. "A lot of people don't. The sports car crowd has its bad element. Just like any other group. We have our stupid asses who cut up on the highway—I've done it myself. But statistics-wise, it's been discovered that on the whole sports car drivers are safer than the rest of the driving public. Does anybody recognize this? Watch the papers. A Buick or a Ford or something like that crashes and smears people all over the highway, and the papers mention the accident, but never the make of car. Let a foreign sports car crash, and they use big black type shouting SPORTS CAR! And they identify it! Why? Because it's *foreign,* and if it's foreign, knock it! Knock it and try to put it in the same category as drunken driving or the punks who run people down in their hopped-up jalopies.

"I could name one ignorant city editor some of the boys called—Ahh, look, you got me on a tender subject, and I could talk all night. I'd better get you home."

"I gather you're a sports car nut," she laughed.

Mart paid and took her back out to the car.

"One more thing. It's really something—to get to that checkered flag before anyone else."

"Why?"

"I suppose for the same reason anyone has in a race."

"If you're having fun, and there's no money involved, what difference does it make as long as you get to drive it?"

"Well, a lot of boys don't care if they win or not. They try to, of course, but they don't feel bad when they don't."

"But you do care."

"Yes."

He stared down the road under the wash of headlights, and they moved swiftly, surely through the darkness.

They were silent the rest of the way. Charlotte directed him to a service station and garage with a cottage in back where she lived with her father.

"This place?"

"Yes."

"Well, it's been nice. I don't suppose I'll be seeing you again." He lit a cigarette and leaned on the steering wheel.

"I think it'd be better if we didn't. I like you, but ..."

"I know. You had a pretty rough time for one evening. I guess it'd be embarrassing to be reminded of it again, and I don't blame you one bit. Better get inside. It's getting cold."

She looked at him for a moment, and then suddenly leaned over and kissed him hard with unsuspected warmth.

"Good-bye, Mart," she smiled but her tone was final. Friendly, but final.

Martin Janis sat there for a while after she had gone, thinking about her, and then turned the car around and headed back for the inn. Anna would be waiting for him.

CHAPTER TWO

THE FOG lay heavy and damp on the ground, slicking the asphalt of the highway until it glistened and sang under the tires of early Monday traffic heading up 101 to Del Mar and Solana Beach or down to Miramar. It was a good sound, and a good time, when the fumes floating up past the nozzle thrust into a gas tank seemed less oppressive than when the dryness and warmth of the sun came later in the morning. Charlotte Greyne never minded that part of the day.

That part of the day—crawling out of warmth and sleep, a hasty cup of coffee, dressing quickly and slipping on the navy-blue zippered jacket...walking around to the front and opening up the station, lighting the kerosene heater inside, breaking change rolls into the cash register. It wasn't bad at all, running the wide push-broom over the black asphalt surface of the apron, and then sitting down to wait for the first car to come in.

Poor old dad. It let him sleep a little longer. He hadn't been feeling well of late.

Charlotte sat down inside and warmed her hands over the heater. No routine this morning. No sweeping. The thing running in her mind wouldn't let her think about anything else.

It was the sort of thing one has forgotten momentarily with the erasure of sleep...a brief moment upon wakening when all is as before, as if Sunday had been like Saturday, and Saturday no different than the calendar days ripped off and crumpled in a waste basket under the table with all its dead time and dead memos scribbled under the date—under the table with its display of auto wax and polishing rags and the sparkplug display card with its flare-nostriled white horse.

But for this Monday, Sunday had been different. By the time her bare feet had found the slippers beside her bed, she had remembered, and with remembrance, a sudden and unlooked-for touch of warmth, and the impression that there had been moments in the night of being half-awake or dreaming...

Martin Janis.

His name, his face, fragments of conversation.

A little cry escaping from her lips, and for a moment a sense of having been trodden upon, having been insulted and pro-faned, and of having been a little foolish.

But now, with the coldness of air and the sounds of morning and the odor of kerosene burning and the roughness of navy blue rubbing the back of her neck, his name came back again.

Martin Janis. A nice name. Good, clean to speak, easy to remember, a nice balance of syllables.

His face. Lean, rough-textured from the burn of wind and sun, sharp-eyed. A good face. Perhaps a touch of hardness to it at moments, but ready to laugh the next, and a softness when soft-ness was felt and needed.

Charlotte looked out at the cars passing on the highway and found herself liking Martin. Liking him more than she wanted to, and more than she expected to. And suddenly there came the sense of shame and pleasure in recalling the touch of his hand on her legs.

Shame—it wasn't his fault, she thought. She had all but asked for it, acting with no more sense than a schoolgirl, as if she hadn't heard the rough talk of the male customers who came in, and seen their knowing eyes, and shrugged off the occasional verbal pass that was made. How naive can a gal be? And she had been blaming him for it.

"Mornin', honey."

Old Pete Greyne sat down and rubbed his hands over the heater. He yawned, his heavy face and frame thick and stooped with sleep.

"You had breakfast yet?" she asked.

"Nope."

"Watch things for a couple of minutes and I'll fix you some."

Pete shook his head. "No. I'll get it. I ain't very hungry. Get me some coffee and sinkers in a minute.... Out pretty late last night, weren't you?"

Charlotte nodded. "Yes. You didn't stay up waiting for me, did you?"

"I mighta known that Canfield character would pull a stunt like that! Got to thinkin' after you left for the races that he sounded a little too much like a polished apple to suit me."

"He didn't keep me out. I didn't come home with him at all."

"Then who's the young scatterbrain who did keep you out to all hours! If he shows up here again, I'll—"

"Dad! You don't even know him. He pulled me out of a very uncomfortable position. Eric Canfield got drunk and—well, Mart. that's Mart Janis, one of the other drivers in the race— well, he got me away from there and we went to a little place up the road and had a nice talk, and time just kind of sneaked away from us." She smiled at him and discovered that there was no longer any misgivings about Mart or any doubt in her mind. "He's a very nice guy, Dad. I like him very much."

Pete Greyne grunted and wrinkled up a bigger frown. He rubbed a hand over the stubble of his fat, red face.

"Don't trust any of 'em. You're an attractive young gal and redheaded to boot. I don't trust any of these characters."

"Well, I don't think you have to worry." She remembered saying good-bye to Mart, and the permanence of it, and felt a pang of regret.

"You're damn right I got to worry about it. I'm your old man, ain't I? Your ma would worry about it if she were still alive. What kind of old man would I be to you if I didn't?"

"I'm a big girl now." A big girl who acts like a child, she thought bitterly. "And besides, I won't be seeing him again. He doesn't live around here, and the only time he comes around is when they have the races at Torrey Pines. He'll have forgotten me by next time. I doubt if he even remembers me this morning."

Old Pete shrugged and stood up.

"Now go get your breakfast, or let me get it for you."

"I'll get it. Here comes a car. You take care of it, and be careful how you count out the change. You know how you are at this time of morning!"

"I'm wide awake."

"You look it." Pete grinned and tousled her hair. "You and that boy's haircut."

Charlotte stepped out to the pumps and greeted the customer. "Yes, sir?"

"Fill 'er up with the Ethyl."

"Yes, sir. Would you move up about a foot?"

Why did she say good-bye to him, she asked herself. He had apologized in a sincere way and they had become friends in the hour or two that was left to them. Why, then, the short and permanent good-bye? And why kiss him? Because you liked him and felt sorry and were touched by his honesty and willingness to admit an error—kiss him and then cut it off as if you were expected to retain some of the outraged dignity in a calm manner for convention's sake? The devil with convention. It was stupid! Stupid because it left you confused, mixed up with what was right and wrong, with what was nice and wasn't nice. Ah, grow up!

"That'll be three twenty-three, sir .... Oh, I'm sorry. I'd better get the windshield."

"No, that's all right. I'm in a hurry."

He gave her a five and she made the change and the car left.

Another car came in, and two more after that, and there was no time to think.

"Okay, daughter, I'll take over now. You better go eat something. Just coffee ain't enough for a growin' girl."

"I'm not growing, except for a few windshield rubbing muscles. But I'm a little hungry. Give a yell if you get snowed under."

Charlotte went around back to the little cottage and sat down in the kitchen after putting bread in the toaster and pouring another cup of coffee.

It's your own fault, she told herself.

You don't have to let a man do that. You don't have to let him do it if it's the wrong time and the wrong place. No, you don't have to play loose and easy. Not at all. But you don't have to shake and shatter into hysterical little pieces either.

She scraped the toast angrily.

There are other women, you know. In the sports car crowd, at the place he used to work, among his other friends. He doesn't have to put up with the ones who act like blustering little Cinderellas. That Anna Barkdale. Did she act like she was made of glass? No! But Mart said that was just for laughs. They were just friends.

Charlotte shoved the toast and coffee away.

Your own fault if you never see him again. Little Charlotte Greyne, the pure of mind! The practical! The levelheaded! Nothing comes at first sight, everything comes gradually with knowing and discovering with both eyes open—and yet it happened, didn't it? You fell in love with him, didn't you? In the space of a few hours.

Always swore no one could possibly fall in love in just a few small hours.

You were wrong.

"It's too late.

He's gone now—unless—unless ...

"All drivers roll your cars to the starting grid. All drivers in the Del Monte Trophy Race, roll your cars to the starting grid."

The loudspeaker system lapsed into a crackling silence and the air was filled with short, staccato bursts from motors, and thirty-two low-slung foreign roadsters moved to the starting positions.

The fog had cleared nearly two hours before, and the sun shone warmly on the Pebble Beach course. There was a bittersweet odor of exhaust still in the air from the two Cypress Point Handicaps—first for 1500cc and below, and the second for over 1500cc. And now, the main event, the even faster cars over 1500cc and modified. Dislodged haybales had been put back and the crowds moved excitedly behind the snow fencing to find points of advantage.

"Clear the track, please. Will Crowd Control please clear the course?" the loudspeaker blared again, echoing over the course. "Folks, in the last race someone squeezed through the snowfence and crossed the road in front of a pack of cars and almost caused an accident. Stay behind the fencing! Don't cross the road at any time, until the word is passed that the course is clear of cars! Believe me, I don't care how small these cars may seem, I have yet to see the man that could outrun any of them. There is nothing in the program that says anything about a footrace."

Martin Janis fastened his safety belt and lowered his goggles, and sat back in the warm sun. He looked up at the small grandstand and the people sitting there. Anna was there. He couldn't find where she was sitting, but she would be there, crisp and cool in some five-hundred-dollar outfit.

Nervously, he fingered the shift lever, listening to the Corsatti Gran Sport's six cylinders rumbling under the long, flat sloping hood. It sounded ragged at an idle, but that was the tuning. Rev her a little and the rhythm narrowed into a thin, smooth whine, a beautifully crisp sound that rose above the huskier voices of the others. Quite a car, the Corsatti. If it were only his and not Barkdale's ...

We'll run away and I'll buy cars for you, like this one and better. Anna had promised that to him. He and Anna would find some kind of heaven. He was sure of that. Themselves, good cars, enough money and no cares. Sometimes love and pride told him that it should be his money that did these things for them and that he shouldn't accept it any other way, but Anna only called him foolish and talked to him and made love to him and made it all right again.

And then there was the impatience again—wondering an uncounted time again when it would all be realized. He grinned wryly. Impatience! Why should there be? He had her now, and he drove the Corsatti as much as if it were his own. But still, Anna without sneaking to hotel rooms, always, and without her having to go back to Ramsey's to wander among the statues.

His hand began to pound the wheel.

"Mart, wave to the peasants and show them you're alive. What's ailing you? Relax." It was Eric shouting to him over the motors.

Eric smiled grandly from the seat of the Hammond next to him on the front positions of the starting grid. The start of a race never seemed to bother Eric.

As for himself, waiting almost induced fear—something that curled in his stomach and sent sweat rolling down the backs of his legs. After the gun, there was no time to think about anything except the business of driving. It was fun, and there was nothing he'd rather do. But waiting—the time of being keyed up, of wondering whether he would drive as well as last time, of thinking soberly of the things that could happen, the countless chances for error, bad judgment, mechanical failure, all the things that could hurt or kill—there was no such thing as getting completely used to it. No race was ever the same, no matter how many times the course was driven. Always something new to figure, to solve sometimes in less time than it takes for a match to spark into flame.

"*Why do you race?*" Charlotte Greyne had asked.

Nobody had asked him that before. He had been asked a lot of questions by those who stood at the side and watched and wished and admired. But never *why,* as if that were understood.

But when you got right down to it, why?

He sat there, fighting the heaviness in his stomach, thinking of these things, and still came up with the same answer.

"*Because I like to ...*"

He wondered what Charlotte was doing now. He hadn't seen her since that one night, several months ago. There was something about her and her questions. She was funny. She was the kind of girl who would ask if he had enjoyed himself. Whether he won or not wouldn't matter to her—ask if he had fun and be frightened about what he was doing, and ask if he was frightened too.

He saw Anan then, sitting low in the little stand of bleachers where she could leave easily and wander around the course later.

Anna had been worried about Charlotte. She hadn't let it show, but he could tell by her voice. *You didn't have to worry,* he thought, *not ever. Charlotte was nice and I liked her, but she's just a kid. You and I have something more.*

At that moment a group of motorcycle cops began circling the course and the crowds quieted with anticipation. These were the last moments of waiting. The starter, named Al Chavez, picked up a flag.

"Al is ready now. He's gotten the word that the course is clear. He's running between the cars, pointing at each driver—if he gets the nod from every one—he has and he's running back. He's kneeling in front with the green flag, rising ... he'll bring the flag down and ... they're off! Please keep the course clear!"

The sudden thundering cascades of sound drowned out the loudspeaker and left the words dangling like a memory.

Martin Janis felt the back of his seat slam into his spine as the Corsatti charged forward. He shifted into second, hearing his rear wheels scream over the pavement; then third, the wind beginning to burn at his face; fourth, and hold it for a while, letting the tach climb with his foot to the floorboard. Turn one coming fast—the first marker he had chosen in practice. A pine leaning out over the road was his cut-off point. Hold it an instant longer than usual, a few feet closer to the turn because Canfield was just at his rear wheels. Canfield was good at sneaking in at the last instant.

Now shift down, brake, shift down and leave Portola Road into Turn One. Canfield lost ground, and Janis blasted out with hard acceleration. The short stretch of Sombria Lane and the same but milder shift down for Turn Two. Now the long, subtle weaving of Drake Road and shallow, screaming Turn Three with the haybale chicanes, and up the hill to the hairpin at Turn Four and Stevenson Drive. Slow to twenty there and accelerate violently down the hill, the long back straight, the hard checking of car at that tricky Turn Six and back up the start-finish straight to finish lap one.

He settled down and began to relax with the business of driving. A hundred miles to go, and Eric Canfield's white helmet and black car were at least seventy-five feet behind in his rear-view mirror. He watched the familiar contours, the racks and bumps in the paving flick beneath, and felt the sweet exhilaration in the quick response of wheel and engine. The Corsatti sang to him with a high, thin, unbroken note—always singing sweet, thanks to Barkdale and his almost fanatical insistence of having his mechanics tear the engine down after a race to clean and coddle its glistening parts.

The laps passed rapidly. Down the narrow roadway lined with haybales and snowfencing and the spectators pressed against it. But he didn't see them. Just the road and going over it rapidly, Canfield holding to a spot forty feet behind and staying there to wait. Not taking on the strain of maintaining a lead yet, waiting until the final laps to really pour it on, waiting until Martin Janis began to tire and show his usual nerves—that was Eric's way. Mart grinned. It wasn't going to happen this time. Not if he could help it.

Down past the pits again, the blackboard raised high for him to see. One minute and fifty-seven on that last lap. Two point one miles to a lap. You're doing fine, he thought, keep it up.

Beyond the start-finish straight, a green Cad—an Allard—snicked into the space between him and Eric. Mart watched Turn One come up. The Allard made the bid and came around regardless. Mart smashed his foot against the brake, swerved to the edge of the road to make more room and waved him around.

The Allard hit the turn and skidded drunkenly, made a sloppy recovery and charged with its excellent acceleration into the next short straight. Mart followed through, swearing against the wind. He knew the man. Dave Taylor. Normally, a good cautious driver in the 1500cc and below category. Bought the Allard just recently and barely had it broken in. Now he was drunk with it, overestimating the car's and his own ability. The noise and dash of it, the newness of it, were inciting him to do a little grandstanding.

Mart followed Taylor for several laps, watching, waiting for a chance to get around, wondering how long Taylor could keep his luck.

Taylor calmed down. Enough to stay out of trouble with the flagmen and stewards. But it was still there, the driving on a thin line of danger, beyond his limitations, doing something that normally would take months of practice and sounding out a new car's individual personality.

Before he could think about it any longer, the Allard drifted into Turn Two, and began to skid wildly out of it, and left the road a hundred feet beyond. Its gleaming green body flipped into the air and landed on its back on the clear side of the road where there were no spectators too close around. Mart was just a short way behind, slowed by the turn when it happened. He saw it burst into flames almost immediately, saw the arm reach out from beneath, vaguely, and stop moving.

Mart's heart pounded strangely and for an instant his foot left the gas pedal and touched the brake. He could see Taylor in his mind, hanging upside down, sealed in what would soon be an inferno. Someone had to get him out—maybe he was dead already.

He saw Eric in the rearview mirror, close on him, slowing, and he started to put pressure on the brake. No! He almost shouted it aloud. No! His foot smashed down on the gas, and he watched in fascination until he saw Eric slow and stop and a bend in the road wiped the image from his sight.

He trembled and wondered at his trembling. Eric had stopped, hadn't he? And the crash hadn't been a total surprise, the way he was driving. Stop shaking he told himself. Calm down! That's it. It's all right now .... Look at those crazy people!

Large sections of the crowd were turning their heads, craning and gaping excitedly and then lunging toward the scene of the crash. Blood curiosity, the pleasure and excitement of seeing something burn, something hurt. They'd never admit it, but that's what it was.

Mart shot down the road until the white flags popped out on the course. Caution now, reduce speed. An ambulance is on the course, coming in from the grandstand area, and the truck with the fire extinguishing equipment.

Well, he asked for it, didn't he?

After a cautious two laps around, the green flags were out again and speed resumed. He drove hard, as before, but not with pleasure. The unexplained fear he had felt was gone now. In its place were anger and resentment. It stayed with him until he took the checkered flag and made the final safety lap.

Instead of pulling to a stop in front of the grandstand to receive the victor's spoils, he stopped at the pit. He climbed out and flung his helmet into the seat. Mike Foster and Joe Crane, his pit crew, were waiting.

"Hey Mart, they're going to want to hang a cup on you down there. What are you stopping here for?" Joe Crane asked.

He ignored the question. "What's the word on Taylor?"

"He'll be all right. They passed the word just a minute ago. Shook up pretty good and singed a little, but all right," Mike told him. "You see it?"

"Yeah. I got a real good look at the whole thing. He was in front of me. The damn fool—he really asked for it!"

Joe Crane looked at him and slowly his eyes began to narrow.

"You didn't stop—I thought you showed up too soon after it happened. You didn't pass him before he cracked up!"

"Hell, no! Why should I stop for a stunt like that?" The look in Crane's face made Mart angrier. What could he know about it?

"What do you mean by stunt?" Crane growled.

"He was grandstanding. That's what I mean. He asked for it."

"But damn it, Mart..." Mike Foster fumbled for words. "He was a little green—aw, look, someone was crowding your tail when it happened, and you couldn't stop. That's what you meant, wasn't it?"

Eric *was* on his tail at the time, Mart thought, but—

"Sure, that's what he meant, Joe. Better to keep on going than have *two* pile-ups."

"There was a *fire,* Mike. A fire! Taylor hanging by his safety belt, knocked out and a fire reaching for him! After this, he can have Barkdale's boys work the pit for him. If it was up to me, Janis, you'd never show up in a race again! There's no rule that says you got to stop, and maybe you had someone riding your tail—but by Christ, I know that spot. There's room to yank out of the way. It's called sportsmanship, Janis. Ever hear of it?"

Mart saw Joe lead Mike away, and he saw the race committee and photographers, the works, bearing down on him. Sunburned old men, jauntily dressed young men, and Anna Barkdale carrying the silver cup, smiling as she always did when he won a race. And he had made them walk and there was talk of modesty on the loudspeakers. Made them walk! Damn right, and they could keep on walking! He wanted nothing to do with it. There was something false about it. He didn't want to be associated with any of it. He glared at them angrily and ducked under the fence. He didn't want to see them, or talk to anyone. Not even Anna, right now—not with her believing a race had been won. What kind of a race was it to talk about or be praised for, a race ruined by a stupid bit of grandstanding?

CHAPTER THREE

"MART, WAIT!" a voice came over his shoulder, and he stopped.

He turned and saw her, not believing. Charlotte Greyne. Charlotte in a light, swishy peasant skirt and white blouse and tanned arms and face, the short red hair burning in the sun.

"Can't you say hello?"

"Sure—sure, Charlotte. I—you caught me by surprise, that's all. What are you doing here?"

"Came to see the race and you. How have you been?"

He looked at her, feeling the anger from the race begin to fall away. He began to smile a little. She wouldn't cram the race down his throat, or heap praises on him. Racing didn't matter that much to her—not like it did to Anna. He closed his eyes for a moment. Hell, he didn't blame Anna. It was her nature, and he loved her. But for right now, for that day, he couldn't face her or any of them.

"Let's get away from here. Too many people."

"But—"

"Come on. I'll explain later."

The award people seemed to have stopped looking for him by then, and he helped her into the car and nosed it into the departing traffic. In a little while they were on the highway and heading for Monterey. He drove fast and didn't try to talk against the wind. He didn't say anything until they reached his hotel. Mart stopped at the desk. The clerk looked up and grinned.

"How'd it go, Mr. Janis? Win?"

"Yeah. Look, there'll be somebody here looking for me. Here is a five that says I've checked out. And this girl..."

"Sure, Mr. Janis. I understand. You ain't even here."

He took Charlotte's arm and they rode up to his floor.

"I want to take a shower before we do anything," he told her, unlocking the door. "Race was hot and I'm full of sweat and dirt. We'll have dinner or something. Have a seat. There's a couple of magazines there. Ice water on the dresser. I'll only be a minute."

"Mart... I didn't intrude on anything? I'm not being a pest?"

"Shaddup and stop talking like that!"

He grinned and closed the door and peeled out of the sweat-drenched dungarees and stepped into a cold, needle-sharp shower. He stood there letting it bite.

He involuntarily thought of Dave Taylor. Taylor had been a steady driver, a winner two or three times in the smaller engine classes—those wonderful machines that made you love them. The cars were like women sometimes. They could turn your head and make you lose all sense of judgment, goad you into doing foolhardy things, showing off, grandstanding as Taylor did. They were wonderful, but the driver was the weakest point in the marriage. The picture of the Allard leaving the road came back. It had happened so quickly, like the striking of a match.

He turned his face into the cold spray and tried to stop thinking about it, but it was still there. He could feel it with him, as if it were just beyond his eyes—it and the way Joe Crane had acted. Eric *was* close on his tail, but—He stood stiffly and let the water come down. No talk about racing, no thinking about it this evening. With Charlotte he'd forget it all for a while. Odd, though, her showing up the way she did. Nice kid. Take her out to dinner and then send her home. Then call Anna and apologize—but don't think about her and the damn race until then.

He listened to the water coming down and closed his eyes, but the rush of spray began to sound like the roar of engines and the darkness of his closed eyes became a winding road. He fought it. It was nothing but water—not a road, not a car, not a sense of fear vaguely in back of everything—just water. But still ... He jerked his eyes open and turned the water off and stood shivering for a moment in the silence and wetness before he reached for the towel.

"I took the liberty of having dinner sent up, Mart," Charlotte told him when he came out. "It's quieter here, and you're tired."

She let up the shade and looked out at the street below and at the water of Monterey Bay already turning dark with twilight.

"Sure am. But I'll be all right in a while. Tell me, why did you come all the way up here? Long way from Torrey Pines."

"I told you. To see the races, and you. Mostly you."

"I had the idea that you didn't want to see me again."

"I know. But I got to thinking about it later, and it seemed so silly."

"I'm glad. You come up here all by yourself?"

"Still think I'm a child?"

"Pardon me. You are five months older now, aren't you!" He laughed with her. "What I meant was, did your father come too?"

"No." A frown bridged her eyes. "Dad died not long after I saw you. I sold the service station and bought myself an MG, banked the rest. I'm just coasting now for a while before I settle down to looking for work."

"I'm sorry about your father. But your coasting, as you call it. That means you have no folks?"

"Oh, I'm all right. It wasn't altogether unexpected. Dad's health hadn't been very good the last couple of years. It hit me pretty hard, but I've had almost four months to get used to the idea."

The dinner was wheeled in then on a cart. Mart paid the boy and they sat down to it.

"Save the bottle until afterwards. So now what? You're coasting and thinking about work. What kind of work?"

"Bookkeeping, secretarial, maybe at the switchboard in some big company. I worked as a telephone operator summer vacations for a couple of years." She made a wry face. "Not very interesting."

"Aw, someone will marry you off before much of that."

"Me? Nonsense."

"Why not? You're very easy to look at."

"Thanks for the nice words."

"How much time do you have for coasting?"

"I've got enough money for several months. But I thought I'd start in a week or two." A smile crept uncertainly to her lips. "I want to take you for a ride in my MG later. Show you how I learned to corner."

"I'll bet you could, too."

"I forgot—congratulations on winning the race."

He frowned and looked out the window. "It went sour. I didn't really win. Everything was slowed down after Taylor crashed." He said it, automatically, without really thinking about it, as if all the emotions about it had drained away any recurrence of feeling.

"They'll want you at the dinner tonight," she said.

"They'll have to get along without me. This is one I'd just as soon forget. Hell, I don't care about dinners. It's just the—"

"Just the winning?"

"Winning when the race has made it hard to win. When you've surmounted all possible odds and still come across the finish line first. Today didn't add up to a race in my book."

Dinner was cleared away, and they sat by the window with a drink, watching the lights and the fishing boats tied up at the pier.

"Want to go somewhere? Show? Drive?"

"No." She shook her head. "Not unless you do. But you seem a little on edge."

"Tension. I'm always keyed up after a race. Sometimes if I sit long enough, talking or reading, or maybe just relaxing with my eyes open, it goes away."

They sat in silence for a while. Charlotte said, "If talking relaxes you, then let's talk." She turned out the light. "Maybe this will quiet your nerves."

"What shall we talk about?"

"Oh, the cars in your life?"

"You make them sound like women."

"If you start talking about other women, I think I shall be very jealous."

He caught the odd tone of her voice.

"Jealous! What are you talking about?"

"I know, it's childish—you've never given me any hope. But I would be jealous of other women. Like Anna…"

"Anna! Now look—"

"You told me that you two were just friends."

"Well?"

"If you still tell me that's the way it is, I'll believe you. If she's more than that, I want to know."

"I don't want to talk about Anna."

"Then I have to assume it isn't just a friendship."

"What difference does it make?"

"A lot to me."

"All right, so it isn't just a friendship. Am I supposed to be ashamed and take up Bible-reading or something because I'm running around with a married woman?"

He told her in anger and expected tears in return. But she lowered her eyes and spoke quietly and evenly.

"I can tell what happened there, and I'm not questioning that. He's much too old for her, but—are you in love with her?"

"Charlotte! Now look, for heaven's sake—"

"Don't stop me. I might lose courage. Do you love her?"

"Yes."

"And Anna loves you?"

"Yes."

"Then there will be a wedding, I suppose."

"I never said so. We might sometime, but we aren't inclined to worry about it now. Does that shock you?" He stopped, suddenly aware that he was shouting. He shook his head. "Look, you're a sweet kid. I like you an awful lot, enough to feel like a heel for throwing that pass at you. But it doesn't give you the right to nose around."

"No, it doesn't."

"Then you have a lot of brass, don't you?"

"No, I'm scared to death."

"Then what are you doing it for?"

"Because I love you."

Charlotte turned away and looked out the window and Mart watched her, not believing what he had heard. She began to cry.

"Now what? Look, what is there to cry about?"

"Because I had to tell you!"

He stood up and turned her around and held her.

"I know. Guess I was kind of dumb. Should've seen it coming."

She tried to smile and wiped her eyes. "I shouldn't have asked. But I never liked the idea of someone trying to bust up a romance, an engagement or anything like that. If you had said there were plans for a wedding, I never would've told you about me."

He drew his hands away and shook his head. "What am I going to do with you?"

"You're thinking here's another female crowding around because she thinks race drivers are glamorous. I guess there are such girls, but I'm not one of them. I'm not impressed by your glamour. Just you. And as long as we've gone this far, I've got one more question. If there aren't any wedding plans, what kind of life—I mean—"

"A car of my own, racing all over the country, money—and her. A free and easy life for both of us. Isn't that enough?"

"No talk of a home, children, working to pay off the furniture, Saturday night movies?" She began to smile, and pushed him down into the chair. "You're a boob, Mart! And in a situation like this, I think all is fair. I'm free to chase you now."

"Now wait a minute—" He didn't get a chance to finish.

She slid into his lap and kissed him, at first gently and then with passion. He felt the softness of her in his arms and the scent of her made him a little giddy.

"Look, Charlotte—you hardly know me. One evening in Torrey Pines, and not a very pleasant one for you at that."

"Can't I change my mind? Can't I think you're something special without you getting suspicious? Mart, I don't know what happened. And I know a gal isn't supposed to say these things. She's supposed to wait for the man to say them, but I don't care. I can't explain it. I always thought it happened in movies and fairy tales. But it did happen. I love you, and I'll do anything in hope that you'll love me someday. Don't look so worried! There's no preacher behind the door—no strings ..."

She kissed him long and hard, fumbling with buttons as she did. He felt his hand being guided to her, touching soft skin and then the warm, round fullness of her breasts. He fought against growing desire.

"No, Charlotte—wait! You don't have to ..."

"I want to—because I love you. That's all that matters." Her legs glistened, rounded and long where she pulled her skirt away. "Please ... Mart ..."

The phone caught him somewhere on the edge of sleep—a sleep full of warmth. The warmth stirred against him.

"The phone," she whispered in his ear.

"I know."

"Better answer it."

"Let it ring. I told the clerk we weren't in for anybody."

"No. It might be important." She leaned across him and lifted the receiver.

"Oh, all right!" He took the phone and growled into it, "Yes, this is Janis, and it's one o'clock in the morning!"

He listened to the voice on the other end, the accented voice and the information it unreeled.

"Is this some kind of gag? Or joke?"

He listened some more, sitting up in bed and not believing what he heard. The notion was too incredible.

"Now look, Mr. Roberti, either you're drunk or you have the wrong party.... Certainly my name is Martin Janis. But why me? I never even touched one, so how do you know? ... Style! ... Yeah and what's that got to do with Taylor? ... If what you say was true, I'd have gotten black-flagged! ... What you're suggesting is crazy!"

He heard a solid stream of Italian invective and his own anger began to creep away.

"Wait a minute—you're really serious about this. You aren't going to call me up tomorrow and tell me it was all a big mistake? ... Well I'll be damned! Sure, I guess I could learn. Sure, why not? Why should I think it over? Yes. Absolutely. And thank *you*. Good night."

He started to put the receiver down when another voice shouted his name from the other end.

"Martin? Martin!" It was Anna.

"Yes, I'm still here."

"The clerk told me you had checked out! Martin—well, never mind. Did you accept Roberti's offer?"

"Yes. I sure did. Great news, isn't it?"

"You've got to turn him down!"

"Turn him down! Anna, it's a tremendous offer. It's what you and I have been talking about, isn't it?"

"Better than my offer, Martin? I know how those things go in my country. I know the procedures. You'll be nothing for months, maybe years. You won't be driving much for a while, and what little you do will be on a team. They aren't going to push their best drivers out of the way so that you will have a chance to really drive. You have to be with them a while, and in the meantime you get nothing but tidbits. Besides this, Scuderia Corsatti is small and not very successful of late. You've got to turn him down. Stay with me, Mart! Stay with me and you will be driving much sooner, independently. Go to Corsatti and you will be nothing for a long time."

"Look, what's a few months? I can learn something. I can't step into the real thing cold like that. Be reasonable. It takes a lot of practice."

"You will get the practice, but you won't have to wait for promotions or prove yourself in a dozen races."

"Maybe not, but I wouldn't have the advice of several experts to guide me along either. I need those experts, Anna. Somebody to show me the ropes."

"If you accept his offer, Mart—"

There was a long pause.

"You still there?" Mart asked.

"If you accept his offer, Mart, you'll go alone. It will be the end of everything between us."

Mart felt something go cold in his stomach. No more with Anna? But why? Why couldn't she understand?

"Damn it, I'm just as anxious as you are. I've always dreamed of something like this, but never expected it to happen. But it takes learning to handle a racer. For God's sake, even the sports car races over there are nothing like these little races here."

"Are you afraid?"

"Yes, damn it! I'm afraid of it."

"Oh Mart, stop and think. Your own car. You and me on the Continent and nothing to hold us back. You winning races on your own—winning them for me..."

"Winning them for you! Is that all you can think about now?"

"Martin..."

"You know, I believe that's all you *can* think about! I kidded about it back at Torrey Pines. I made a joke of it because I came in second instead of first and you acted funny about it and I didn't really believe you could be that way. Sure, I joked about it and you made it all into a pretty story, and all along your only real interest in me is my driving. Sure, Martin Janis, a pretty good driver and a possible way of getting back into Europe's high society where you broke tea biscuits as a little girl."

"Martin, let's not be childish. What difference does it make? We have everything."

What difference? What kind of ego could ask these things of him? What kind of ego could ask him to do something that was close to suicide? Sports car races, the professional kind—perhaps that would not have been too much to ask. There was understanding there, confidence, something he knew or could know. But this other—no one did that, not cold, not without training, not without an expert to teach and watch and warn and correct. Otherwise, it would be a quick way of dying. Anna knew this. Anna knew racing as well as he did.

His mind kept repeating the thought, hardly able to believe. What kind of ego? What difference did it make? Why sit there with the phone glued to his ear and try to find explanations to the whole thing that would make everything all right? Face it, he told himself. The truth was begging and scolding and whispering in his ear right now. He closed his eyes and his voice exploded into the phone and cut her short.

"You better find someone else. I'm taking Roberti's offer—and I'm damn grateful to get it."

He slammed the phone back on the table and sat looking at the darkness of the room. Anna and himself—through! It hurt. It made a sickness inside and he thought of calling her back. But it was no use. Nothing could be changed.

"That was Anna, wasn't it?"

"Who else?"

"What was all the argument about? Or am I being nosy again?"

"A man named Roberti—he tried to reach me at the dinner. I've been invited to join the Corsatti people as a team driver."

"In Italy?"

"Yes. Italy. Sign on with them, train in their racing cars and sports cars—and then, professional driving all over Europe. All the big races I've ever read about."

She was quiet for a moment. "Are you going to?" Charlotte asked. "Really?"

"I've always dreamed of it. It seemed beyond thinking or hoping. And yet it's happened. I'd be a fool if I didn't. I'd be a damn fool."

"How soon?"

"Within the week."

"I see ..." Her voice saddened in the darkness.

He took her in his arms. Thought of Anna came to him and all that had existed between them. Gone now. Anna wouldn't be back. She was too proud, too strong. It was hard to realize. And it made an emptiness inside.

He drew Charlotte closer. He needed her now—someone to take the sting away. And she was so sweet and trusting.

"Come to Italy with me, Charlotte. Please. I need you."

"Is this a proposal, Mart?"

He thought of speed and cars and the countless things that happen, the things that touch quickly and leave the moistness of fear; and he thought of this wonderful young woman standing at the edge of a course somewhere in Europe, a place full of strangeness to her, watching the cars, waiting for him, alone except for him—depending on, attached by bonds of marriage to a man who could in one shattering instant become little more than fragments in a cloud of smoke .... What would happen to her? She was too young, and he liked her, but—yes, *liked* her. That was another thing. Liked her a lot, but ...

"No," he told her quietly. "It wasn't a proposal. I'm sorry. I went off half-cocked. I couldn't even pay your way. I couldn't go myself, except that Corsatti is footing the bill. And besides, I don't—"

"I can pay my way, Mart. Am I still invited? Or do I have to follow you?"

"But that marriage business..."

She kissed him softly. "Maybe someday you'll want it, but right now, I don't care."

He made love to her—and yet, now, behind everything, like the breath of something touching his shoulder, there was the wondering about something else beyond a continent and a sea, the hinting of a possible mistake, the ghost of inadequacy. How could they know he was good enough? How could he know himself?

CHAPTER FOUR

THE small Italian freighter, *Humberto,* rolled with the cold Atlantic darkness, the harbor of New York far behind and little more than a fleeting image in the mind. The lights of other ships passed in the night and grew more frequent. The sea lanes narrowed and Gibraltar loomed against the sky and was left behind with its British and Spanish lights winking in the darkness. Along the coast of Africa and the warmer waters, the screws churning beneath the surface, a pulse of time and distance and motion touching the night, and someone not being able to sleep.

Martin Janis walked slowly around the deck and found Charlotte leaning against the rail staring out into the darkness at the rolling shadows of waves.

"What's the matter?" he asked. "Afraid you'd get caught coming out of my room in the morning?"

Charlotte tried to smile, but she didn't look up.

"I can move down to your room," he joshed her. "That way, I'm the one they raise eyebrows at."

"Silly, it works out the same either way."

"You spent a lot of money just for appearances, and I'm *sure* these Italians would've talked if you hadn't gotten a separate stateroom. Don't you think you ought to use it now and then, you shameless wench?"

"Cut it out, Mart. I don't feel like joking tonight."

"What's the matter?" he asked.

"Couldn't sleep."

"I know. I heard you go out."

"Sorry if I woke you up."

"I wasn't sleeping much. Getting excited, I guess, thinking about getting there tomorrow."

A little frightened too, he thought. That feeling inside. The kind that comes when a roller coaster dips sharply down and leaves you gasping, the little butterfly business that hits while waiting in the office of a dentist. No, those were little things. This was something bigger—a loneliness, a wanting to be good, to do the thing right, and wondering if he could. A good driver, or only a young man with promise?

"Mart, how will it be? I mean, when a man does this sort of thing—how does he start?"

"I'll be assigned to a car. Maybe a month of practice, and then a tour as a reserve driver for a while to get the experience before I'm a full time member of the team. I guess it depends on how fast I learn the ropes. I only know what I've read and what little Roberti told me. But basically, that's the way it ought to work."

She nodded and stared back out at the waves. "Nervous, aren't you? You've seemed tense lately."

"I don't know. It just doesn't seem to penetrate. Why should they invite me? I've had some good wins in the States. I suppose my technique adds up to what they want for a start. But still, sometimes I wonder if they're right. I'm scared to death I'll try out and not make the grade, and we'll be coming back on the boat."

"Is it bad?"

"Dangerous?"

"Yes."

"Well, there isn't such a thing as safe auto racing!"

"More dangerous than sports cars?"

"I'll be driving the Corsatti Gran Sport part of the time. Don't forget Le Mans and Monte Carlo, and the Mille Miglia. I'm almost certain to be driving at Le Mans. That's next month."

"What about the others?"

"You're worrying again."

"I just want to know, and you're avoiding it."

"Sure, driving a Grand Prix racer is more dangerous. Look, when Eric and I were taking our cars out to Pebble Beach or one of those races, we raced for fun. We had hot little cars that could squeeze out a hundred and forty-five miles an hour in a pinch, and sometimes we did some pretty wild things with them. We raced on Sundays, and sometimes we teased Olds 88's on the way home."

He laughed quietly, remembering, and put his arm around her. "All for fun, and not as dangerous as you might expect. But Grand Prix racing—professional. It's for money, a lot of money, and kind of a big advertising thing for the outfit you're driving for. Some of the cars can go better than two hundred miles an hour, and others hit only a hundred and eighty-five, but make up for it with superior brakes and cornering. But it's all dangerous. It has to be. There's more speed, and more reason for winning than just pleasure."

"I don't think I like it."

"But honey, they're going to train me for it. It isn't as if I were just stepping into it cold. They've got a lot at stake—a reputation that isn't helped by a lot of accidents. And besides, think of all the money tied up in one of those little cars. I don't know what a Formula One Corsatti costs, but I suppose it's in the neighborhood of twenty to thirty thousand dollars. They aren't going to turn me loose with one just any old way. Now come on, all this drink out here is making you gloomy. Let's go back down to the cabin."

He helped her down the companionway and down the slightly pitching stairs. They walked aft to their cabin where there was a faint booming of the ship's screws underneath. She stood there, listening, with her eyes closed, leaning against him. Mart opened the door and turned on the lights and smiled at her.

"Come on, cheer up."

"But why you? You didn't ask to drive for them. You were satisfied with the racing you were doing."

"You were there when I got the call from Roberti."

"Yes, but—"

"What is there to say, Charlotte? Corsatti hears about me, sends a man to look me over. The scout likes what he sees and makes the invite. That's all there is to it."

"Yes—yes, I know that. But why not Eric? Eric has had as many wins, hasn't he?"

"I've wondered about that too. Evidently my style was a little sharper—it isn't just winning races you know. Technique counts more than sheer speed. Eric's car is a little faster. The times I've beaten him, I think, were due to technique. And besides, he's considerably older than I am. That might've had something to do with it. And—"

"And?"

"He said I had a greater desire to win."

"You didn't tell him that."

"No, of course not."

"You're acting mysterious, Mart. How would he know?"

"Why, by watching, naturally. Let's forget it. It's silly."

"By watching! But all the drivers are trying to win."

"Forget it, Charlotte. It doesn't mean anything."

"I would, except that you seem to be worried about something."

"All right, all right. It's because I didn't stop to help Dave Taylor when his car crashed at Pebble Beach and caught fire. Eric stopped, but I kept going."

"Mart! But why."

"I don't know. I was too busy driving to think about it. Besides, Eric was close on my tail. He might've rammed me—but it doesn't make any difference. I wouldn't have stopped anyway."

"Why not? Why wouldn't you?"

"Taylor's a nice guy, but he was grandstanding, driving recklessly, and no matter what it looks like to the spectators, there's no room for recklessness in a race. What happened, he asked for."

"That may be, but it isn't like you. Not at all!"

"Why get excited? It didn't kill him."

"No, Mart. But—"

"*But!* It's happening already, isn't it? First, you spend a big chunk of dough for a separate room so that somebody on the ship won't say, Hey, Giuseppi, you know that redhead? She's putting out to that American driver, and they aren't even married! Sure, you worry about being seen with me, among people who think it's the most natural thing in the world. And now, this horrible person you're in love with begins to look like a killer." He sat down and nodded his head. "The expression in your face is just like Joe Crane's was when he found out!"

"Mart! Stop it!" Her face was suddenly red.

"Okay, I'm sorry," he snapped. "But it's the truth, isn't it?"

"What if it happened again? Would you stop? Maybe you were just confused. We all do things like that. Maybe it wouldn't happen again."

"I wouldn't bet on it." He said it almost angrily. "I can't be responsible for the crackpots in the crowd."

"But you just can't do things like that."

He laughed at her and the sound was hard and flat.

"I never told you what I did to my big brother, did I? Never told you how I goaded him into riding a coaster down a hill when we were kids and how he smashed against an apple tree and was killed. I made the ride, and I knew he was a coward, and I made him do it too. How do I look to you now? Go on, say what you think. What do you think of a boy who does that and before the mourning is over is thinking of ways to go down the hill faster? Sure, I took a brand new bike up there and rode it down and wrecked it. Maybe I'd do anything to race. Maybe I'd trade you for a chance to do a few good laps around a course."

She bowed her head.

"What about Anna? Would you have traded her?"

Mart thought of Anna. She was far away now. But every time he closed his eyes in the quiet of the sea, he could see the raven hair and the dark eyes, the slender, compelling length of her.

"I'm sorry. I don't know why I have to bring her up. I guess I'm jealous of her. She's so beautiful, and she understands all this and I don't. But I know one thing. What happened to you and your brother could have happened to anybody. You didn't know he was going to be killed. You were teasing."

"Then what about Taylor? Maybe if I hadn't kept my speed when he got in front of me, it wouldn't have happened. Maybe he wouldn't have felt like he was being pushed. Maybe it was another dare. I dare you to stay in front of me. I dare you to ride the coaster down the hill. Maybe I made him crash, and then on top of it, didn't even stop for him. Ever think of that?"

She looked at him and began to cry.

"I—just don't believe—you could be that kind of person."

"Why not? I don't feel sorry for the damn fools that get out on the roads and start cutting up at speeds they can't handle and in cars that were never designed to be safe over forty. They've been told and they've seen others like themselves get mangled, and yet they keep on. Of course I don't feel sorry for them. So why should I worry about Taylor? He was grandstanding and in doing so ruined a race for everyone else."

Charlotte still cried and he saw the anguish in her face. He sat down and with the thing spent in himself began to wonder at his own likeness: a driver had crashed out of foolishness, and he had not stopped. Simple, and yes, not very sporting. But the worrying he felt seemed to go beyond all that.

"I'm not talking about what happens on highways." Her voice was tight and unhappy. "I'm not saying Taylor was right—but I just can't believe you'd stand by and let anyone ..."

"All right ... all right." He felt sick inside. "Maybe you're right. He might have lost his life and there's no right or wrong in dying."

"Maybe I shouldn't be judging. I'm not a driver, but—"

"I've been avoiding it, trying to forget, making up a lot of excuses for myself. Sure, Eric was right on my tail and there could have been another crash, but he was slowing down and so was I. He was anticipating it. It wasn't like I had a novice on my tail who was too wrapped up in what he was doing and couldn't see what was really going on. I could've stopped and I don't know why I didn't. Really. I don't! It was almost like being afraid. Maybe a crash reminds us all that it could've been us instead of someone else and we don't want to look. I don't know. Look honey, I wasn't aware of daring him to stay in front of me, or of pushing him. In fact, I think I did slow down a little just before it happened. I've tried to figure it out, but I only get confusion or crazy answers. I tried to forget the whole thing. It isn't unusual. Puzzled my folks for years before they died—this desire to go fast being stronger than fear and regret over accidents and death. That's what it looked like to them."

"You see?" She tried to smile. "That proves it. You don't know why you didn't stop. A mistake, that's all. We make them every day of the week. You like to win your races. You wouldn't be much of a driver if you didn't. But you won't do it at the risk of some one else's life. You're too gentle."

He held his head in his hands, trying to face it for the first time, not trying to ignore it anymore. But he wasn't sure that she was right. Maybe he wouldn't stop next time....

She took his hand.

"Don't you think we ought to get some sleep? Busy day tomorrow. It's almost two. Come on, what's done is done. You can't correct old mistakes. You've got a future to worry about, and what's Mr. Corsatti going to think if you come dragging into his office with bags under your eyes?"

He looked at her bright, young face and pushed his lips into a smile. He couldn't stay gloomy around her.

"A guy can't even have a decent worry around you, can he?"

"Not if I can help it! Now better get your beauty rest."

He buried his face in her breasts and held her for a moment.

"All right. We'll get some sleep."

He started to take off his shirt. "There's something else that bothers me, Charlotte."

"What's that?"

"Well, you're inclined to worry an awful lot."

"I try not to."

"I know, but look. Even if it is a sport, professional racing gets pretty rough. Some of it isn't going to be pretty. Things happen. You know, bad crashes and things like that."

"I suppose."

"I was thinking maybe you'd be better off if you didn't go to the races. If you didn't watch, it wouldn't bother you."

He lay down beside her and pulled the blanket up and listened to the pulse beat of the ship, bringing them closer and closer.

"I'll be there to root for you. It wouldn't be right if I wasn't. I just don't understand sometimes why you want to get so involved in it...."

He lay there in the darkness with her and wished he could explain why he wanted to and had to.

"Where did it begin? That little ranch in California, where he was born? There was a hill....

The hill rose two hundred and fifty feet above the valley. From its grass-blown top could be seen the Janis ranch and its martial rows of prune trees, the apple orchard and the field of corn. And beyond, the Elmer ranch, and the shake and tarpaper shack of old man Canby. Beyond the Janis orchards, the county road twisted like a gray snake through the valley. Above, blurred with summer haze, the Santa Cruz range with its mottling of redwood, pine and buckbrush. Over the small years, the hill had become Robbers' Roost, King's Hill, and the high and sacred mount of a child's dreaming.

It was always for himself, that hill. Never for his bigger brother. Something had happened with him. Tom was scared of everything. Always hanging around the house. Always tattling or spying, staying close to his mother, following her with his fat white face and watery eyes.

But the hill. It wasn't gradual, the thing that happened to it and himself. One minute it was still the old place of pretending, and the next he was tying a shoelace and looking up at it, and the hill held a different kind of promise.

He made a coaster, and because it was a typical boy's thing to do, his father made Tommy get in on it. His father didn't know about the hill, nor did his mother. The hill was meant for coasters. It didn't occur to him to mention it—he could only look up at the hill, and feel a quickening of his pulse as he walked toward it, pulling the coaster behind him.

"Where are you going?" Tommy asked.

"What do you care? You'd be chicken anyway."

"That's what you say. Where are you going?"

"To the top of the hill. Still want to come?"

"All the way?"

"Sure, all the way!"

"I'll come. I didn't say I wouldn't did I? I'm coming."

Mart led the way through the orchard and up the hill. The grass once green from winter was burned with July and yellow. The only green now was the taller, acrid smelling tarweed that drags at pants legs and sticks with its tiny points, and blackens the faces of grazing animals. The smell rushed over them in waves, and they felt the sun beating down. Tommy puffed and blew hard behind him.

Tommy always was soft, and Mart remembered that Tommy had been frightened or nervous over smaller adventures than this, and he was frightened now, in the way he followed, his eyes watering and nervously aware of the diminishing size of objects below. It must have been some small and sickly pride that kept him from running home.

Three-quarters of the way up, Mart felt a cooling breeze. It was almost always there. It riffled the grass and blew against his sweat-dampened shirt, and he could begin to see a long way off. It was dad's land, but this was his hill, his place. He smirked at Tommy and turned and kept on going until he reached the top.

"You're crazy! You'll get killed—you'll be going a million miles an hour before you reach bottom!"

Mart turned the coaster around and pointed it toward the orchards below, toward the truck road that ran between them. He got down on the boards and held the coaster back with his toes.

"You watch, chicken. It'll be your turn when I get back."

He lifted his feet, and felt the wheels turn.

The ground was rough, but the grass took up most of the shocks and he hung on and steered, and felt wind beginning to push against his face. Faster and faster it dropped, tarweed lashing across his face and the road below a wildly gyrating blur.

Halfway down now, and the hill dipping more sharply. The coaster swooped down, half flying, and his chest ached with the jarring.

His eyes watered and he could hardly see. Then *whoomph!* he was on the bottom and there was a sick-sweet thrill in his stomach as the coaster shot along the flat. He was too low to see the truck road, but he could see the division between the two orchards where it ran, and steered toward it. He cut its deep dust for fifty yards and stopped.

"Boy, ain't you a dandy!" He looked at the hill and the small figure standing on top.

Quickly, he pulled the coaster back up the long slope, and stood panting by his brother.

"It's almost like flying. You'll like it."

"Me?" Tommy was pale and shaking.

"What's the matter? I did it, didn't I?"

Tommy shunned the view at his feet.

"Nothing to it. All you do is point it and hang on."

"I don't feel very good."

"You chickening out?"

"No. I just don't feel very good, that's all."

"You're scared! Heck, it's better than a roller coaster. You ain't going to fall off."

White-faced and uncertain, Tommy settled down on the coaster. Mart put his foot on it and gave a little shove.

"No!" Tommy shrieked as the coaster shot down the slope.

The coaster and the frozen figure of his brother grew rapidly smaller with speed and distance. The coaster lurched and plummeted until it reached the bottom and zoomed out across the flat with Tommy still holding tight, making no effort to steer.

"Tommy!" Mart screamed at him. "Steer it! Hey!"

He stood up and began to run down the hill when he saw the coaster careen into the apple orchard, bounce twice and smash into one of the trees.

He stopped and stood still, down below where the breeze touched the hill, with the sun beating down on the silence, seeing the tree trembling yet, and the apples rolling crazily on the clotted ground. Moving closer, he could see Tommy lying still with a patch of sunlight plucking at his hair ....

There seemed to be a fog, a shrouding mist through which they walked and sat down stunned in the living room. There was a closed door they couldn't help looking at, not quite accepting what lay beyond it. His mother and his father and himself. But not Tommy. Tommy was in the other room. In the dark.

His mother began to cry then, hard, racking sobs that shook her whole body. His father stared at the bedroom door, not moving a muscle. And Mart sat frozen, upright in his chair. *Tommy is dead ... Tommy is dead! Dead,* a new word, a play word suddenly real and yet not real. Tommy dead? Why? A few minutes ago standing on the hill in the sunlight, and then dead there among a hundred fallen apples. Dead. What did *dead* mean?

"It's your doing! That's what!" His father was standing in front of him, his face blazing white. "You killed him!"

His mother broke in. "Oh, Adam, no! How can you say such a thing?"

"Only someone crazy would think of riding down that hill!"

Mark sat there, terrified and unable to move. His father came closer, the muscles of his mouth working spasmodically.

"Adam, no! It wasn't his fault!"

"Your son is stretched out dead in that bedroom!"

"Yes. My son..." Her face looked terribly worn and tired and hurt, but she sat down and talked to her shoes very quietly. "Nobody told them to stay off the hill with the little coaster."

"What's common sense is common sense, damn it! Mart killed his brother! Because he didn't have sense. Because—"

"No. We killed him. Mart, you go crawl into my bed and try to rest. I'll be in to see you in a little while. You aren't to blame."

Mart walked slowly and dazedly from the room, closing the door behind him. He stopped and leaned against the wall in the hallway, and couldn't help but hear them talking.

"Elizabeth, you're talking crazy!"

"We killed him. Adam, we didn't bring him up right. You know yourself Tommy was kind of—well, you know, a sissy. A little too soft. He should've been outside a little more, played with the other kids, gotten a few knocks. He was always too nervous— you've said so yourself. We brought him up to be like an angel, and an angel is a pretty sickly thing walking on earth."

"We brought him up no different than Mart."

"Mart's different."

"Aw, hell, it's the same blood, ain't it? Naw, he's just got a crazy, mean streak, that's all!"

"Oh, no! Not crazy or mean—just different. Don't you see? Adam, didn't you ever take a dare when you were a boy?"

"I don't remember. I suppose I did."

"Sure you did, and that's all Mart did. He took a dare, from that hill and somehow got away with it—somehow, someway, maybe something in him—I don't know, but it was a triumph and he wanted Tommy to try it too. Only Tommy wasn't able. Maybe Mart goaded him a little and maybe Tommy finally got enough boy in him under all that fright to make him try it too. He just didn't make it."

The porthole moved slowly up and down, and Mart watched it remembering.

There was the hill and the coaster and the times he sped down the county road on the new bicycle that came later, and the trip down the hill that collapsed the fine spoke wheels. He remembered staring at the ceiling of his room, even after the fight with his father over the ruining of the bike, and wondering how to go faster still.

Maybe it began there on the hill, or with the succession of broken-down heaps he bought for a song after school and the war, and raced on the back roads away from town.

He didn't know. He only knew that for as long as he could remember, he had wanted to drive, to drive fast and race. Study the subject, read about it, work in garages and gas stations, hang around the midget tracks talking with auto enthusiasts until that day when the Mercedes left the station in Morgan with a peculiar kind of thunder.

Perhaps it had begun then. Perhaps that day everything in the past had run together and suddenly it all had a purpose.

He had to race. It was as simple as that. There was nothing else.

Why? Because he wanted to, but it was no answer. Why was one man built to carry, and another to chop and another to punch, and another to add and subtract and multiply, and another to walk out on a stage and believe for the moment he was someone else? Because they want to? They want to, but that isn't the whole of it.

He tightened his arm around her in the darkness and knew she was afraid and that he was afraid too. Afraid and impatient ....

"There you are, Mr. Janis," Rudolfo Roberti said in his precise but accented English. He turned his blue-chinned, dark face toward the wind and breathed deep. "Italy."

Martin stepped out on deck and stood at the rail as the ship moved slowly past the moles of the outer harbor into the old port of Genoa. He saw the warehouses and shipyards, fishing boats sleeping on the dark green of the water by the quays. And above, the city itself rising from the foot of the Apennines. A city of castles and walls and cathedrals built on hillsides, grays and browns of stone with a flash of color here and there in the stirring of an awning or a window curtain, in flowers, or in something a little less ancient than the whole. A sense of quiet beyond the industry of the waterfront.

"Old," Martin observed.

"Oh, Genoa has its modern sections," Roberti shrugged. "But the antiquity is very beautiful, Mr. Janis. You do not have this in your country. Your country is very young. This is where the great Columbus was born. There is a square in the city where his home still stands. It is all very beautiful."

"Well," Mart nodded, "what's first on the schedule?"

"First we must see to your train tickets. I'm afraid there will not be much time here. We must get to Turin without delay."

"Provided by Corsatti again?"

"Of course. Corsatti always provides transportation for his people. Especially when they come as far as you have. There are very few of the rich who wish to risk their luxurious lives in racing. It is unfortunate that you did not tell me of Miss Greyne. Corsatti would have taken care of her passage too."

"We aren't married."

"That makes no difference. Wife, mistress, whatever. Corsatti sees to his drivers, Mr. Janis."

"It doesn't matter. She would've been too embarrassed anyway."

"Embarrassed? You Americans are strange in some ways."

"I suppose. All right. We catch the train to Turin. And then?"

"In Turin, my friend, you shall find a suitable hotel, and then go to the address I shall give you. I suggest a taxi. It won't be hard to find, that way. It is on the road between Turin and Rivoli. The Corsatti establishment, of course. The factory and testing ground. There you will find Corsatti himself."

"He sounds a little frightening. Corsatti! Don't you have a first name to soften it up?"

Roberti shrugged. "If Corsatti has a first name, no one knows of it. He is Corsatti. You will not even have to have him pointed out. When you see Corsatti, there will be no mistaking him."

"He is expecting me tomorrow?"

"That is right, Mr. Janis. Now I must tend to the luggage."

Mart watched at the rail as the ship moved in closer, more slowly now, feeling the excitement within. The home of Columbus. Interesting, perhaps, and a brushing with the ancient; but the land today was the country of those other men, the big racers. How many? Tazio Nuvolari, Felice Bonetto, Rudolf Caracciola, Maglioli—and now himself. He laughed at the idea. Comparing himself to those men. They were real drivers, born not with the pampering sedans of Detroit, not raised to be unconcerned about such things as springs and steering and excess weight and the ability of a car to sit hard in a turn, not learning to drive and not really driving. His smile faded. These were the gods. The mighty and the incomparable masters of road and machine and speed. He wondered if he could ever be one of them.

"What are you frowning at?" It was Charlotte.

"Was I? Maybe a momentary case of cold feet and wondering if I'm good enough!"

"Silly. If they didn't think you were good, they wouldn't have made the offer."

"I know."

"You'll really show them what a good driver you are, and I'm going to be very proud."

"Kind of cheerful, aren't you? What happened? Last night you were seeing crashes all over the place."

"Maybe everything looks better in the daytime. I'm still a little scared. But I believe in you, and love you. I think that makes the difference."

She kissed him, her youthful face tanned and happy from the trip across. He looked at her closely, smiling, but behind her eyes he could see the trace of worry.

CHAPTER FIVE

THE desk clerk, a thin, sick-looking but energetic little man named Piero, led them to a room on the third floor with loud and excited and mostly unintelligible acclaim for his establishment, the Hotel Parigi. He opened a door and whisked across the floor of a dark and old room and opened the window and blinds and pointed proudly outside, emphasizing that if one leaned a little to look beyond the brick wall facing the window, one could see the street, Via Venalzio, and even a part of the great Via Pacchiotti where traffic rolled noisily toward the center of Turin, or out toward the hills and Alpine passes. But that was all—none of that which seemed to be a city of monuments and squares, of great buildings and splashes of color sitting there below the mountains. Martin wasn't thinking of that at the moment. There were other things to think about; and the room was only five hundred lire a day.

Piero left them, and Martin sat down in the easy chair, and immediately jumped from it with a yell. He ran his hand over the seat and began to laugh.

"I've been shot down! There's a spring sticking through!" He sat down on the bed and looked around, his eyes finally falling on Charlotte, apologetically. Other things to think about or not, it couldn't be ignored.

"Pretty bad, isn't it?"

Charlotte sat down beside him.

"What do you suppose he was thinking—about us, I mean?"

"Now look, Charlotte, how many times do I have to tell you? It doesn't matter. You're not back in the States. Hell, the only thing they'll notice is you acting as if you were doing something shameful, if you don't cut it out."

"I'll probably get over it, Mart."

"I hope so. I said the hotel room is pretty bad."

"I don't mind. I can do wonders with a scrub brush and a little paint. Maybe a couple of travel posters or something over those rips in the wallpaper. We'll manage all right."

"Well, this is just temporary. Until we've got more time to look around, and get more money. Maybe it will be only a couple days or a week, and we can move over to one of the first-class hotels. It's just that we don't have much, even if my way was paid, and you mustn't dip into what you have. Save it in case of some emergency."

"I know, honey. Stop worrying about it. I don't mind. Really!"

He pulled her to him and kissed her gently. "Okay. I'd better get out there, then." He kissed her again, got up and looked around the room with a grim smile on his face. "You wait. If they can make a driver out of me, I'll buy you a gondola in Venice when I win my first race. See you."

Charlotte stood up and looked around the room and began to frown. Beyond the ancient brass of the bedstead, there were faded and dirty roses amid Roman columns from floor to ceiling. It had two bad tears in it, and the ceiling had cracks and a brown stain on the plaster from a leak, and indeed, there was one section in a corner with no plaster at all, but bare boards and chicken wire showing through. The walls showed a photograph framed in cheap gilt of Vittorio Emmanuel, and a faded print of a chariot race. No carpet on a dirty, bare floor.

She pushed open the door to the bathroom. Her heart sank farther. A grotesque tub with gargoyle feet and a homemade shower standing precariously over it.

She turned on the spray, tentatively, and listened to the pipes rattling down the walls and beneath her feet. And she looked at herself in the mirror. The glass was dappled and muddy with age.

Her eyes stared back at her in the dim, flickering yellow light, until she turned and ran from it, slamming the door and hurrying for the window and the bright warm sunlight of Italy that she could see by leaning a little and staring beyond the brick wall.

But in a minute she smiled a little and turned to face the room.

"What's the matter with you?" she said to herself. "It's just a room in an old hotel. Just needs more light bulbs and a little cleaning. A few bright flowers would do wonders. Besides, it won't be for long. Maybe we won't even be staying here tonight. You're just tired, that's all."

She stretched out on the bed and closed her eyes. It wasn't bad at all, resting in the darkness of her own eyes, trying not to think about it. Listening to the sounds that seemed muted and faint with antiquity. It was old, all right—old with the gas jets still mounted on the walls, and the rather high ceiling and the once fancy molding of the woodwork. There were old sounds, voices at the end of the hallway or from the floor below, perhaps, a million miles away in another time and dimension. A distant rattling of the plumbing sounded, and a horn down the street, the cry of a child; from somewhere came the odor of something cooking. And the knowledge of a man and woman above somewhere, the sound of her shoes dropping on the floor, a high, animal laugh and the sounds of struggling dying into the fast metronome squeaking of a bed.

From the next room over she could hear music—rasping music that drowned out the bed; tinny, worn and scratching, the distortion of running down and being wound up again. Strangely, classical music. Not Caruso crying with the sadness of the clown, not something that came with the dimming of the lights at La Scala, or sung with passion on the wandering waters of Venice, or in the tomb of an imaginary Egypt. A symphony of some kind. She didn't know. She didn't know much about music. She liked it, but she could never keep the composers and titles straight. She went to a concert once in Los Angeles, but got so excited at watching the musicians and waiting for the cymbalist to bring his discs crashing together that she never really heard the music.

The symphony scratched on, a serious thing, a grim undertone to it, a sadness and a violence, or what was left of it coming out of that ancient instrument. But still, a feeling of gloom listening to it, and no release from it after the final chords because the music began again. The same music, from the beginning . . . .

It had to be music about death.

There was no escaping the finality of its theme.

She tried to shut it out of her ears.

What was Mart doing by now? Mart and those frightening cars he talked about. Surely he wouldn't be driving one today. It was too soon. That's what he had said on the boat. Just looking around today, most likely.

But what if he did?

The music began to creep into her mind again.

What if he was?

Mart was a good driver. One of the best, or they wouldn't have asked him to join the Corsatti team. Sure, he's a good driver. That's why he came to Italy, to drive racing cars. Why act as if it had been a secret all that time? What difference whether he starts acquainting himself with the cars today or tomorrow or next week? He's not a brutal or reckless driver, taking all risks and chances for the purpose of winning—even though he thinks he's cold-blooded and only wants to win. He's too gentle inside to be that kind of man.

What kind of a man, though, really?

What makes him tick? Where does it begin?

Does such a man have to come into the world accompanied by violence and danger—or was that merely superstition, the stuff from which old wives' tales come?

When she had asked Martin where he was born, he had told her, and the whole story came to be so vivid in her mind.

It was raining that night. Raining in sharp, spraying gusts. The trees were black, and the canyons and hills were black, and the sky a boiling thing beyond seeing.

Three in the morning. Time, circumstance, the dark secrecy of a bed months before—all funneling down to a narrowed instant, one minute chosen.

The town of Morgan, fifteen miles away in the California hills.

Adam Janis had placed Tommy in the care of a neighbor, and was driving Elizabeth to town, to the hospital. Elizabeth sitting on the seat of the Model-T truck—the pain and death-whiteness of her, the withdrawing of her eyes and mind into a private, unreachable void.

They never made it to town. It happened at the side of the road, with Adam facing his wife, himself, and the storm that crashed across the roof of the truck.

He had never done it before, and no book or quiet authoritative voice could have told him how. There was a calf, once, one night out in the barn, in the straw by the sputtering glow of a lantern, but that was something else and a long time ago and he was blind to time and the rest of the world, deaf to the raging that twisted across the small circle of his flashlight, too involved to remember fear and squeamishness over what he was doing—unaware of himself and of the fact that at any other time, in daylight and time of calm, if he were asked, he could not know the first thing about what had to be done, or what was wrong and what was right. All of that somewhere else now, left somewhere....

It was just Elizabeth, a circle of light, his hands, and the rain on his back as he leaned into the truck.

Martin Janis had come into existence, into a night full of doubts and dangers, flirting in the first minutes of his life with something akin to the long and unknowing sleep he had just left ....

Charlotte, remembering what he had told her, thought about it and closed her eyes. A driver because he was born on four wheels, not concerned with danger because he was born in danger? No, nothing as superstitious as all that. It couldn't be. But if the answer wasn't there on that night, or with the coaster and the hill, with the new bike ruined there later, where was it?

What kind of a man ...?

A good man to love, and good in his loving. She felt a little worry, and conscience, over the lengths she had gone to, but it didn't last long, and it didn't matter .... Her man now? She wasn't always sure—Anna was so beautiful. Anna fit into the world of cars and racing. Anna was far away now, but did that mean Mart had forgotten her? Charlotte shook her head sadly and stopped thinking about Anna.

Still, what kind of a man?

He eats like any other man, has to shave in the morning, wants a woman like any other man, likes whiskey and martinis, a good western now and then at the movies, a certain song on the Hit Parade, but doesn't mind the classics; thinks Grace Kelly is too flat-chested, and he loves cars, lives with cars and for cars, dreams of cars and talks cars, designs, motors, performance figures. He races cars, wins races, and is going to make a profession of racing and winning races.

A man who likes to race cars. As simple as that?

No.

Why did a man have to go fast, and faster and never be satisfied with fast enough?

Why did he find satisfaction and yet not satisfaction enough in a car that would grip the road and whistle through a turn faster than any machine or man had a right to without skidding and crashing?

Why the loud whine of an engine...why compare it to music...what was wrong with the beautifully silent, muffled engines of the modern passenger car?

And why no mixing of marriage with driving? They were as much together as a married couple, and his wasn't the only dangerous profession, and there were other drivers who were married. What was it in driving that he saw and she didn't see, that wouldn't let them marry?

What was he actually looking for? Sometimes he seemed afraid—and yet he still looked for it.

They speak of the moment of truth in the bull rings of Spain. Maybe that was it. Maybe there was such a moment in a speeding car, a moment when all the forces working on car and driver converged to a point just blow disaster, a moment when Death brushed the sleeve and the driver could keep on driving—keep on and laugh and say, I know you are here, with me, somewhere here in the sound and the speed, in the wind that rushes over my face like fire...but it isn't time. You are not good enough to catch me yet.

What was he looking for?

CHAPTER SIX

THE walls of the inner office at Corsatti Fabbrica Automobili were bare. It has been said that once pictures adorned them, as in the outer office where the secretary worked. Pictures of the great road aces of the time lining the walls in a great cavalcade of fame, momentos of membership in the racing fraterinity, the specialized breed. That was twenty years ago, but for twenty years now, just the bareness, the nail holes.

There is one picture in the room and it stands in a simple frame, a round pewter frame maybe four inches high, on the desk. It is the likeness of a child of ten years, a boy named Carlo Corsatti. It has not moved in the twenty years since the boy, then twenty-three, died in Belgium in an inferno of oil and petrol and twisted metal a hundred or so yards away from a turn that hissed in the rain near Malmedy; and it is twenty years since Corsatti himself, in a tormented rage, whipped through the office and tore the pictures down and burned them right there. The dark spot, the slightly charred section of floor is still there, partly covered by the desk.

Corsatti sat behind the desk, his massive body slumped in the chair. Before him was the schematic of an engine, but his eyes were closed and the giant's face relaxed. He would have appeared to be asleep if the cigar in his hand had not been sending twisting ribbons of smoke toward the ceiling.

The intercom on the desk buzzed softly in the quiet room. He let it ring once more before he reluctantly reached out and touched the switch.

"Yes, Miss Baroni?"

"I am sorry to disturb you. There is a man here who wants to speak to you. His name is Martin Janis. Mario says Mister Janis has been told you are expecting him. Shall I send him in?"

"No. He is the new driver. You know the rule. Mario knows the rule. There is no reason to talk. Have Mario put him to work immediately. There has been no change in method around here. And since Mario seems to have forgotten, you may tell him that the young man will be completely in his charge as before. I do not want to be disturbed again today."

Corsatti flipped the switch and tried to feel the anger his voice had held. But there was no anger, just concern, worry of things to come, a fear. His eyes fell on the picture of his son.

It was not an easy thing, what he was doing.

To sit there, to not greet the newcomer, or associate with the men of the *scuderia,* or talk with them on the subject of the grand sport or any subject. It was hard to limit contact with these men to pure business and pure necessity.

But when you see your own boy find his ending, see him sitting there like a charred black statue while the flames lick around him, and know that you put him there and sent him off to drive your fast cars—that is something no man can forget.

It had to be this way. Stay away from them. Let them drive your cars, let them enter races—you have to do this, but keep all emotion away from the schematics and stay away from them and make the cars safe, and then safer still. That was his only life—to make them safer for the veterans, and for the new ones like his son had been, like Martin Janis was.

Corsatti sat there for a moment, smoking the cigar, wondering what the boy looked like.

His knowledge of Martin Janis existed solely in a collection of statistics. The fact that he was twenty-five, in assumed good health and had distinguished himself in a product of the Corsatti plant with an unusual number of wins.

It was true that the American sports car races were amateur and tamer than the European equivalent. And it was true that a good sports car driver did not necessarily become a good driver of Grand Prix racing machines.

But with so many wins, one becomes interested, and when interest exists and one is in need of new blood, one checks and double-checks. Observing, asking questions—all of this done by a competent person. In this case, Roberti.

And it was there. It was confirmed.

Martin Janis had good style. Good, clean style. No waste of effort and motion, every ounce of concentration and co-ordination and purpose focused to bring the car over a course in the least possible distance and time. And a will to win. That part bothered him a little. Roberti knew a good driver when he saw one. A will to win was necessary to driving a race, but that drivel Roberti had mouthed, the misdirected praise of Janis passing up a fellow driver rather than jeopardize his standing in a race—that was something not to be considered lightly. To be sure, he wanted a man to drive with the desire to win. It would be pointless any other way. But he did not want a man who would leave any of the other members of the team at the side of the road to die just for the sake of catching the checkered flag. That part bothered him about Janis.

But there were so many circumstances facing a driver, so many ways to hold the mirror—perhaps no time to stop, no room with the competition closely pressing unless an even worse accident is to be risked. Or perhaps the thing happened too fast. It is for the driver to judge what he can do with the world rushing past him at a hellish pace, not the man who watches, standing quietly and safely in the warm sun. Too many ways to hold the mirror. To judge him badly for a single act would be jumping to conclusions.

No, Martin Janis had a remarkable record, and a very good technique in driving the three-litre. He was worth inviting on the team, worth bringing all the way to Italy, worthy of a trial in a formula-one racing car so see if the skill continued to exist and grow.

Corsatti shifted uneasily in his chair. He thought for a minute, and then touched the intercom switch.

"Miss Baroni…"

"Yes, sir?"

"Oh, never mind. You can leave now if you wish."

"Thank you, sir."

He waited for a moment and then opened the door to the outer office. The girl had gone. He walked to the outer door and opened it a crack. He stood there quietly, watching Martin Janis and Mario going over an engine.

He was like Carlo.

He looked like Carlo, and probably talked like him. The face, the nationality, the difference in coloring and stature meant nothing. They were still alike.

Impatience written all over the boy's face. Impatience, a hunger in the set of the mouth, the eyes. The eyes of a driver, a race driver, are different somehow—different as the mariner's eyes after years at sea are different from the landsman who looks at the earth around his feet and within the span of his arms. And the angle of Martin Janis' head, the cut of his jaw—they too were different, as if speed and win shaped a man, or as if drivers were born, adapted to the business of speed before they left the darkness and warmth. It couldn't be pinned down to one dimension or one formula, or anything concrete.

Martin Janis looked like what he was.

And he reminded Corsatti of his son.

Corsatti closed the door and went back to his desk.

"All of them," he muttered. "All of them remind me of my son."

Remind him of Carlo—their fears, their trials, their pleasures and every way they moved. Like his son. They are all alike in most ways. Get to know them, love them, fear for them, share lives together on the grand tours of Europe; eat from the same table, send them on their way in search for women—in search of brief respite from the tension of the profession.

This was all done with. Finished.

No more. Only the requirements made by business and racing.

Martin Janis wouldn't understand. Mario would tell him about Carlo. And how long Corsatti had been in the business, and how impossible it was to leave to a less reminding life.

Martin Janis would merely grow used to the idea, become accustomed to the fanatic who insisted on such trivial things as knowing the engine before driving the car, and seeing races before driving in them, of working in the pits for the added experience and discipline. Youth seldom saw the value or had patience for such things.

Corsatti lit another cigar.

The more a man knew about his car—every inch of it—the better chance he had of getting through the seasons unscathed. The reading of the tachometer and oil pressure and the water temperature gauges and all that was not enough. To know the stresses and strains the car will take in every inch of her, what she will do and what she won't do, the little messages she cannot send to an instrument face or transmit to the seat of the pants—to know the whole thing before sitting in the car, to know a car as a doctor knows a patient of long standing, that is when you drive it better.

There had been those who complained. Most of them had complained about the learning of what seemed trivial. But make the cars well known by the drivers, and perhaps the drivers will grow older.

He had made the cars marvelously safe, and he devoted his waking hours to make them even safer.

But you cannot eliminate all the danger, so stay away from them. Conduct only affairs of business with them. Do not become attached.

Do not become friends or brothers; none of that.

It is bad enough when something goes wrong, when a car loses its grip on a turn and plunges to oblivion, when a tire goes at the wrong moment, or when a brake shoe grabs, or a piece of metal fails. You eliminate the faults as much as you can in the making of a car, and they are close to perfection now. The car exists. But the man driving them is far from perfect, no matter how many times he has won a race. The car exists, but the man does not.

Do not become friends and brothers.

It hurts and tears, rips the soul asunder, tortures you at night, because they remind you of the son you cherished. It is an unholy thing when they die.

Stay away from them.

CHAPTER SEVEN

MARTIN JANIS heard the voice of its product before he saw the dirty brick buildings of Corsatti Fabbrica Automobili, which was not far from the road leading from Turin. Before him was a road. At first glance it could have been any one of a number of roads winding through the hills of Northern Italy, the roads that did not fight and conquer the hills and mountains as they did at home, but curved with them and over them until the pavement became a tortuous thing. But beside this particular road was a sign that warned that it was out of the ordinary. Martin Janis could not read it, but with the name Corsatti mentioned twice, its meaning became obvious. But clearer than in any other way, the purpose of the road was revealed in the smell of burned castor hanging in the air. And the voice that came from the direction of the hills was not an ordinary voice.

Martin Janis listened in fascination. It rose and fell like the road and sounded like a number of things. Behind the hills, it sounded like an angry insect. When it came into the open, suddenly breaking from somewhere over there, it became a terrifying rotary saw about to break loose from its mountings and go slicing into the air. The voice became a scream. And at that moment, Mart saw it, the blood-red of its shining body—a red dot in the distance, growing fantastically, plummeting toward him, a crouching thing seemingly burning the air around it until it too glowed red—at that moment the voice became a bellowing and a sharp cascading of wave after wave of deep throated harmonics. The red was a blur in the sun now...and then suddenly it was gone, leaving the wind to slam against him in its wake.

He stood there for a moment, a trembling in his chest, a wondering and a longing, before he turned finally to walk toward the trees and the brick buildings behind them.

There were Corsattis inside, three-litre Gran Sports like the one he had driven in the States, and a few of the *monoposto* formula-one machines like he had just seen on the track, and a few he had never seen before—wicked, low-topped *due posti* sport coupés, a sleek four-passenger Gran Turismo—all in various stages of repair and disrepair or construction, and the whole setup was like no garage known to him before, no shop he had ever seen. The place was immaculate.

He wandered in, looking for the face and stature of a man who would be, unmistakably, Corsatti.

A short, heavy mechanic, with a face that seemed massive and undecided between happiness and a great sadness, straightened up over the polished workings of a three-litre and looked at him.

"Signor Janis?"

Mart nodded, and tried to think of something to say that would make himself understood.

"Do not be uncomfort. I speak your English. Excuse the oil." He extended a short, thick arm and grinned out at him from under an unholy wedding of car grease and gray, curly hair. "We just return from the Mille Miglia where our own Benito Taglio win in eleven hours twenty-seven and ten. Ah, the *tifosi*, they loved him! But now there is much work. ... I am Mario Felice. In the racing I am—crew—the..." He swept the grease-blackened hand in a manner with encompassed the cars and other mechanics.

"Crew chief and head mechanic?"

"Yes, those are the words. We talk a while, and I begin to remember words."

"I'm glad you know as much as you do. I was beginning to feel lost. Look, Mario, I'd better see Corsatti. Where can I find him?"

"Ah, you do not need words with Corsatti. We begin here."

"No, you don't understand. I'm supposed to see him—wait, I see his name on a door over there. Is that his office?"

"Yes." Mario Felice nodded with a shrug of his bullish shoulders.

"Fine. I'll see you later."

He walked over to the frosted glass door and stepped in. He entered a small office of paneled wood that led to another office beyond. There was a taint of cigar smoke in the air. The walls were lined with row upon row of framed photographs—cars with their drivers sitting in them, cars frozen in a slid through a turn, and cars grouped in combat on some deadly speedway.

At the desk, to one side of the other door, sat a dark-haired, proud-looking woman with cold eyes and a stiff but not necessarily cold mouth. Mart glanced over her handsome proportions and nodded.

"Hello. I would like to see Mr. Corsatti, please. He is expecting me."

"Corsatti?"

Mario stepped in and spoke rapidly to the girl in Italian.

"I help," he explained. "She not know the English."

The girl asked a couple of questions, her eyes studying Mart from hair to shoe leather. Mario answered and shrugged. She pressed a button and mentioned Mart's name. A deep, impatient voice fired back angrily and mentioned the name of Mario Felice. The girl shook her head and resumed her typing.

Mario took him by the arm and led him back into the shop.

"You see. We begin here. No words with Corsatti. That come later perhaps. Words with Mario. You understand?"

Mart looked back, irritated, at the frosted glass, and wondered what was going on.

"Not quite. A man in Italy hires a man living halfway around the world to come to Turin and drive his cars for him. When the man gets to Turin, he doesn't even see who hired him. I'm supposed to understand this. Is he a mystery or something?"

"I explain to you. With Corsatti, no talk until he ask to talk. I tell you why when there is time."

"I just start driving, eh?"

"No."

"No? What do you mean?"

"With Scuderia Corsatti, first comes motor." Mario spoke gropingly, and as he searched, the words began to come easier. "With Corsatti, we know motor before we drive. Know inside, outside, what every part do. Start at beginning. It is habit of Corsatti."

"I know how engines work."

"You know Corsatti motor?"

"I drove the three-litre in the States, didn't I?" He avoided mentioning the fact that the old man Barkdale had always seen to the condition of the engine. He never had to touch it—but certainly he knew what made it tick.

"Ah! You take it apart, into pieces?"

"Well, no ... but—"

"Signor Janis, you know this engine?" Mario pointed to a gleaming eight-cylinder job mounted on a test bench.

"No. Of course not."

"Two-point-five litre for the formula-one racing. You must know. With Corsatti, we know the—"

"Yeah, I know. We know the motor backwards and forwards before we drive. Okay. How long does this take?"

"Two weeks, perhaps. That depend."

"How fast I learn, huh?"

"Yes."

Mart glanced around at the shop, feeling disappointment. He hadn't expected to step into a car the first day, but—

"Two weeks is a long time."

Mario smiled unhappily at him.

"I know—the impatience. Always with the young, the impatience. But Corsatti knows. He believe to drive right, must know first what makes car go, what suspension, how it work. Also he say to us if the motor die in some race, like Mille Miglia, and your mechanic is sick or hurt, can you fix or do you drop from race—is important. For certain, most of time it is for us in the pit. It is not often you have to fix yourself, and sometimes you cannot. The trouble is—is—too deep in motor. But that is luck, Signor Janis. It is still important you know these things."

Mart turned and stared at the door with Corsatti's name written on it. What kind of man was he? What was this fanatical devotion to details that seemed to be presenting itself the first thing, in the first minutes—to put to work immediately and without question a man he did not care to see and greet, to sit in his office without curiosity about the man he would soon entrust with several thousand dollars' worth of racing machine. He shook his head, wondering, and then turned to Mario. He grinned and slapped the mechanic on the shoulder.

"Okay, Mario. I got a girl waiting for me back at the Parigi Hotel. You want me here first thing in the morning?"

Mario shook his head.

"We begin now."

"But—" Mart looked at the clock. It was almost four.

"Time has no importance to Corsatti. Only work."

"Okay, we begin now," Mart sighed. "Where do I start?"

"Wait." Mario turned and shouted to one of the mechanics. The man nodded and reached into a locker and pulled out a pair of coveralls.

Janis peeled out of his coat and pants and slipped them on.

Mario led him to the test bench. This one held the three-litre Gran Sport power plant.

"We begin. I touch, and give Italian name, and you remember. You give English so I remember. Make easier later. See?"

"Let's go."

"Yes. *Il carburatore.*"

"Carburetor," Mart responded.

"*Magnete.*"

"Magneto."

"*Candela.*"

"Sparkplug."

Sparkplug, camshaft housing, fuel pumps. It went on, Mario checking and remembering, the words coming back, and Martin becoming familiar with the Italian equivalents. The external parts of the motor, the suspension, and then Mario straightened and touched another with his foot.

"*Lo scappamento?*"

"Exhaust."

Mario nodded and they went to a dismantled three-litre motor and went through the process again. Then for a second time, a third and finally a fourth. They went over the engine completely until Mario was satisfied. It was nine o'clock when he crawled out from under the Gran Sport, going over the clutch assembly.

"We do fine now. Tomorrow we work. You go to your woman now."

"All right. Brother! I'd forgotten how many parts went into one of these babies. How do I get back to town at this hour?"

"Oh, *scusa!*" Mario dug some keys out of his pocket and pointed to a three-litre standing near the entrance. "Yours to use."

"Compliments of The Corsatti again, eh? Say, Mario every minute your English is getting better. Where did you learn?"

"I have a brother in your country. He's the butcher, in Brooklyn. I live there a while and learn. A little time to remember and I will find all the words. Soon I speak as good as you. With you I practice, and soon we talk like brothers."

"What did you do over there? You were born here, weren't you?"

"Not far from Mantua. I went as mechanic to races. Long Island—1936. The Vanderbilt Cup Races. I like what I see, and stay with my brother Guido. But soon, I become sick for Italy, and for this." He pointed to the cars.

"1936 Vanderbilt—now wait—by any chance were you mechanic for—" This simple little man of Italy with the graying hair and great patience, with quietness of word and kindness who was born near Mantua—a sweet chill swept over Mart and for a moment he felt as if he should be on his knees to make this man and this little factory a shrine of a kind.

Mario knew what he meant and nodded.

"Yes. But you go to your woman now. We talk of this some other time."

Mart took the Corsatti and drove it up to the road and headed for Turin. He felt strange inside, and it was only by luck that he turned off Via Pacchiotti at the right corner and found Via Venalzio and the Parigi Hotel. There was a strangeness, a lightness and reverence inside him—a feeling of having for an instant brushed very close to something big, a presence of something terribly great. Mario had worked for Nuvolari, the immortal, Il Maestro . . . .

Mart went up the stairs from the lobby to the room he and Charlotte had taken and sat down on the bed. Charlotte emerged from the bathroom, broom in hand.

"How did it go? You were gone a long time."

"All right, I guess. I didn't see Corsatti. They put me to work learning the engines, inside and out. I'll be at it for a couple of weeks before I even begin to think about driving."

"That's not so bad," she said with obvious relief. "At least they aren't rushing you into anything."

"The head mechanic speaks good English. Turns out he worked in Nuvolari's pit when Nuvolari went to Long Island."

"Nuvolari?"

"I've mentioned him to you—the greatest driver of all time. He—I'll let Mario tell you about it sometime. Right now, I'm tired. Didn't realize it until I sat down."

"Coffee? I made some to wake me up. Fell asleep after you left."

"No." He settled back. "What's the music?"

Charlotte laughed and shook her head.

"I see it's started again. That's been going on ever since you left. Same record. I think it's an old lady. She evidently has just that one record and an old phonograph. She keeps it going like it was a fixation—I don't know. Maybe she's just lonely and has nothing else to break the silence."

"*Death and Transfiguration,*" Mart murmured sleepily.

"What?"

"*Death and Transfiguration.* Strauss. Barkdale had it in his collection. I used to listen to his records by the hour, waiting for his mechanics to finish on the car. Only thing to kill the time. I don't know why I remembered it. He had hundreds."

He stood up and peeled off his shirt.

"Shower work?"

"It works, but don't let the plumbing scare you. Rattles like a truck of garbage cans." She shrugged. "Never heard such strange noises. That funny little phonograph, things peeping and bumping in the alley below the window, the pipes, and voices down the hall that seemed miles away, and some woman upstairs—well, the bed squeaked. Weird! But I guess we can get used to it."

"When I start getting paid, we can do better."

He went into the bathroom and stepped under the spray and drew the curtain.

He stood there letting the water pour over him. In a moment, the curtain drew back and she stepped in with him.

"Soap my back?" she asked. "That's something in the way of luxury I miss when you aren't around."

"Sure." He turned her around and ran the soap over her tawny skin. "Makes you purr like a kitten. Sometimes I think you're half cat." He put the soap down and held her quietly.

"Happy?" she whispered.

"Real."

"You sounded like the small boy who shook hands with the president when you talked about Mario working for that race driver."

"Well, it felt strange, knowing—you know, when a sports figure steps down, like Babe Ruth or Bobby Jones, any of them, there are the others to step in and take their places, and when you get right down to it, they're just as good. Hell, look at Dimaggio. But no one ever stepped in to take Nuvolari's place. No one could and no one ever will. He was kind of a god when he lived, and still is to those who remember."

"I suppose he was someone that everybody else tries to imitate."

"Maybe they try, but it doesn't work. Nobody knows exactly how he drove. It was something in him, rather than something in a book. They say he had a pact with the devil. Well, maybe he did. He had a technique that defied all the laws of physics, and he beat his cars until they disintegrated beneath him—cursing, yelling, driving to win, going until he was ready to drop and they had to pry his fingers from the wheel and lift him bleeding from the car."

"Bleeding?"

"Yes. That was the strange part of it. He was a man who lived for nothing but driving, knowing nothing else, so fanatical about driving and winning—any kind of a race—hell, he was a poor loser. Don't go making up pretty pictures about him—an ugly little man who never lost one gracefully with a smile and hope for next time. He *had* to win. Anyway, it's impossible to keep those fumes from the motor out of your lungs. Most people aren't bothered by it. But his lungs always hemorrhaged."

"He didn't quit?"

"Well, eventually he had to. There was no other choice. He drove until he couldn't make his body work anymore. He died in bed one day, just a couple of years ago. They buried him in his coveralls with his helmet and steering wheel. Something like a Viking funeral. As if there might be cars to drive and race where he went."

"I wonder about a man like that sometimes. They puzzle me."

Mart Janis held her in his arms and listened to the water whispering over them. What made them tick? What kind of man?

That question again. Where did it begin?

"Marti" she screamed at him. The hot water!"

They scrambled out of the sudden icy spray in a stumbling rush and stood dripping on the bathroom floor. He reached in and turned it off, laughing at her shivering, shocked nakedness.

He handed her a towel and began drying himself.

"I think I'm going to do all right, Charlotte."

"It's good to be confident. I'm glad you have someone like Mario."

"He'll be a lot of help. Probably more than anyone else around there. And I forgot to mention something else."

"What, hon?"

"I saw one of them today. One of the Grand Prix machines. It was out on the track. I guess that's where I'll get my practice. It was going like hell. You could hear it for miles, and when you saw it, you weren't really seeing it because it was going too fast and was gone. Like a woman screaming—that's the way it sometimes sounded—or a big buzz saw, or sometimes like one steady note of music. It's a beautiful thing, Charlotte—a real wicked litle beauty!"

Charlotte dropped her towel and stared at him for a moment. She shivered and it wasn't from the cold water.

CHAPTER EIGHT

TIME moved swiftly at first. Martin Janis learned his motors. He learned them inside out, backwards and forwards, according to the wishes of a man with whom he had yet to speak. He learned how they operated, and how to repair them. But time then began to drag slowly and painfully. Damn, he could have repaired them blindfolded and up to his neck in ditch water, and he kept looking to Mario Felice for the word that this part of his training might be over.

The original two weeks were over. Two weeks, and then another two, and still no signal from behind the frosted glass door, and nothing but a smile and a suggestion of patience from Mario. Always patience, and the motors, over and over again, until he saw each individual valve clicking open and shut in his sleep.

"Soon," Mario would say. "Soon, we drive."

And one did not get close to Corsatti. The shadow behind the wall, a voice in the distance, a presence activated and deactivated in a small box operated by the cold-eyed Miss Baroni…. A faint remnant of cigar smoke, or perhaps an overcoated figure sitting in the distance on the hill overlooking the test track…. A glint of light from the lens of binoculars.

Sometimes he wondered if Corsatti had forgotten that a Martin Janis existed.

Sometimes he felt that he was being deliberately shunned, a grease monkey dancing on the end of an unseen string, and he tossed at night, planning on how he would break past that

Signorina Baroni in the outer office and step into those holy confines and shout into Corsatti's god's eyes, *drive or nothing!*

Sometimes, when he had finished with the engines for a while, he would wander down to the track and watch the team drivers working out. Taglio, Brocco, Brusetti.

Benito Taglio, the number one driver. The small, brilliant, arrogant little old man of thirty-seven who drove not by the book but by his own sweeping, flourishing, dancing style that seemed more of a violent courtship of car and road than a racing stance. But this ugly little hawkfaced man was used to winning races, until Mercedes brought out new models and found supremacy. He had become bitter, and it touched everything he did.

Achille Brocco, the fat, bespectacled steady—the cold, good position holder, the precision driver who placed his wheels on the same black streak of rubber every time. He spoke to few. A book and quiet music rather than boisterous celebration or drinking away the tension after the races as the others did. The quiet one, always in the background.

Valerio Brusetti, the thin, hollow-eyed boy. The weeper, the crying shouter of insults and imprecation, the good driver who rode with a scream behind his teeth. The neurotic, the worrier and the drunk after the driving was over; the man who was forever afraid of what he was doing, but stubbornly fighting it and the good sense that told him to quit.

This was the team, the drivers for Corsatti. A small team. Martin Janis would watch them at practice, waiting for the day when he could join them, smarting under the cordial but condescending way they greeted him. Obviously he was not one of them, not proven yet, this American, this clumsy child who had been forced upon their Olympian heights.

And sometimes he sat up at night, while Charlotte slept, and stared out the window down at the alley and thought of going home, back to driving Ramsey Barkdale's car. Back to the things he knew at Pebble Beach and Torrey Pines, and Reno; and the people he knew, people he could speak to on even terms without running into a cold, solid barrier of language. Oh, most of them at the plant could speak enough English to get by in a simple conversation. But there were things, so many things he could not get across. They thought differently, these people. Where was the American's patience? To work for Corsatti is an honor, no matter what kind of work, a privilege to help keep the shop immaculate, to wipe up the grease that falls on the floor. All drivers have started this way. Patience, friend. Patience . . . .

At the end of the first week in June, Scuderia Corsatti was in France for the Grand Prix D'Endurance de Vingt-Quatre Heures at Le Mans.

On the evening of June 11, Martin Janis sat in the Corsatti pits with Charlotte and watched the cars charging past. The twenty-four hour race was only a few hours old—a short time since the drivers began the race at four P.M., with the unique starting of lining up on one side of the pavement and running across to their cars and entering the dreadful scramble of machines that follows. The Germans were not so fast in their running, but they did not have to be. Once their cars were in motion, they quickly took command. Schiller and Hoff were ahead first and second for Mercedes. Hunsley and Morris held third and sixth with the XKD Jaguars. Benito Taglio's Corsatti Gran Sport held fourth against a hotly pursuing Ferrari. Achille Brocco was seventh, and Brusetti followed at his heels. And then the field of Ferraris, OSCAs, Cunninghams, Alfa Romeos, Hammonds, Frazer-Nashes, Austin-Healeys and the rest.

And standing over near the pumps, a figure of gloom in the darkness of coming rain, Corsatti, quietly and silently shredding his temper to bits. The race was young yet, young and subject to all the whims of chance that could come in the twenty-five hundred miles or so that would be covered. But the Germans had been having it too good with the new Mercedes too often and too long—the methodical Germans, the outfit that sent more than twenty-five men to the Mille Miglia to aid their drivers with every kind of convenience and facility, the thoroughness that resulted in their driving forty-five thousand miles in practice before the thousand-mile race began. Taglio had won the last one, but it had been another of those whims of chance that brought him into Brescia ahead of the white cars.

Mart Janis sat there staring at the back of Corsatti's head, growing angry and beginning to fidget, no longer engrossed in seeing the Le Mans race for the first time.

"I can't go this route any longer," he told Charlotte. "I'm going to put the word to him now. I'm ready to start driving his cars and he goddamn well knows it. If he wants a glorified mechanic, he can get someone else."

"Mart! Remember what Mario said. He said part of your learning is to watch a few races, just like working with the motors was."

"To hell with what Mario said. He's holding back too. Look out there! Those are sports cars. The team is driving the same car I drove for Barkdale. Maybe I don't expect to start driving in a Grand Prix racer right off, but damn it, this is something I know about. I could be on Taglio's tail, or even past him at the rate he's gone so far. I'm good enough for that, and they know it, but did I get invited out to practice? No! Well, either I get started driving for this outfit, or we put an end to it here and now."

He slid off his perch and walked over to where Corsatti stood. The man ignored him and continued to stare blankly at the cars whipping past and at the first curtain of rain beginning to fall.

"Mr. Corsatti."

Corsatti swung around and looked at him. The huge face towering over him with its massive jaw and long thin nose, the eyes that burned through him without seeing.

"Listen, this little game has gone on long enough. I know you're busy with a race, but if we don't settle this now—I'm ready to drive, and you know it. I've been working on your damn motors long enough. I'm a driver, not a mechanic."

"Mario!" Corsatti bellowed.

Mario hustled over and took Mart by the arm.

"Come, Martin. We talk of this later."

"No, damn it! Take your hands off!"

"Are you crazy?"

"Sure, just crazy enough to be fed up with the whole damn works!" He swung at Mario and flattened the old mechanic on the wet pavement. He brushed past the other mechanics, past Charlotte, and ran away from the race area until he found a ride into the town of Le Mans.

He stumbled into some underground place, not knowing where he was in the dark and raining streets, just some bistro on a side street, and not caring. He slumped at a table and ordered a bottle. He began to drink and watch the clock go around.

Twenty-four hours the races lasted. They wouldn't be finished until the next afternoon. Well, let them go. Let Mercedes get the checkered flag. Let Corsatti stand there and eat himself out inside. He didn't care, not about any of them.

These were sports cars, not Grand Prix racers. Sports cars running at Le Mans. He and Charlotte and Mario had gone out and looked at the course before it was opened to practice. There it was, the thing he had followed in magazines, the familiar names and turns. He knew them—almost as if he had driven there— Pontlieu and Mulsanne, d'Arnage, Maison Blanche, Tertre Rouge, the famous Dunlop tire with the track sweeping under it, six grandstands ... Hell, what was the use? Sports cars. The one thing he knew and he was sitting it out. Anna could have made it different for him. If he had stayed with Anna, he would've been driving at Le Mans. Maybe not this year, but certainly the next. Sure, she would've made it different, but she was gone. She was gone, so to hell with sports cars and racing machines. Up their noses with the whole works!

The last month echoed at him. Where does it start? What kind of man? Damn silly questions! Just the kind of question a woman would think up. Charlotte Greyne—that kid he'd left standing at the track. She had a frame on her. A real frame that got all over him when he looked at it, but still a kid with questions.

Who cares about where it starts, and who cares about what kind of man? A crazy kind of man. A crazy kind who goes shooting around in back of a roaring engine, trying to kill himself just to go faster, to turn faster, to win, to have some silly fool jump out at him in the final straight and wave a checkered flag in his face and say he's a hero.

They're crazy. Short life if they're good, dead quick if they aren't, and scared all the time. Scared of headaches, scared when there hasn't been enough sleep, scared when they sit down in their cars when someone unwittingly wishes them good luck, scared of not winning, and scared of the things they had to do to win. And yet not knowing anything else, not wanting anything else. What kind of a life was that!

Well, there wasn't going to be any of that.

No more cars for him. No more racing.

Back to the States for him. The States and a quiet return to some simple job. Maybe back to the box factory, the simplicity of a box factory. That's what Felice Bonetto should have done, gone back to whatever he was before he drove, but he didn't go back and look what happened there in the Mexican Road Race. The skid at a hundred and fifty, the pole at the edge of the street.

And that German, von Delius—he should've had a box factory. That camelback bridge on the Nurburgring that left the cars airborne—that's what got him. Von Delius coming down to touch the rear of the car in front of him, and turning end over end, and not stopping until he was a quarter of a mile off the track and dead.... And you, Nuvolari. Even you were crazy. Driving until you were near dead, bleeding your lungs out until they were rotten and you had to stay in bed until you died there, hungering for the sounds, the speed and the smell of castor oil hanging blue in the air.

What kind of life was that? What was there to driving fast, with an engine roaring in your ears?

Martin Janis slumped over his table, the dream world around him spinning and weaving like a green, underwater scene ... voices coming to speak to him about what kind of man and where did it begin, and aren't you afraid, and have patience, and why don't you go back to your little hill in California? ...

The hill wouldn't be as high now, and the ride never again as fast, gone now like the winds that touched its grassy slopes. And the farm, perhaps gray-wooded with age and deserted with blowing dust and shriveling orchards, perhaps gone too. Elizabeth Janis was dead of a thing that had eaten within, for five years—or was it six? And of Adam there was no guessing where wandering had taken him after the drinking began. He could have been anywhere or dead too, and the memory was all that was left of anything.

Or maybe some other family lived there to pick the apples and the blue prunes on the ground, and maybe some kid and his brother were riding down the hill on boards with wheels from their own baby carriage, or trying it on shining new bicycles.

Like he had done with his own bicycle.

Yeah, that bicycle. It was a crazy thing to do. He remembered he was given the bicycle as a gift, and also because the war with Japan was on, and his father couldn't get enough gas for the truck to haul him back and forth from school every day.

It was not an ordinary bike, not the kind a boy took and discarded the fenders and fitted with a foxtail and balloon tires. Nor was it the kind loaded down with headlights and tool kits and speedometers. It was one of the light, thin-tired English racing bikes with the handlebar brakes and everything reduced down to the barest essentials.

It was another part of a strange relationship.

Martin Janis and his dad were not close. It was a silent thing. Adam never felt right about Tommy's death and the circumstances that brought it about. They never talked or played or went adventuring like they used to. They merely existed in the same house. And yet it could not be said that Adam did not love his son. The love was buried beneath doubts and pride, and embarrassment and shame and a little bit of anger that flared unseen now and then. Perhaps the bike was the man trying again while he didn't understand, trying to be close again; his way of trying. Purchases for Mart did not come often, but sometimes they were a little better than they had to be.

But that bike! The first time he rode it he felt the wind on his face, and the cooling of the late afternoon in the shade of the trees over the road, and the last of the sun was a brilliance that seemed part of speed and motion and the exhilaration he felt.

The long, gleaming spokes flashed and hummed, and the deep red paint became a bit of fire in the afternoon. He bent low over the handlebars and pumped harder and faster, making the wind and speed a thing to taste in his teeth, and when the road dipped downhill for a long way, he let it coast, swooping free, and shooting up the next rise, pumping hard against the lightness of the bike. When darkness came, he was far away without realizing it.

He hadn't been satisfied to leave it at that.

He couldn't sleep that night. He watched the shaft of moonlight creep across the floor, and listened to the crickets outside. He could remember not being able to take his mind off the red bike and where it sat in the barn, in the warm musty darkness where dew couldn't settle on it.

No, he was never satisfied. He got dressed and went outside. The night was warm and clear, with a faint touch of haze to soften the moon. His eyes touched the hill. It stood tall and round, touched with night silver, seeming to breathe with the swaying of its grass in a gentle wind. He stared, as if transfixed, remembering the roller-coastering ride down its slope on the wheels of a buggy—little wheels, and two boards, a rope to steer. He felt a sickness, remembering then, but still the thing was nagging at him.

It took only a few minutes to push it up there, and it seemed all right. The bike had brakes, which was more than the coaster had. And he could steer better, and there was a seat with springs to soften the ride, and the grass wouldn't be whipping at his eyes. Not like the coaster—faster maybe, but at the same time safer.

Like a bat out of hell, that's the way it was coming down. Brakes useless on that grass, coming down, and the wheels collapsing in the field at the bottom and the dogs milling around, yawping and howling in excitement over the apparition that had come skating down in the moonlight. And his father, aroused by the noise, coming running across the field and catching him there, bawling the bejesus out of him and asking him if he had forgotten Tommy and what happened on that goddamned hill.

Yeah, that hill. Like any hill, there might be kids coming down its slopes on coasters or brand new bicycles, and whatever else they could find. If there were kids there, it almost had to be that way—that, and perhaps a Gus Brodie to learn from. Maybe not, though. Gus Brodies, the old back-alley mechanics, were getting scarce.

But if nothing else, there would be a hill and wheels to shine in the sun of a good day. And it wouldn't stop there. That would be the danger. They were fools if they kept going, if they didn't stop and stay satisfied with that little hill. That little hill! It had been a killer too....

Mart staggered out of there, up the stairs and into the rain, away from the checkered tablecloths and the guttering candles and their waxen bottles making castles with the light. He wandered a while and then sat down on a step, feeling the rain no longer, and fell asleep. Home tomorrow! Tomorrow we go home....

"It's him!" a voice cried out, and it was terribly cold. A rough hand shook him in the darkness.

"Lemme alone," he moaned and tried to find the numbness of sleep again, to get away from the cold that was reaching his bones.

"Mart! Please. Come out of it. Oh, Mario ..."

"The French drink! You see what it does to a man." The man who so often swore by the deep red of his native wine sounded as if he were thundering to every cloud in the cold rain of France. Red wine could never make a man this unhappy.

"Wake up, Martin." The big hand slapped across his face several times. "You wish you were dead. You stay here longer and you will be dead. Up! Up on your feet!"

"Okay ... okay." Mart sat up and blinked his eyes at the rain. Charlotte stood over him. Charlotte and Mario danced in a double image.

"Well, look at you." He blinked his eyes at Charlotte. "You got four of 'em now. That oughta be real interesting."

Mario put his heavy shoulders against Mart's weight and the two of them helped him to a Citroen parked at the curb.

"Poor Mario," he said between his chattering teeth. "Poor Mario, you've come down in the world. Riding in sedans. Fixed head sedans. Now ain't that too damn bad!"

"Shut up, my friend. We get you to your hotel and a hot bath."

"Why bother, why do you care after I plastered your kisser for you, Mario? Who cares? I got my walking papers, didn't I? What's all this Citroen business?"

"Shut up and get in the car before I plaster your kissing—what did he say, Charlotte? Ah, forget it! You watch while I drive."

Mart rested gratefully in the soft upholstery and drank in great gulps of the warm air flowing up from the car's heater.

"You might've caught pneumonia," Charlotte scolded him.

"Well, don't give up hope. I may yet."

"What did you want to go do all those things for anyway?"

"You know as well as I do. I'm no longer working for the great Corsatti now. The Corsatti has given me the knife. We are going home and work in a box factory, you and I. Mario, why don't you try a four-wheel drift around that next corner?"

"But you haven't been fired," she informed him.

Mart opened his eyes and rubbed his jaw and laughed.

"I haven't? Well, The Corsatti just hasn't had time to get around to it yet. He will by the time the race is over."

The Citroen stopped in front of their hotel.

"Besides, I've already settled the question. I don't want to go back. I don't want to be a grease monkey hopping on the end of a string. I don't even give a goddamn about driving. What do you think of that? Why did you stop, Mario? Keep going. This is my last ride in a foreign car. I want to enjoy my last ride. Say, Mario, what's the Citroen business all about?"

"You are home, my friend. Charlotte, you run up and turn on the hot water while I carry this son of a goat upstairs."

"Didn't you hear me?" He lurched out onto the sidewalk and took a swing at Mario. Mario ducked it and caught Martin in the stomach with his shoulder and lifted him. He carried him that way into the hotel and up the stairs and into the room.

Mario dumped him, clothes and all, into the tub.

"I see you in the morning or maybe after the race. I get back to the pit. I should not have trusted my men to be alone this long."

"Give those Kraut drivers hell, Mario!" Martin laughed until his head hurt, then he stared morbidly through the rising steam at the wall. "Like I said, kiddo, tomorrow we go home!"

Charlotte ignored him, and brought him a glass of hot tea.

"Drink it."

She turned on the hot water and allowed it to run into the tub until he felt as if his skin would shred off. He yelled at her.

"It won't hurt you. Stand up and give me those clothes."

"Say, getting pretty bossy aren't you?"

"Give me those clothes and stop talking so much. I don't want to hear another word about going home. You make me mad."

"What are you complaining about?"

"Me? Complain? That's an odd one, isn't it! When have you heard me complain? All these weeks sitting in a little hotel room or wandering around with nothing to do, lonely because you've got long hours, wondering how many more dirty little hotels there will be. Maybe I should have complained. Maybe I should have asked for a small consideration here and there. I've even kept myself from asking a real old question because it sounds too much like a cliché and because I hope that once you get started driving maybe you'll get around to it."

"Get around to what?"

"To tell me we'll get married one of these days."

"I suppose you're going to run crying from the room about what a beast I've been. Reducing you to shame, and what are all these people going to say? Oh, my! Never seen the gal that didn't arrive at that stage sooner or later!"

She looked at him and shook her head.

"I'm getting pretty used to the whole business. It doesn't bother me as much as it did, and I'm not going to cry. I've been happy with you, and it won't be any different if you don't want a wedding. I'd like one, and maybe I could stop wondering about Anna then—what she meant to you after all this time. I'd like one, yes, but I wouldn't leave you because of the lack of one. All I want you to do is not go fuming and fussing all over the place and hitting your friends. You're going to drive us both crazy if you keep it up. Now, please, give me those clothes and get back down into the water."

"It's too damn hot," he said quietly, and began to remove his clothes.

"No, it isn't. You've got to stay in there until we drive the chill out."

He sank back into the hot water and soaked for a long time, until he began to grow sleepy and all the aches and pains and chill had finally vanished. In a little while, Charlotte came with a big towel and helped him out.

"Dry off quick and jump into bed. I've got it warmed with a hot water bottle."

He did so, without protest, and got into bed. He watched her with half-closed eyes.

"You're a pretty good kid. Sometimes I wonder where you get the patience to stick with me."

"All right, now that you're away from slippery tubs and such, I'll tell you something."

"You're pregnant! I can tell by that cow's expression in your eyes. I knew it would happen sooner or later."

"No, that isn't the case. Damn it, now listen. What would you say if I told you that as soon as we get back to Turin your driving practice begins?"

"I wouldn't believe you."

"It's true."

His eyes opened wide and he sat up in bed.

"What?"

"Mario told me after you ran off tonight."

"My words with the boss paid off, eh? Well, what do you know?"

"Nothing to do with it. The decision was made a week ago, when we were still on our way here."

"Why didn't they tell me?"

"I don't know. Maybe they were too busy getting ready for this race. How would I know about it? All I know is what Mario told me, and that he was just told himself tonight. Now go to sleep and keep covered up."

CHAPTER NINE

T HE first day of practice for Martin Janis dawned bright and clear and still, with a touch of coolness to the air. It was the kind of day when everything for driving seemed perfect. Visibility had that fine, faraway razor's edge. It was cool enough to take some of the bite out of the engine heat that forever plagues a driver in the cockpit of a Grand Prix machine. And the stillness, the very content of the air, seemed to hold the right ingredient, the proper balance of moisture to bring that extra degree of crispness to the engine and a little more speed.

Mart had felt it when he woke just before light and slid out of bed and poked his head out the hotel window. Yes, even in that dark gray alley, he could feel the rightness of the morning. Without waking Charlotte, he dressed quickly and swallowed a quick cup of coffee, and slipped out into the hall. He ran down the hall, down the stairs and into the street to the car.

He had seen those days before, on the California coast, when it was a pleasure to drive anything. He grinned with the thought and the anticipation. Today, he wasn't driving just anything. Today, it was a car smaller in dimension than anything else he had ever driven, a car all business, all engine and very little else.

He remembered the first time he broke a hundred, an honest, magic hundred, in a little modified MG. The exhilaration and the thrill, the moment never to be forgotten. And later, the wild but respectful journey into the realm of a hundred and forty, and the fantastic world of meteoric landscapes. The tightness it brought to the throat as the wind slammed across his face like a warning, as if it were a twilight world to be entered only briefly, a dark place where man played and was not meant to play, where something could reach out and touch with a cold sting. He was aware of that chill and yet the dark realm again and again, as if he had to. The thought was sobering. Now the little devil he would drive today....

A racer, but not the same as the racers seen on the ovals in the States. He had known the difference before coming to Italy. The sports car magazines were full of statistics and figures and photos. One could know from reading that the Corsatti, for example, and all the other European racing machines were different from the Indianapolis type. The Indianapolis car was at best an oval racer, and as such, would never make out on a tight-turning road course against the European's superior cornering and acceleration. It was simply not made for it.

The European racer was made for average roads. Hairpins in any direction, up and down hill, for long straights and the extreme braking needed at the end. It was everything. The wonderful machine. He knew it before coming to Italy, and he knew every nut and bolt on them now. But it was facing him now. The actual driving.

In a lot of ways it would be no different from the three-litre Gran Sport. The basic principles of driving were the same. But it touched close to a hundred and ninety miles an hour. There would be times when he would use that speed. And there was, among other things, the matter of learning to go through a turn at a hundred and fifty.

Mart pulled in beside the shop and turned off the motor. He got out and stood smoking a cigarette, savoring the beginning of this day and the time for which he had been waiting so long.

"You are early, my friend. Impatient, eh?"

Mart swung around and found Mario opening the door to the shop.

"Yeah, I'm impatient. Who wouldn't be? How soon do I start?"

"As soon as we can fuel and push her to the track. How long have you been here? All night?"

"Just a few minutes," he grinned, and saw the other mechanics coming to work. "Woke up early. There wasn't much point in sitting around at the hotel staring at the wall and biting my nails. I thought I might as well come on down and wait here."

"Always the impatience." Mario punched Mart in the shoulder and laughed. "Well, be patient just a moment more."

Mario pushed one of the cars out to the fuel pumps after throwing some coveralls on the seat.

"I prepare this one myself. I work into the night to be certain that when it talk to Martin Janis it talk like a woman."

"Yeah? What did you do, put a governor on it?"

"Ha! I speak of Italian women, my friend." He turned and shouted into the shop. "Maglio! *Ho bisogno di benzina!*"

An answering shout came back.

"Maglio will fill the tank. Listen to me, Martin. No speed today. Slow. Get the touch, eh? Get the touch first."

"Not even on the straight?"

"Not even on the straight. Martin, slow, like a woman— you do not say *scusa*, signorina, and knock her down on the floor. No. You love a little first. So! With the car it is the same. *Capisce?*"

"Okay, Mario. I'll take it easy. Where are the others?"

"What others?"

"Corsatti, Taglio, Brocco, Brusetti. I thought they'd be down here giving me pointers. They're the experts. And Corsatti, it's his investment, trusting me with this car. I thought he'd be down here sweating like an old lady."

"Most of it you will learn yourself, my friend. That is why we do it slow. You have the experience from the three-litre to build on. It is not so different. Just the speed, and the touch on the wheel, and the way it sits on the road. We used to have the leading driver get the new ones started—Bruno when he was alive. But now it is Taglio, and Taglio has been champion, but he is not a good teacher. And Brocco and Brusetti—for that matter, all of them, there is the language, my friend."

"Corsatti speaks English," Mart reminded him.

"Corsatti has given me the job of teaching you."

"That makes you a pretty big man around here."

"I have my importance now and then," Mario laughed. "But you will discover that mostly it is up to you. You learn the feel of the car, drive it for each day like this woman we speak of, and we talk, and soon you see how to do this and how to do that. You will see that it is the machine that does the real teaching."

They rolled the car out on the track, and Mario started the motor with the electric starter before climbing up to sit on the fence. Mart tightened the helmet and lowered his goggles. He tested his safety belt and looked out over the long, narrow, torpedo-like hood, listening to the eight cylinders drumming at the quiet morning air.

He touched the accelerator, and his heart stopped as the car charged forward with the velocity of an express train, yawing from side to side from wheel spin, as if the surface of the track shone with glare ice. He clutched the wheel and backed off the gas a little, straightening out awkwardly and moving briskly down the road. He grinned weakly and raised his arm in a wave to let Mario know it was all right. Mart sat tensely, like a woman taking her first driving lesson.

The first two lessons to learn had already presented themselves. Easy ones to overcome, but something new just the same. That accelerator was too touchy to play with, with the weight of one's foot. Gentleness or there was wheelspin at almost any speed. And second, that steering ratio was direct enough that only the slightest of movements brought an immediate and definite response. Too much brought oversteer.

"Cut it out," he muttered to himself. "Relax. Just relax. A nice drive in the morning sun. Sunday stuff, remember—that's it."

Gently he took the car around the track, easing into the turns and out, learning the sensitive steering and the throttle under his toe, making himself familiar with the short throw of the shift lever. The engine bellowed crisply and surely, waiting for any demand he might make, sounding like all the music he had ever heard.

The sound seemed to take on a new note, and the new note came too rapidly and too loudly, and before he could realize what was happening, another car shot past him at high speed. He flinched at the howling image, startled at the unexpected company, and almost left the road. He hadn't seen who it was.

Mart settled down and regained his pace. He made another lap and watched for the other car to catch up with him again. Now that he knew the other was there, it was all right, but he marveled at the speed with which the other had passed him.

The other car caught him again, farther down the track than before. Mart watched him coming in the rearview mirror, coming like a red blur. He moved to the side of the road to allow him plenty of room. There was the blurring image and then the sound coming in sharp, high-pitched waves. The car came closer and Mart crowded the shoulder of the road.

"Damn it! Get over! Can't you see?"

He tried to wave the other off, but it kept coming and Mart swerved to avoid him just as the car passed with only inches between their wheels. Mart felt the wheels grab the shoulder and the car lurched and fishtailed for fifty yards, drifted broadside down the road, turned around completely and nosed up over a low embankment on the other side.

Mart took a shaking breath and turned off the ignition. He removed the steering wheel and got out to look at the front of the car and underneath, what he could see of it. There were only a few scrapes. No real damage. But he trembled with anger and the reaction from the close call, and fear—fear of realizing how close it had come and anger with himself for suddenly feeling fear over such an incident. And then he knew anger at the other car!

He couldn't see Mario from there, or the rest of the track and the other car, but he could hear it coming.

In a moment, the other car came around the turn and howled to a stop. Benito Taglio threw his gears into neutral and sat there laughing at him. Mart began to see the humor of it, too, until Taglio made a small but definite gesture.

Mart stepped over to the car and with a quick turn of the lever, had the steering wheel off.

"Get out!"

Taglio sneered at him and climbed out.

Mart grabbed Taglio's collar and brought one from over his shoulder. Taglio crumpled and lay groaning on the pavement.

Mart pulled him off the road and climbed into the Italian's car, replaced the steering wheel and threw it into gear.

He took the car around for five more laps, never touching over sixty, waiting for his anger to cool. He saw Taglio limping across the field to where Mario sat, and kept on going with his practice. He didn't think anything would be said. He turned his attention to the car, slowing down for a turn—like a woman, Mario had said. Love a little first. He would love it a little, yes, but it was all there waiting, with its hungry, surging power, waiting for an ounce or two of pressure on the throttle.

Gradually and cautiously, he began to let it out a little. He didn't try anything in the corners. Not yet. That would be the most important part of driving it. Learning what it would and wouldn't do in the turns. To find that fine hairline between a drift and an unwanted skid. No, no fancy cornering yet, but he let her out to a hundred in the straight, and it was like a bright, shining thing.

It was beginning to feel good.

After a long while of it, he sneaked one four-wheel drift on a back turn and whooped with pleasure. It was a beauty, that car. He was certain now that there wouldn't be any need for much practice before Corsatti would say he could enter a race. Maybe only as a reserve driver at first. But even so ...

He laughed into the wind with sheer joy and shot past Mario at a hundred and sixty, exulting with the scream of tires as he braked at the end of the straight and drifted into a turn. Next time around, Mario waved him out.

"Slow! You go too fast!"

"But the car felt good. Mario, it's like I've been driving it all my life. Damn, Mario, what a wonderful hunk of machinery!"

"I know. I know. But that is enough for today."

They walked toward the shop.

"Mario, you know about Taglio?"

"Yes."

"I guess I shouldn't have hit him and taken his car. But if you want my opinion, he asked for it."

"I thought as much. As long as there was no damage and no one hurt, I think we don't have to say another word about it. But watch Taglio. He has a temper, and pride, my friend."

"Well, I'm glad to hear you aren't passing it off as a sense of humor. I damn near flipped that car back there."

"And hereafter, when Corsatti or myself says go slow, you go slow. When we say go fast, you go fast. Even if someday in a race he signals you from the pit and tells you to fall back, that is what you are supposed to do. Even if you feel like you are about to win the race, you fall back. That is part of being a team. You see?"

"Sure. I just forgot myself out there."

Mart remembered how Mario told him about working for Nuvolari and he took the scolding without resentment.

"If you do not learn right, it is like cutting your throat. There is no room for mistakes in this racing. One mistake and you are out of the race with no chance of getting back in and placing in the front. Or you are out of the race, dead or crippled."

"I know. But I can't get over how natural it felt to be driving that car. Like it was tailored to me and no one else. But what you say goes," he said with reluctance. No one can tell you how a car feels. You find that out for yourself, and only you know when you are really ready.

He looked once more over his shoulder at the car sitting down on the track, already impatient and looking forward to tomorrow when he would practice again. As he looked, a glint of light caught his eyes. He looked up at the hill in the center of the track and saw the lonely figure of Corsatti standing there, with binoculars in his hand.

"He's been watching."

"He always watches new drivers. To see how they do. A good sports car driver does not always make a good racing car driver."

Martin felt a dryness in his throat. "Honestly, from what you can tell this early, how did I do?"

"Do not be nervous, my friend."

"Then why doesn't he come down in plain sight and watch, like you did? Why is he always off in the distance somewhere with those damn glasses of his? Why doesn't he ever say anything?"

"You make something of nothing, my friend. He can see the whole road from there, that is all."

"But he never—"

"Martin, do not try to be friends with him or become acquainted with him. The others are acquainted, but only because they have been here a long time, but even they are not what you call friends of Corsatti. Let him call you when he is ready, talk to you when he is ready to talk."

"But why? What's it all about?"

"Corsatti has a fear for young men such as you. I should have told you sooner, I suppose. He had a son named Carlo, some years ago, and that son was killed in Belgium on a rainy day at a hundred and fifty miles an hour—a brake seizing on one wheel. Every young driver that has come since has been a reminder. He does not wish to be close to any of his drivers for fear he will find the anguish of another crash, that is all. Since his son died he has been this way. And since then, he works himself near to dying, improving the cars he builds, making them safer. He is never satisfied. There is no room, or time, for anything else. Now go home and spend some time with your Charlotte. Show her Turin. Come in early tomorrow and we will practice more. And Martin…"

"Yes?"

"You did well enough."

Mart hung around for a while, watching the mechanics. Mario thought he had done all right. What had Corsatti thought? Whatever the somber-looking head of the Corsatti factory thought, there was no indication in his face. Nothing in his fierce, massive countenance when he walked through the shop and into his office. Not even recognition. Mario thought he had done all right. Mart walked out to the car, uncertain now and wondering. Mario wasn't the boss.

CHAPTER TEN

MARIO FELICE watched with satisfaction as Martin Janis' practice continued regularly each day, for longer and longer periods of time. His agility picked up swiftly. More and more, the car seemed to be the most natural thing. It was astounding how it began to look like a part of his delicate threadings of nerve and muscle, part of his thought and motions. It was there sooner than anyone could have expected. Exactly when, what moment it happened, the division betwen newness and precision occurred, would have been impossible to know. But the accomplishment was in his face like the flush of wine. It was good, and yet—and yet there was something there that wasn't right. Mario had tried to touch it many times at night in thinking or while working over one of the motors. But it was an illusion, a gray shadow that vanished upon study, as if thinking were a sudden ray of sunlight.

He was thinking of these things on an evening not too long before the Grand Prix and Twelve Hour Race at Rheims. He had finally and laughingly consented to intrude on Martin's and Charlotte's privacy long enough to have dinner with them at the Palazzo Torino. He was such an old man, and they were so young, and he felt that they would grow quiet around him. But they had not. Indeed, Charlotte had at moments, seemed almost overly attentive to Martin. To be sure, they were in love, but her actions sometimes seemed to be a thing of worry, almost as if there were another woman in the picture. But he let the moments pass and enjoyed their company.

They were all drowsy with good food and enjoying a smoke. Charlotte stared dreamily into her empty plate.

"Mario, do you think I could ever learn to cook these—this—"

"Again, I pronounce—*abbacchio alla cacciatora*. Anchovy sauce over fried sucking lamb. Well, why not? You are a woman."

"Your women learn so early, when they're still kids. I can barely fry an egg, let alone something like this."

"You learn. I have not seen Martin grow thin."

"That's because we eat out most of the time."

"Let's stop talking about food," Mart cut in.

"Food is not important?"

"Only when I'm hungry."

"Ah, these young ones..."

Mart grinned at him. He lit a cigarette and spun the stem of a wine glass between his fingers.

Mario, what kind of a man was Nuvolari? You promised to tell me about him. Remember?"

"There is not much I can say."

"But you worked for him."

"For a short while, yes."

Mario stared at the guttering candle, his eyes far away. Martin seemed to be a lonely man, lonely in his eagerness, looking for help in knowing the gods he wished to emulate, lonely with anxiety and the secret comparisons he would make with each added bit of information thrown to him like a rattle thrown to a child. He remained silent for a long time, remembering and feeling a little sad, and yet glad that there was something to remember now that those times were gone. The times of the man of whom Martin was asking.

It would be hard to know any of these men. Sometimes it would seem they were like gods in their own paradise. And perhaps to know them in the way you wish to know, you would ride the Thousand Miles with them—the Mille Miglia—know what they feel at the start in Brescia, down to Verona and Padua and

Ferrara, how they die for every mile and mountain and turn down the unholy coast of the Adriatic from Ravenna to Pescara. Balance terror against their desire to keep on and try to win as they turn north again.

Popoli, to Terni and down to Rome. Be with them when they leave Siena and the Apennines rise before them as from a bad dream with bad roads and fog and cold, and fatigue and shattered machines threaten to fling them into some deep mountain gorge. But there is no slowing down. To slow is to lose, and to lose is worse than what tears at their sanity now. Think with them through Florence and Bologna and Modena to Piacenza and Cremona and Mantua. Perhaps pray with them to the moment they are lifted nearly dead from their machines back in Brescia when it is all over. Then, perhaps, you might know.

"I think I started it, Mario," Charlotte told him. "I asked Mart once. What kind of a man, and why does he race? He can only say because he likes to. But a man doesn't go out and risk his life just because he *likes* to. There has to be more."

"I don't know. You ask a big thing."

"Well, what do you know of him?"

"Nivola—or as the world knew him, Tazio Nuvolari—was a small man, about my height but very thin. He had a face like that of an evil bird, a lonely face that sometimes had a begging to the eyes, and a face full of hunger. One leg was shorter than the other because of an accident. He was the most profane man I ever met." Mario smiled quietly. "I have seen him going fast through the turns, going after someone, beating his fists on the sides of the car, cursing at the top of his lungs as if it would make the car go faster. He was not calm. He knew anger in every race. He drove better than anyone and still he was not satisfied. He drove like something inhuman.

"I was not on his crew at the time, but I remember once he found cars wrecked in front of him. He was going very fast and it was raining and there was oil all over the road in that spot.

Nivola had maybe an inch to spare for his car to pass through, and he did not slow down. He worked his wheels back and forth faster than one could see and went through without touching. It was greatness, even for a man who had been a driver since he was a small boy."

"I read about that one," Mart commented.

"Yes. There isn't much more you can say—no way to answer your question … except for maybe one incident."

"What was that?" Charlotte asked.

"It happened when he was still racing—eh—" He groped for the word and couldn't remember. *"Motocicletta?"*

"Motorcycles?" Mart suggested.

"Yes. He had broken this leg and had been told to stay in bed for a long time. And no racing for a while. Tazio could not stay away from racing that long. It was not his nature. He raced anyway. He had the big cast on his leg—he had friends carry him down to the track and put him on the motorcycle—and he found as long as he could keep it moving, he could stay on, and as long as he could stay on, *he could win.*"

Mario swallowed a half a glass of wine, tasting the bitterness of the vine in it.

"Perhaps that is part of the answer. He had to win. No matter what, he had to be a winner—you understand? There was no other way for him to finish a race. He was a very bad loser, Nivola."

Mario saw Charlotte sit back in her chair, and he could see that she was not satisfied. And there would be no telling her. No one knew to tell her or themselves. What kind of man, why must they race? Only fragments that would never fit to make a whole.

"Well, I've intruded long enough. I will leave now. We work again tomorrow, and I am old enough to need my sleep."

"I suppose we all ought to get to bed. Can't practice with a fuzzy head." Mart paid the bill and they went into the lobby.

"Mario, soon we'll be going to France for the races, the Twelve Hour especially."

"Yes."

"Will I have a chance to drive?"

"That will be up to Corsatti."

"I'll do all right, you know."

"There is a new driver coming. An Englishman from the Jaguar team. There would not be enough cars—but perhaps. There is always a chance. But be patient in any case. Your time will come. Good night to both of you."

Mario left the hotel and made his way down the street slowly, wanting to walk a while. Martin Janis. What was there about the boy, the young one who drove so wonderfully so soon? What was it that was wrong with the boy who idolized Nivola? The talk of Il Maestro was as nothing. Martin had too much respect for Nuvolari's skill. He would not dare even try to imitate him as some had. If anything, he was too self-critical, a worrier, and indeed sometimes almost afraid—afraid of something. But that would not be it. They all had that. It was something else, and Mario could not touch it.

Anna Pavanne had just come down from her rooms at the Palazzo Torino, where she had taken a short rest and a quiet meal by herself, when she saw Martin Janis and Charlotte Greyne cross the lobby and leave through the front entrance. She smiled and followed them slowly. There was no hurry.

Indeed, though she had been in Turin only a few hours, it had not been difficult to locate Martin. A Miss Baroni out at Corsatti Fabbrica Automobili had been most helpful.

It would be good to talk to Martin. It had been a long time. Not that there was love there, or the pain of being parted—nothing so naive. He was a wild pleasure in bed, but no more than that. It was his driving, the excitement of it, and knowing there was greatness there. She wanted that, to be a part of it.

She thought of the cheap hotel where he and Charlotte were living, and of the weeks that had passed, and the natural course of things in that time that would have had to be at Corsatti. She knew Martin Janis well enough to know that he might be ready to change his mind and behave sensibly by now.

Anna emerged from the hotel and stopped. She saw them standing on the steps, and heard them talking. There was an unhappy slant to Martin's shoulders as Charlotte asked him a question.

"It's this new driver, isn't it?"

Martin nodded.

"Mario said there was always a chance. You might still drive at Rheims. Cheer up and look at it that way."

"Yeah, look at it that way," Mart snorted. "Might! One chance in a million!"

"I warned you about that, Martin," Anna spoke down to him.

"Anna!" Mart's voice was a whisper of disbelief.

"Surprised, Martin?"

He just looked at her.

"Oh, I know I was pretty angry when you left. But I thought about it a lot after you were gone, Martin." She walked down to them. "You're headstrong, and sometimes like a child. You do not know what is best. So I came to find you."

Anna's eyes left Mart and touched on Charlotte. The girl's face was frozen, as if in sudden fear and despair. Anna smiled.

"I believe we met at Torrey Pines. Miss Greyne, is it not?"

"Yes … we met briefly there." Charlotte was trying to be calm

"Briefly. It could not have been. I do not remember the names of the young people that easily."

"You were involved with six or seven drivers at the bar, or was it outside on the lawn before the party began? It's been so long, Mrs. Barkdale."

Anna smiled at the acidity of her tone.

"Miss Pavanne. Anna Pavanne. I am no longer married."

Mart waved a hand uncomfortably and nodded toward the door.

"We can't stand on the steps all night. Let's go in and have a drink."

"That is a fine idea, Martin," Anna said. "I came up from Rome today. I stopped there first after the flight across to replenish my wardrobe—such fine shops in Rome—but it was a long trip from there to Turin. Or at least it seemed so. I am a little tired."

Anna hooked her arm in Martin's and led him back up to the door, leaving Charlotte to follow with a trembling anger in her face. She was such a child, Anna thought, and the clumsy way she had attempted to insult her had only been amusing. It was obvious what Martin saw in her. But that was all she could offer, and it was not enough. Not for a man who could be champion.

They took a table in a quiet corner of the taproom and ordered drinks. Anna took a long cigarette from her golden case and held it for Martin to light. Nothing was said. But she could see the tension buiding up in Charlotte, and the discomfort Martin was feeling. Anna smiled and let it build. She sat there with the long cigarette, knowing she was dressed in the finest Rome could offer. It would bother Martin, she knew. The casual carelessness of her new hair-do, her profile in that dim light, her shoulders and an ample portion of her breasts rising softly from the fabric like dark ivory. It would make him think.

The drinks came and Anna toyed with hers delicately. Martin tossed his off quickly, and Charlotte let hers turn to water.

Yes, go ahead and worry, Martin. Sit there and look at me and want me. Sit there and remember how it was before .... And you, child, believe me, it will not be pleasant to see your face as you watch this thing you have woven with Martin Janis slowly pull apart. I can almost be sorry for you.

"I suppose you would like to know all about Ramsey?"

Mart shrugged, but curiosity was written all over him.

"Ramsey was unhappy, of course. Very unhappy. You know, he put the house and all the things in it up for sale—your car, too—and he said he planned to find a small apartment somewhere. Something with just a bed and a stove in it. No pictures, no statues, no garden. Nothing. He said he had no desire to look upon beauty anymore. Isn't that silly? I think he'll change his mind .... But really, I had to leave. The place was like a museum. I had to come home. Be with my own people, and of course, see you and talk to you, Martin. Naturally, there was a large settlement. I was sorry, but ..."

"You accomplished what you wanted to do, didn't you?" Charlotte flared, her face flushing. She spilled her drink.

Anna smiled.

"*Cameriere!*" she called, and a waiter came and changed the cloth. "Yes. It is no secret. I accomplished what I set out to do. I am quite wealthy now. But I can still feel certain regrets, can I not? But enough of that. Tell me, Martin, how are things?"

He shrugged. "You heard me on the steps. I'm up to here in practice. I haven't driven in a race yet."

"And you are unhappy. It is not like the days when you drove at Pebble Beach and the rest. You were very happy then."

"Why not? I didn't sit on the bench there."

"And you were good. You were the best in the country."

"Maybe, maybe not. That would be hard to say."

"You are good, Martin. You could be a champion. This is my country. As a girl I went with my father to watch the cars go by as they reached Rome in the Mille Miglia. I have watched them drive at the Targa Florio, and at Monza. I have seen most of the great drivers, Martin. I know how they drove. This may sound strange to your little friend here, but this is a big thing in Italy. I know road-racing as little Charlotte knows football or tennis. Yes, I know how they drove, and I know you would be one of them, if you did not bury yourself with Corsatti."

"Corsatti makes wonderful cars."

"Certainly. But that does not mean you have to be their mechanic or their hired hand, an apprentice. Corsattis can be bought. And so can the excellent Ferraris and the Maseratis. And they can be driven independently. Races can be won in them, and the driver's name made known, and the team invitations that come then are worthwhile. To come from the bottom takes long, Martin, when it isn't necessary."

Mart remained silent and slowly turned his glass.

He was thinking of Rheims. How he wanted to drive there. Anna could see it in his face.

"There is a lot to learn." He said it half-heartedly.

"You don't really believe that, do you, Martin?"

"I don't know …"

Charlotte couldn't sit still any longer. She stood up and half-crouched over the table.

"Of course he believes it. Why don't you leave him alone?"

Anna smiled slightly and sipped from her glass.

"My dear, you are only a child. Please do not try to understand these things."

"I don't care what you call me, but we just had dinner with someone who knows more about Mart and driving than you'll ever know. If he thought Mart was ready to drive in a race, Mart would drive in a race. Leave him alone. Go pick on some other driver. Mart's not going out and kill himself for you, just so you can satisfy your dirty litle ego … *Look, there goes so and so the famous driver, and look who's with him! Anna Pavanne!* That's all you want. I'm going back to the hotel, Mart. Are you coming or are you staying here?"

Anna interrupted with a laugh.

"I think it would be a good thing for all of us to say good night. It is getting late."

"I'll see you to your hotel," Mart offered.

"That will not be necessary. I have rooms here. When will I see you again? How about tomorrow evening?"

"I don't know. There's a birthday party for one of the drivers tomorrow night."

"Oh? Would I be too forward in asking if I might come? I would enjoy a party and a chance to meet some of your friends."

Mart hesitated and then nodded. "All right. If you like."

"Good. Well, good night, Martin. And think about these things we have talked about, won't you? And see that your little friend gets a good night's rest. I don't think she is quite herself."

Anna stood up and walked beautifully from the room.

Mart sat there for a moment.

"Mart …"

"Yeah. I guess we'd better get back to the hotel."

They went to the car and drove back in silence.

Back in their room at the Parigi, Charlotte undressed quickly and got in bed to wait for him. She watched him slowly undressing, almost absent-minded in his movements. She watched his face, studying it, trying to see what he was thinking. Unhappy because Anna had followed, or unhappy because he wasn't with her now, or angry because she didn't see things his way, or angry because he hadn't done things her way. Charlotte didn't know.

She could only feel a helplessness. She did not know what to do. She could not even think clearly now, and she was afraid. It had happened. Anna had followed, and she had almost known that it would be that way. And Mart—she didn't know how to cope with it.

In a minute, he turned out the light and crawled in beside her to lie staring at the ceiling.

"Mart … what are you thinking?"

"Nothing."

"Did you have to invite Anna to the party?"

"I don't see how I could have done otherwise."

"By telling her no."

"Let's don't talk about it now."

"Are you glad she came?"

"I don't know...."

"You were angry last time you talked to her."

"I don't want to talk about it now."

She tried not to hear the hesitation in his voice. She tried to pretend that the vagueness in his answers was not there. But it was there, and fear was something that came close to shouting.

Charlotte rolled against him and flattened her breasts against his chest and kissed him desperately.

He held her for a moment, but then released her and shook his head.

"Let's get some sleep."

Charlotte sank her head in her own pillow.

He hadn't acted like that before. There had always been a little love before sleep.

He felt far away tonight.

Sleep ... not for her that night. There could be no sleep where there was fear.

She began to cry, and the crying was silent. She would have been ashamed to let him hear it. Maybe Anna was right, sitting there smiling over her drink. Too much of a child....

CHAPTER ELEVEN

BENITO TAGLIO staggered to his feet and stood precariously looking at the faces he knew so well. He swept his glass around to each of them in a grand toast. Achille Brocco, Valerio Brusetti, Mario Felice, that to-be-damned Englishman, Robert Morris. He stopped and drank deep, ignoring Mart Janis and the woman with him.

Martin Janis! You do not belong here. Oh, I have seen the way Corsatti has looked upon you from the distance. Under your tender, child's skin he believes he has found a great talent. Bah! Better that you should tend goats like Mario's twisted little father.

Today, I am thirty-eight years old. Thirty-eight, and perhaps the great Corsatti has found a tremble to my hand, or a mist before my eyes, and perhaps he believes I find the great speeds more than they used to be. To think that I, Benito Taglio, who have won more races than I can remember, must soon step down to raise fat children and tend to the grapes of the vineyard or perhaps die—that I must have someone to take my place! Perhaps this boy—this—this...

I have seen you practice, Martin Janis. I have seen you move the machine around the track by yourself and make a fair thing of it. I have heard that you have won many races in your country, but what kind of races are they to compare with the Grand Prix of Italy or Belgium or France? A drive through the park! Yes, you practice well, and you move your machine down the track with grace and speed, but by my Christ you will lose that boyish fever in your eyes when all the great drivers of Europe begin to come down on you.

Thirty-eight. You will be lucky if you live as long. It perhaps is old for driving. But I have, just a few weeks ago, won the great Mille Miglia—twelve minutes in front of the new Mercedes, in the world's most dangerous race. Perhaps Corsatti will not know such a win again until we get the new motors I have been begging for. But the Mille Miglia! Does that sound like an old man? Does that sound like a trembling of the hand and a mist before the eyes?

No, there are many races left for me. You are strong enough to knock me down and strong enough to turn the wheels through many turns, and young enough to have your whole career before you, God willing it is yours to have—but you will never replace me. Never! Better you should tend goats than try to be of my world ....

He drank again and looked down the length of the table, at the faces grouped around a great gathering of bird and pasto and soups and wine there in the large dining room of the Palazzo Torino. Taglio began to laugh, knocking over a bottle of red wine. He watched the stain spread on the cloth and laughed harder.

"What of it?" he shouted. "There is plenty more. I thank you for a beautiful celebration. I congratulate myself on being alive for another year. And Corsatti will see more races won. To assure these victories, I will personally spit in everyone's carburetors. I hope you will be so generous as to do the same for me. And now, my friends, you Achille, and you Brusetti, and even you Signor Morris, though you are a pale Englishman—I toast the races that have been and the races that are to be."

He named them one by one, drinking to each and remembering the many victories and the defeats that marched across Europe. Starting in a time that was dimming now, down to the present, interrupted only by the great war.

He had come a long way, from the son of a maker of shoes and boots, from poverty among the gray buildings of Naples. A long way from that first, wheezing little Fiat, and driving taxis in Rome, and getting hired as a mechanic in the Corsatti Fabbrica Automobili. A long way from the night he deliberately left the shop door unlocked so that he could sneak back in the darkness and push one of the machines down on the track and drive and drive, not knowing Corsatti had come back to look for some papers. A thousand years since the miracle of getting caught at it, berated, and then told he was good enough to join the team.

He finished the toasting and bowed to the cheers around the table. Taglio sat down and stared moodily into the glass before him.

"It has been a long time, Mario."

"Yes, my friend. A long time. Many years. You have done well."

"I will continue to do well. Perhaps if we get new motors I will win enough to get the points and become champion again."

"There is talk of a new motor that will give us as much speed or nearly so as the Mercedes. Perhaps you will."

Taglio frowned and nodded toward Martin Janis.

"I think he is here to replace me. I have seen Corsatti's face."

"You are wrong, Taglio. You are wrong. You know the team is too small. We need more drivers. That is why he is here."

"I don't know, Mario. Corsatti shows an uncommon interest in this child."

"Corsatti has spoken to you of him?"

"No, but my Christ, Mario! How long have I known Corsatti? That great bull of a face says nothing to those who do not know him. But I can see what is there—the expression of a man who has found a prize of some kind."

Mario shrugged and smiled.

"Martin Janis is going to be an excellent driver, but that does not have any connection with the fact that you are thirty-eight years old or that most of your career is behind you. It is usual for a man in Corsatti's business to have each driver on his *scuderia* a good driver. Of what use would it be to have one good driver, as yourself, and the rest unable to ever do better than tenth place?"

"Damn you, Mario," Taglio muttered. "You always have to be so damn logical."

"I think, my friend, that you are merely jealous."

Taglio snorted and pounded the table.

"I have the scars and ill-knit bones of many races, many victories and a share of defeats. Why should I be jealous of an unmarked child who has not even the calluses of a wheel on his hands, and who has not even driven in a real race yet?"

"Do not be angry, Taglio. We are all jealous of those who just begin, those with their lives and professions still before them. We would all secretly trade."

Taglio shook his head and scowled into his glass. He drank some of it quickly and wiped his sleeve across his mouth.

"No. I have thought of that part of it. It is just that I do not like the idea of there ever being someone better than myself on this team—whether I am still here to drive or not."

"You are just sad from drinking, my friend."

"A man goes to all the trouble, the work, the half-killing of himself following a dream up high enough to where he can carve the initials of his name where everyone can see and always remember—it is not a happy thing to have someone come along and knock it down and carve his name higher. Well, he will never get past me. Do you understand? He'll never get his wheels past mine."

Mario chuckled and patted him on the shoulder.

"You will feel better in the morning," he said quietly. "Well, we have a new guest!"

Corsatti himself came in then and stepped slowly up to the table. He looked around at the faces, with his hat in his hand. He accepted a glass of wine and sipped at it for a moment.

When everyone had quieted down, he started to speak.

"The last car has been put on the truck. All is in order, and tomorrow we shall be on our way. I must remind you all that the plane will leave from Caselle Airport at exactly nine."

Taglio only half listened as Corsatti spoke. He heard them laugh at something he said, laugh at the words that came from a wooden face. He frowned, watching Martin Janis strain eagerly listening to the great man and to the Englishman's translation. Janis—pale, unmarked child! *It is not in you to drive as I drive....*

Corsatti left, and the party resumed, noisily, with the knowledge that not much time was left. The hour was late, and the time to catch the plane early.

"You will feel better tomorrow. Perhaps a bad head, but better, and you won't feel so sorry for yourself, and perhaps you will not resent our new man so much. Why not try to be friends with Janis?"

"Friends!"

"Certainly. It is easier that way. Go over to him now and offer your hand.... Oh, he is leaving. Well, no matter. Charlotte is staying. He will be back. When he does, take my advice."

Taglio watched Martin Janis leave the room. Friends? It would be an obscenity upon obscenity. Never!

You clumsy young pup! I am thirty-eight—thirty-eight! There are many races yet. Your wheels will never pass mine. Oh, you need not worry. I will not run you off the road to see the end of you. I do not need to kill or to maim to be rid of you. But by the time I am finished with you, you will be running for your mother and crying like a child with fear. You will leave on your own accord. It isn't for you to drive as I drive. There are many races for me. Many races yet....

Martin Janis stared drowsily toward the high ceiling in the dining room of the plush Palazzo Torino. He had eaten more of the food and downed more of the rich red wine than he had intended. Charlotte had hardly touched any of it, and for the whole evening she had sat there with a frown around her eyes.

"You still wondering about Anna, for heaven's sake?"

"I can't help it," Charlotte said. "Like she was up to something."

"Hell, forget it and enjoy yourself. Maybe she had to go somewhere. I don't know. She wasn't here when we came and she left no word. It doesn't have to be a mystery and it doesn't mean she has to be up to something. In any case, it's got nothing to do with us. Now come on, drink some wine."

"I don't know...."

He tried to let his mind drift away from it. He didn't want to think about Anna. He didn't want to torture himself with visions of her when things were as they used to be when he drove Barkdale's car. He didn't want to think of her offer. But none of it would leave him. There was still love in him for her, he knew. His dreams were often troubled with her, and thoughts of her turned up in the strangest of places—sometimes where he wouldn't have thought there was room. In the middle of a howling, drifting turn... yes, and even in the darkness of a room, a voice, a body, a faint outline of a face when it was the voice and body and face of Charlotte.

And the offer Anna had made. He couldn't just ignore it. It was too great a thing. Cars of his own, racing now instead of wading through the drudgery of apprenticeship and training with Corsatti for a few long months more. But—

Yeah, *but!* There was the catch. A few months more at the most. Wouldn't it be silly to be premature, go independent because he loved someone, and perhaps be maimed or killed for the lack of one final stage of polishing, of perhaps one final hour of Mario's critical instruction? He didn't know. He only knew that no matter how much he loved Anna, and no matter how impatient and bitter he was becoming at Corsatti's, the *but* came into it.

Just like a kid, he thought. Just like a kid. Talk big, and bluster and fight, but when the decision is there to be made, you back off and say *but!* Hungry to do it, but scared. Martin Janis, scared and hungry. He pushed the whole thing from his mind and emptied a glass of wine. He thought about Rheims instead, for which even now the bright red Corsattis were being rolled silently into the big vans and tied down for the trip.

Corsatti was entering two Gran Sports in the Twelve Hour Race, and three racing machines in the Grand Prix. For the Twelve Hour, there were two drivers for each car, to be driving as teams, one spelling the other until the twelve hours and some twelve hundred or more miles were done. Four drivers, three on the regular team. Mart had seen a chance there for his entering, to appease the hunger he felt. But sitting next to him at the table was his reason for losing hope. Robert Morris, the young and able British driver, had signed on that day to drive with Corsatti for the rest of the year.

For a time he had felt antagonism toward Morris. But it was senseless. Now, he only felt envious of the thin, hatchet-faced boy with the slightly stooped back. He found him likeable and friendly. And his presence gave Charlotte and himself someone they could talk to easily in English, someone besides Mario who sat down the table from them, between Taglio and Brocco. Besides, Morris knew enough Italian to act as interpreter for them.

"I have great admiration for the three-litre Gran Sport," Morris was saying to Mart, "although the XKD Jaguar will make a better show of it. When the Corsatti is peaking, the D Jag still has a little left. The Gran Sport's cornering is what fascinates me. But the formula-one Corsatti—we have nothing to compare with it. That's the real reason I signed on. I want to spend a season getting the touch of one and comparing it with Alfa and Ferrari and Maserati."

"What does it matter? Mercedes has us stopped."

"Yes. Maybe so. I have my own private theory about that. The right man could take the Corsatti in either category and beat the new Mercedes. The Merc's margin over Corsatti isn't so great, and in one department they are inferior. Perhaps you haven't seen enough of them to notice, but while they have the edge on speed, something has happened to their suspension. It is too unpredictable. It has become a shade unwieldy. Mercedes is not going as far into the turns before cutting off. They're hitting the turns a little slower than they used to. The right man taking advantage of Corsatti's cornering ability just might make a show of it. It might be just the right combination."

"Who? Such a man doesn't exist, to my knowledge."

"Perhaps. There is no way of knowing until someone tries it."

"Are you going to?"

"No. I'm afraid not. I'm too much of a conventional driver. I've won a few races, but it was all by the book. Perhaps some-day—but I don't have the experience. It would take someone with a great deal of nerve and imagination."

"What do you mean? Damn, Morris, they refer to you as the prodigy, the young British lion."

"The journals again. Well, maybe I am what they say. I can write my own ticket, certainly. But each man knows his own limitations. This I feel is mine. When the book drivers fall behind and no longer win the races, I will fall with them. But there are always new drivers coming in, dying, being crippled, making the grade, winning their first race and beginning their climb to the top, perhaps becoming another Ascari or Fangio. Perhaps becoming this driver who could win over Mercedes with a slower car with pure nerve and imagination. Maybe you could be that man, Martin. Who knows?"

"That's a good one. But instead of Corsatti holding his breath waiting for that, I suggest that the engines be beefed up a little."

Benito Taglio stood up and, weaving a little with his hungry, falcon's eyes glittering over the candles, made a little speech. His voice rose and fell with a quantity of gestures.

"He is congratulating himself again for being a year older, a year still alive. He is also toasting the races he has driven, and the races to come. He will also spit in everyone's carburetors, and hopes that everyone will be so kind to do the same for him...."

The toasting began. Le Mans, Grand Prix of France, Belgium, England, Italy, the Mille Miglia; the races at Monte Carlo, Monza and Targa Florio, Silverstone.... He could hear Taglio mention each one and recognize the names like familiar faces.

"He left one out," Mart said when Taglio was done. "One of the big ones, and I don't see how he could forget."

"I don't think he did. Which one?"

"Germany. The Nurburgring. Maybe I lost it in the Italian."

Morris put his glass down and shook his head.

"No. The Nurburgring is there. He didn't mention it, but only a part of it. It is what he fears the most, and perhaps what all of us have feared at one time or another. You will meet them someday."

"What? You're talking like a funeral director. A part of the Nurburgring. Which part?"

"As you come down out of the Schwalbenschwanz and Galgenkopf, down out of the high places, there are two bridges which have to be taken at a hundred and sixty or more if you have any intention of winning at all. These two bridges have humps in them that put air under the car. It's a terrifying thing."

"I've read about them. That's where von Delius was killed."

"Yes, von Delius in his big Auto Union coming down to tick the rear of Dick Seaman's car. And others have died there, too. The Ring.... We drive a fraction over twenty-eight kilometers per lap, fourteen miles roughly, for a total of three hundred and eleven miles. One lap would be enough to show you. But drive the whole distance and the course becomes something you'll never forget. I believe it is the best—or the worst in Europe, perhaps equalling the Mille Miglia for pure challenge. But those bridges! For a lot of us, the bridges are like the mountains a man can climb but in a lot of ways never really conquer. You never feel quite right about them, never feel secure with them, or confident as you can with the other parts of the course—Karussel, Wipperman—after practicing them."

Martin saw the bridges in his mind. Low bridges, he imagined, low and not very wide, and not imposing at all, not dangerous-looking until you noticed the rising of of the pavement to meet them, and the pavement dropping abruptly away again. He could almost hear the engine racing insanely as the wheels left the ground, the roar of the engine as the wheels touched again and brought the tach down.

"Mart ... Mart!"

"Uh! I'm sorry."

"When is the next one?" Charlotte asked.

"Nurburgring? Last of July. Why?"

Her face was turning white as he spoke the words. Her hand began to tremble, spilling the glass of wine it held.

"What's the matter?" Mart asked her.

"I'm afraid it's my fault," Morris said. "I shouldn't have talked like that. Miss Greyne, please pay no attention to what we say here. We all have our private frightening places. Because some of us are afraid of the bridges at the Nurburgring does not mean we are all afraid of them or uncertain about them. Mart may find no trouble there at all."

Charlotte shook her head and smiled a little. "That's all right. Please, I'm just a worry wart."

Mart laughed at her. "Look, you seem to have the idea that I'm going to be driving in it this year. Corsatti isn't going to start me off in something like that so soon. Now cut it out and enjoy the party."

"All right, Mart. I'm sorry I'm such a baby. Those things frighten me, that's all."

"These things worry us all a little, Miss Greyne," Morris tried to help. "It is the babies who do not have sense enough to worry, and for what it's worth, I've seen Mart in practice and I think he'll be able to handle things admirably."

A shout came, and Corsatti himself stepped up to the table. He still wore the overcoat, holding his hat, and smoking the inevitable cigar. Corsatti's face was somber, even with the drivers shouting and cheering for him and pressing glasses of wine on him.

Corsatti accepted a glass of Cinzano and shook hands with Taglio. He sipped at his wine like a man who was standing all by himself. Then he looked quietly at everyone and began to speak.

"He says the vans have been loaded," Morris translated, "and are on their way, and reminds everyone to be out at Caselle airport at nine in the morning. The charter plane to take the team to Rheims leaves at nine, promptly. He also reminds Valerio Brusetti and anyone else who is frightened of airplanes that liquor and altitude do not mix and the supply isn't going to last long enough to provide courage for the race anyway." Morris chuckled. "Even on the rare attempts at something other than business, the man does not smile."

Corsatti put his glass down without proposing a toast and glanced around the table. His eyes stopped on Martin for a moment. Corsatti gave an almost imperceptible nod, made a slight bow in the direction of Charlotte and then walked out of the room.

At that moment, a waiter came over and whispered to Martin. He nodded and turned to Charlotte.

"Hold the fort for me. I'll be back in a minute."

"What is it? Word from Anna?"

"Yeah. Probably wants to apologize for not being here."

"Do you have to go?"

"I'll only be gone a minute."

She tried to smile as he turned and left the party.

CHAPTER TWELVE

MART took the elevator to the fourth floor. He followed the door numbers until he found the right one and knocked.

"Mart?" A voice called faintly. "Door's open."

He turned the knob and stepped in. The room was dim, and she was not there.

"Anna?"

"In the bedroom, Mart."

Slowly, he walked into the bedroom. The lights were out, but the windows were thrown open and the lights of Turin came in softly.

He did not see her at first, not until his eyes adjusted to the darkness. Anna stood at one end of the window, looking out at the city. He could hardly see her face. Just a white robe and bits of light catching her eyes.

"I'm sorry about the party, Martin."

"I wondered what happened to you."

"I wanted to go to the party when you spoke of it yesterday. I was home, among my own people, and there were going to be drivers there. Drivers are magnificent and I wanted to meet Benito Taglio. I have seen him drive."

"He is still there. It's his party, Anna."

"I know. But something happened."

"Something wrong?"

"No. Just one of those evenings. All at once, I did not feel like a party. I did not come back to Italy just to come home. There have been a couple of moments when I've almost forgotten that, and wanting to go to that party was one of them. Seeing Rome for a few hours did it too. But it's you I came for."

"Look, Anna, I've got to get back to the party."

"Martin, do you still love me?"

He felt the strange excitement of her sweep strongly over him. The way it used to be—he could smell her perfume in the room, and sense her touch there. She always left something in a room, something indelible and indefinable.

"It has been a long time, Martin."

He saw the robe fall open, and Anna standing in the light of the window, and her long, full body gleaming.

"Anna…"

She came to him slowly and made him sit in a chair. She sat on the arm and leaned over him, her nearness crowding his senses.

"Do you still love me?" She asked the words slowly.

Mart, in answering, pulled her to him and kissed her.

"You don't love that girl, Martin. I know you don't. I can tell the way you talk to her, and in the way you still look at me. Martin, put an end to this foolishness and come with me. Forget about the races at Rheims. I can have any car you want delivered here in a day or two. Then we can go to Monte Carlo for a few days just to be by ourselves. There will be time to drive the car and get used to it by the time the Grand Prix at Aintree comes around. Please. Monte Carlo, and then England where you can show the world who is going to be champion."

He shook his head and buried his face in her breasts. "Let's don't talk about it now…."

"You're naughty. Is this all you can think of?"

"When you invite me up into a dark hotel room and start taking things off? What else would I think?"

"Once, nothing."

"What do you mean by that?" He started to let her go, but she held him there.

"I want you to be a champion, Martin. I know you can be a champion. Now."

"You forgot about points. Race by race they either start adding up, or they don't. For a whole season. No one becomes champion winning just one race or a half dozen."

"I know. I am talking about your skill. You can drive like a champion now. If you will leave Corsatti. Next year you would have the points. Don't you see? Don't you want me, Martin?"

"Enough so that if you don't stop talking I'll blow a fuse."

"Then do as I ask. Drive for yourself."

"I get it. That's why you didn't come to the party. Use yourself as bait. Keep the candy out of reach until your boy behaves himself."

"Don't be angry..."

"Angry! I'm sore as hell!"

"Aren't I worth it? What is wrong with what I want for us? Think about it. A season of racing each year—not for just a small silver cup as before, but for money and glory and the right to call yourself champion of drivers—and then my world the rest of the time. Venice, Rome, Paris, a villa at Monte Carlo, the right people. Be one of these gods, Martin. Why hesitate?"

For an instant, he was almost ready to surrender, to agree to her terms. But that sense of inadequacy came creeping in as it had at times before. It all seemed like a mistake. Martin Janis, the winner of a few amateur road races, professional driving? The great road courses of Europe? Grand Prix racing? Want to do it, be impatient—but at the same time wonder a little and find comfort in the teachings of Mario Felice.

"I can't. Can't you understand that once and for all? I just can't. Goddamn it, Anna! Be patient and let me get there in my own way, or let me alone and stop torturing me like this. Sometimes I wonder what you're made of."

"I'm a woman, Martin. And I like greatness in a man. I would never be satisfied with a man who was content to be mediocre because it would make me mediocre."

"Maybe you've picked the wrong man. Ever think of that?"

"I've got the right man. I know I'm right about you."

"No, you aren't. You're only fooling yourself. You've seen some of the big races. You've seen the drivers. And because you've seen the way they drive, you think you have the whole thing down pat. Well, you're wrong. You haven't ridden with them. You haven't driven yourself. You couldn't begin to know all the things a driver faces, the things that can happen, and the way it tears at his guts, and how long he can take it. It isn't just driving against a few other cars, like I did at home. You're up against big boys here. I don't even know if I have the guts to go out and face them and pretend I've a chance to come in better than last. I don't know any of that yet—and if you can't see that, you better go find yourself another boy."

Anna stood up and drew the robe about her. She smiled at him.

"I can be patient for a little while, Martin. One of these days, real soon, you'll be impatient one day too many, and then you'll come to me."

"Don't hold your breath." He hurried for the door, not looking back.

"I'll be waiting, Martin."

He slammed the door behind him and ran to the elevator, and when it was slow in coming, took the stairs down and back to the party.

"You were gone a long time," Charlotte said.

"Anna made her apology, and then insisted I have a drink."

"You look pale. Is something the matter?"

"No. Must be the wine catching up with me." He managed a grin. "Nothing to worry about."

The celebration had begun to slow down. Taglio was still talking heroically. Brocco, who had remained at the party only out of deference to Taglio, very soberly left. Brusetti stared into a half-empty bottle, gloom etching out from the shadows of his eyes, looking very near tears. Mario looked around at everybody, but not really seeing. He seemed to be thinking about all the other celebrations where the drivers got together and talked and enjoyed each other's company away from the tensions of the track. Morris looked bored.

"Shall we go home?" Mart asked Charlotte.

"I don't want to take you away."

"It's pretty well over with. We might as well go. I'll pay my respects to Taglio and then I'll be ready."

"I thought you and he didn't get along."

"I know. But I'd like to try. Doesn't do the team any good to have fighting in the ranks."

Mart walked over, around the table to where the sharp-faced Italian sat, now silent. He nodded to Mario and touched Taglio on the shoulder. Taglio looked up, frowning.

"Congratulations on your birthday. Miss Greyne and I must leave now." He offered his hand while Mario translated.

Taglio looked at the hand, sneered at Martin, and turned away.

Martin flushed angrily and started to grab him by the shoulder, but Mario caught his eyes.

"Forget it, Martin. Perhaps later something will happen to make you two friends. Maybe later. But right now, he is drunk and he ..."

"Sure, Mario," he nodded. Taglio was drunk, but he also had not forgotten the incident on the first day of practice.

Mart went back to Charlotte.

"Let's go. I'm ready for bed myself."

Charlotte finally drifted off to sleep, and Martin lay awake, staring through the darkness at the window and the curtains that stirred gently with a night wind. She had worked a miracle in this place. It wasn't grim any longer. They were used to it. And with the splashes of color and a few repairs and a little living, the hotel room had become a home. They had decided not to move, at least not yet, with traveling coming up.

Rheims.... Rheims with racing cars and sports cars. And not much chance of driving, at least since Morris arrived. Mart would watch it as usual, helping in the pit. Then there would be more practice in England, since that was the next stop on the schedule. The British Grand Prix at Aintree. Maybe he might get a chance there. Or maybe not until next year. But there was no use even thinking about it. There was even less patience, thinking at night when thoughts and wants filled the whole mind. He felt the impatience and thought of Anna's offer, and for a moment it seemed easy. Take her offer and *drive*. But he couldn't. There was something there that was frightening—something he couldn't do.

He listened to Charlotte breathing softly and began to relax. He stopped thinking about anything. He was tired and was near sleep. He let himself fall into the darkness. And in that softness and on the painless edge of sleep he began to hear the young Englishman's words come out of a twilight of blue and shadows—of Karussel and Wipperman, and the two bridges waiting for those who shot down from the Schwalbenschwanz, over the Galgenkopf, the two bridges and the pavement rising to meet them, the sound of a motor racing insanely as the wheels left the ground at a hundred and sixty miles an hour....

CHAPTER THIRTEEN

T HE Twelve Hour Rheims International Sports Car Race
began at midnight, following that day's Grand Prix. For some
obscure reason, repairs to the track had not been made until the
very last minute, forcing the juxtaposition of the races. But it was
an ideal thing for the small Scuderia Corsatti. It allowed the team
to enter full strength in both events, sleeping after the French
Grand Prix and entering fresh into the Twelve Hour—entering
with angry hope for a chance to atone for the way Herr Schiller
and his comrades had swept the 305 mile GP race in a nearly
impossible two hours and thirty-seven minutes.

And now, with the flag dropping on the Twelve Hour, the
cars roared away to sweep under the Dunlop tire and into
the first turn, their lights streaking like comets in the darkness,
the object not to beat each other to the checkered flag, but to
cover the most distance during the twelve hours. It was a gruel-
ing matter of speed and endurance. Mercedes immediately took
command. Behind them were Corsatti, one to keep the pace and
the other hanging back in reserve, then Ferrari, Jaguar, the Alfa
Romeos, OSCAs, Austin-Healeys, Maseratis—all of them touching the night with a high whining and then scattering with speed
and distance. At the end of the first lap, as they came around
the last treacherous turn at Thillois intersection and into the
straight, a flash of fire and smoke billowed into the air.

It had taken three minutes plus to cover the five miles of the
course. And as they flashed by the pits to finish the first lap, a car
was missing. After three minutes, death and the smell of smoke,

Corsatti checking them over, gloom in his face, a slumping in his coat.

"Who was it?" Mart asked Mario. "Looked like one of the Jags."

Mario checked down the list of drivers and found the number that had been missing after the first lap.

"Yes. Osbourne."

"Corsatti probably wished it was Schiller or Hoff."

"He would like to see all the Mercedes team licked, but not that way."

"We'd be ahead."

"Yes, but not by good machine and good driving. He wants to win by being the best, not at the expense of drivers."

Martin looked at the overcoated figure standing there with the stopwatch and shook his head.

"Well, what the hell, Mario. People are going to get killed in this business. You told me that every time Corsatti sees a young driver he's reminded of his son, and he never mingles with them because he's afraid they might get killed and he'll get torn up by it again. Now he's even shaken by the crash of a man on another team. Why does he stay with it? Why doesn't he let the *scuderia* fold and devote his time to just making pretty little sedans and coupés, touring cars and stuff instead of racing and sports cars?"

Mario shrugged.

"Perhaps it does not make sense to you. But you must remember Corsatti has been in the business for a very long time. Back to the days of the great Bugatti. In forty, forty-five years, he has built his cars, enlarged his little shack to the factory you see today, had a son born and raised in its shadow die in one of his cars in a foreign land. The cars were not as safe then. There were others who died before his eyes and it was enough to wish blindness. Sometimes I think if his son had not died, Corsatti would have left the business of building racing machines. Or perhaps he would have had a chance to become hardened to it—that is a necessary thing in this business.

"But his son died, and because of that he will cry and rage when a member of his team dies. He will brood and mourn the loss of a man he has never known. It will be the same if Osbourne who crashed tonight is dead. But he cannot leave. He can only go back to his office and blame himself and die a little inside. The driver is never perfect. The human element—it must be allowed for in the design of a racing machine. There will always be men who race, and as time passes, it gets faster and faster.

"Corsatti would be deserting something if he left. He has to find ways of making them safer and safer. This is his life. To do this and then test them, display them by entering races each year and trying to beat the other Italians, the Germans, the English and all the others. This keeps the factory going, and there is the hope that others will copy the safety features. This is for his son and for all of them. It is some sort of purgatory."

"I guess so—only, he had better start winning races soon."

"Maybe next season will be better."

"New engines?"

"There are designs on the boards. A smaller, lighter motor for both racing and Gran Sport, but with more power. And perhaps the disc brakes. We may have them for Germany this year, with luck."

Mart considered it with excitement. A lighter engine in itself was good for reducing weight and improving handling characteristics. If smaller and lighter, and still putting more power to the rear wheels, with the added advantage of disc brakes to put them closer into the turns before shutting off—

"Enough to catch Mercedes?"

"Enough or nearly so," Mario told him. "It is the only way we are going to win, if we are to win at all."

"I don't know. I'd like to try it."

"Driving against Mercedes?" Mario smiled reprovingly.

"Right now."

"They are experts. You are but a small wet chicken, my friend."

"Even so, those are sports cars. No one has tried me yet."

"You are thinking of the many times Nuvolari beat the enemy with a slower car merely by driving better and going on sheer nerve."

"No, you're getting the wrong idea. I'm not setting myself up to be another Nuvolari, but I just think the Corsatti could get closer to the Germans, maybe even catch them, without the new motor."

"Forget the idea, my friend."

Mart sat back on an oil drum and watched the cars scream by. A moment later, Morris came in with the white of the fabric showing in a rear tire. Mart and Mario and the other members of the crew leaped to the car, jacked it up, knocked the wheels off, refueled, filled the radiator, changed a plug, put new wheels on and sent Morris back into the race. It took thirty-one seconds.

Mart went back to the oil drum then. Corsatti was placing third and sixth now and the race was only a couple of hours old.

"You look angry." Charlotte came over and stood by him. She had been out in back, napping in one of the cars.

"How does the race usually go? The Germans! In the GP they showed speed and endurance for three hundred and five miles. We showed endurance and steady position holding. In this race, they are showing speed and endurance and will cover more than twelve hundred miles before they are finished. We're showing endurance steady position holding. I'm tired of the steady, half-baked performance!"

"What was all that smoke down there a little while ago?"

"One of the Englishmen. A Jaguar."

"Was he hurt?"

"I think he's dead."

"That's terrible." She said it quietly.

"Well ...?"

"Mart!"

"Now what's the matter?"

"You sound so cold about it!"

"What do you want me to sound like?"

Her face was white and she was shaking, and her eyes were full of hurt and surprise.

"A man gets killed and you shrug it off like he had been an insect. What am I supposed to do, smile and agree with you? Is that what your Anna Pavanne would do?"

"Look, he knew what he was doing. Nobody asked him to drive in this race or any other race. Nobody made him become a race driver. These things happen. He knew it, I know it, everybody knows it. There's no point in worrying about it. Mourning is a waste of time."

"Maybe he had to be a race driver."

"Don't start bringing up that silly business again. And while you're at it, quit dragging Anna into everything."

"Don't shout at me like that. I don't have to stand here and listen to you."

"No, damn it, you sure don't."

"You know, you were right after all! I know why we couldn't get married as long as you're a driver. It's because you're cold and hard, and you don't really need me at all. You never loved me—any woman would've done as well. You just can't be bothered—no sentiment, no feeling, just something they strap into a car to make it go. I should've seen it when you didn't stop for Taylor at Pebble Beach that time. Other people don't matter. You and Anna—you're perfect for each other. Go to her. She's right there in the grandstand. I suppose you'll pretend you didn't know she was there too. I don't care. Go on, go to her. I should have left a long time ago."

"Thanks for telling me. I'll take your suggestion."

Charlotte ran out the back way. Mart watched her go and turned his eyes to the grandstand. He hadn't known Anna was there, but there was no great surprise in finding it out. There would be no finding her now. But it didn't matter. Anna would find him, and he felt no discomfort or anger about it.

Charlotte—little Charlotte, always shook up and confused. Argue about somebody crashing and suddenly she was talking about marriage again, and saying he was hard and cold. If she had looked at the crash a little closer, maybe she would've seen why he didn't have the heart for marrying anyone—that death was there on the course always, and that a man couldn't stay in perpetual mourning. Mart shook it away and concentrated on the race. She didn't understand like Anna did. Maybe Charlotte was right, after all. Maybe he and Anna were perfect for each other.

The cars went by screaming, or stopping at the various pits to take fuel and tires or quick repairs and then rocket into the race again. Alfa Romeo, Mercedes, Jaguar, Ferrari, Talbot—their racing colors, once deep reflections of brilliant color in the lights of the straight now streaked and smeared with dirt and oil and the damage of flying pebbles and near disasters. And with the other things that happened in the time of racing. Breaks in the rhythm of a motor, smoke and flame coming from an exhaust, expensive noises coming from under a hood, silence and an exhausted driver pushing his car into the pit, a shake of the head from some chief mechanic and the car is retired and the driver looks angry and sad as the other cars go by with the strength of their motors chiding. The gods of petrol and castor, of rubber and pavement, of speed and chance, of gleaming moving parts of polished steel, turning their thumbs down on a car and smiling at their fast little toy and saying we are tired of you.

Another pillar of smoke and fire, this time near the little stand of trees before the road plunges into the Garenne de Gueux, smudging dawn and horizon with darkness of burning oil and rubber and paint. And Corsatti watching the cars closely again.

The three minutes of waiting.

A careful check of all the cars.

Robert Morris comes by and Taglio breathes easier. He and Morris have been trading off since the race began, spelling one another while the other napped or sipped coffee and tried for a moment to close his eyes against the rapid turns and dizzy whirl of headlamps he still saw and felt.

A second passed, and then two, and then fifteen.

Where was Brusetti?

Corsatti began to pace back and forth, trying to listen to the garbled reports of the loudspeaker echoing down the straight.

"Brusetti?" Martin asked Morris.

"Must've been—everyone else seems accounted for. No, look, there he is! Something's the matter."

Brusetti came down the side of the straight in an erratic manner. He narrowly kept out of the other cars' way and skidded into the pit, nearly overshooting and taking Mario with him.

Brusetti was sick. The whiteness of his face, the vomit on the right side of the car, the way he staggered to a bench and sat with his head in his hands attested to that. He spoke in brief, agonized phrases to Mario. There was a brief discussion between Mario and Corsatti. Mario came back and stood in front of Mart.

"You're driving. You and Brocco on this car. Brusetti was right behind the Talbot when it crashed. It hit his nerves."

Mart whooped and was in the car before they could finish with it. He waited impatiently among the rushing mechanics.

"Take it easy, my friend," Mario advised. "Do not be excited."

"Hell, this is old stuff, Mario. These are sports cars."

"You forget, this is professional, and not like your little races in your country. Now remember, do not try to pass the Morris-Taglio car. Let them fight with the leaders. You will drive close enough to Morris and Taglio to take over if something happens to their car, but no more than that."

"I know, Mario. I heard the instructions before the race."

"Yes, but I know your impatience," Mario said and turned to hurry the mechanics a little more.

"Don't worry," Mart muttered with mounting irritation.

"I repeat. Drive where we tell you to drive and nowhere else. If you feel like there are too many chains on you, just remember it is often those who hang back and save their cars who come in to the last hours of an endurance race. It gives you a chance to put on speed at the last and catch up on the distance while the others may be blowing themselves up. And who knows? You might win."

The crew stepped back then and Mario nodded.

"You're off. I spit in your oil!"

He shot into the race and accelerated with everything the car had to offer.

He joined battle with the madly rushing cars and their terrifying voices, and there was no fear, no sweat, no case of jitters as Mario had anticipated.

He shot under the Dunlop tire and hit the first turn with morning light growing around him. The wind burned like ice over his face, and the excruciatingly high sweet voice of the Corsatti tore at his ears. His first chance to drive—not the first race, not the racer he dreamed of, only part of a race, but just the same it was sweet and long in coming.

He settled back and began to take stock of things as he swooped down the section of the course that was the Route Nationale 31, the long straight ending in a sharp bend near the Thillois intersection. There were several cars to catch and pass before Brusetti's original position could be regained.

In going past the pit, there were no instructions for him on the blackboard, no urging for him to make better time. He was the baby of the team, the still wet chicken; they did not expect him to be of much use. Let him drive a while and try and retain the position Brusetti had held while Brocco took his much needed rest—a few cars back from the leaders where only a medium effort was required of car and driver, waiting for the last laps or the chance that the other Corsatti might get knocked out of the race for one reason or another. But the way the spells at the wheel would more than likely work out, Brocco would be in for the fury of the final laps. He frowned and sat harder on the throttle.

He nudged the wheel to the right and drifted into the straight towards the shadows of Garenne de Gueux. He passed a Talbot and then a Ferrari. Quickly, he moved around the lap and the time was fifteen seconds better. But still not good enough.

He bore down harder and passed the trailing XKD Jaguar, seeing its tail fin glinting with the light of the first sun, whistling after his next goal with the tach needle nearly in the red.

He passed the pits again. The blackboard told him to hold his position. He was where he should be now, and Morris was in and Taglio taking over. He flicked on past and noted one other thing: Schiller was in the pits with the first-place Mercedes.

The other Merc was due soon, if he remembered right; cashing in on some of their mileage advantage to refuel and re-tire. The margin was big and no great urgency was needed to protect it. But he was fresh, and who knew what might happen if he let go the reins of his nerve?

Mart whipped around another lap and then another, until he'd lost count of how many he had made; he'd passed another XKD and a Ferrari, and then had noted that Taglio was coming up to resume his position after the pit stop. Schiller, too, was back in again. Mart wondered what the reaction would be in the pits if he went after Taglio. Hell, he knew what the reaction would be. Well, he thought, up your big nose with your damned blackboard, Mario.

Then another Ferrari was going by, and Taglio, too, quickly passing. Mart whooped and took up chase, breathing Taglio's acrid exhaust as if it were a beautiful perfume. Down the straight they hurtled, past the pit again and Mario frantically holding up the board. Slow down, it ordered. Not on your life, buster, Martin muttered, and swallowed against the dryness of his throat. Not on your life. Work up to the front, get miles covered, start shaving away at time and distance.

He flicked past the Mercedes pit and saw that the second Mercedes, which had entered the pit on the last lap, was still there. What was going on? Mart couldn't believe it. A Mercedes breaking up under the strain? That part of it didn't matter. What was important was that if it stayed out long enough the mileage it had marked up so far would be passed by the Corsattis. He would be in third place. And if he could pass Taglio, he would be in second, within reach of Schiller himself.

There was no doubt of it. The different classes running, the categories of engine size from small to large, were scattered all over the course now. The big 3000cc cars had lapped the 750's and the 1100's and 2000cc jobs until they were all intermingled in their rushing, and the untrained observers might have a hard time telling who was leading. But the Corsattis and the Mercedes had stayed pretty well bunched together. Martin knew exactly where he was. With a little luck, he'd be going after Schiller himself. Pull that off, and he wouldn't be sitting out races anymore.

He waited, staying with Taglio until the moment was right. Like the rest, with maybe five hours left, Taglio wasn't all out yet.

When the long straight was opening up before him, the Route Nationale 31, it was time. He pulled out to the side and took on more speed. Taglio was watching him closely, and as he came close, swung over and blocked Mart's way. Mart felt the tires bite in and squeal as he hit the brakes and swerved to avoid the other car. He swore against his teeth and watched the tight-shouldered little Italian pull away a little. Taglio could have caused them both to crash with a stunt like that. Wheels tangling, the cars tripping—both of them could have got it. Taglio knew it.

So that's it, he thought. You're counting on me to scare off. What happens if I don't scare?

Mart grinned tightly and pushed the speed up a little and duplicated the maneuver. Taglio swung over as before, scowling angrily. But Mart kept on coming, watching the distance between the wheels grow smaller and smaller. It was hard to keep from slowing or swerving away again. He saw Taglio's face, the intentness of it and the sudden paling as wheels touched and screamed. Abruptly Taglio pulled away from it, and Mart jammed his throttle to the floorboard triumphantly. He saw the tach needle hit the red zone as he pulled into the clear.

He saw a little excitement in his pit as he passed to start the next lap. Well let them get excited, he thought. Let them watch a driver with a little ambition and wonder why they waited so long to let him drive. Spare the engine? Hell, maybe it would quit before noon ever came, and again, maybe it wouldn't. Maybe he could set things up before Brocco took over again, get the number of laps up to what the Germans had and more, and maybe Brocco could hold it there. Maybe at noon, when it was all over, Corsatti would have covered enough laps on the record sheets to go to England with a win in his pocket.

Schiller was visible ahead now, and Mart opened the Corsatti all the way, slowing only for the turns, and slowing a little less than the Mercedes. He was gaining. He was fresh and the German was not and was leaning on a time advantage. The worst of the race was over. It was daylight, wasn't it? It might add up to be all in his favor. If he worked it right.

He drew closer to the Mercedes, close enough to see flecks of grease and dirt on the silver skin, close enough to see the man himself. Schiller, a cold, efficient, ruthless part of a team that was cold, efficient and ruthless. Mart grinned. You're being hard on him, he thought. Probably a nice guy at home, or in some beerhall, with a nice blonde wife and fat blond children. But in the car, all the cars, it was a different thing, and Mercedes was supreme.

He was close enough now to see the pale blue eyes when Schiller glanced back over his shoulder. Mart nodded.

"One minute, Herr Schiller!" he muttered into the wind.

He hit the turn coming out of the Garenne de Gueux with Schiller just a breath in front of him, and felt the rear end swing around. With a startled cry, he tried to correct, but the Corsatti was going too fast; he corrected too much and the Corsatti spun around completely, skidded off the road backwards and turned over in a drainage ditch. His head snapped against the cowling and blackness and silence enveloped him.

CHAPTER FOURTEEN

ORSATTI watched the second hand jerk around the dial of the stopwatch in his hand, ignoring the ache in his legs that came from supporting his tremendous bulk without rest since the Twelve Hour at Rheims began. Morris was doing well as usual, the steady fast laps, the daring of darkness and road, hitting his stride quickly and holding it. But it was not making a dent in the damnable lap times clicked off by the Mercedes team that in the end would send their total mileage soaring above every other team's.

Wait until the new motors were placed in his cars—maybe they would find supremacy once more. Brusetti was not doing well. Night driving always did this to him. The times on the laps were fair, but the driving was erratic and tense. Brusetti was fine on a hard, dry track in the light of day, but let it rain or get dark, or have a little too much oil on the road and his style went to pieces.

He saw Brusetti streak by then, twenty seconds slower than his previous lap, and cursed under his breath. Ought to put Brocco back in—but you can't drive a man into the ground. Brocco has to have a breather. Took a good load of the French Grand Prix the day before. No, Brusetti has to stay his time, and you can't push him. You can't push him beyond his limit—a life is more important than a race—but it is still hard to stand there and see the product of Corsatti eating the fumes and wind of the others.

He saw the flash of light then. The flash, and then the flames, and the black smoke illuminated by the flickering red glow.

Mario, he saw, was standing frozen, watching, his heavy face tense with worry and fear. Poor Mario, Corsatti thought, this old son of the Mantuan hills; he should have stayed with the goats of his father instead of listening to the cars that spoke to him down on the roads. He is happy here, yet not happy. Like me, these are his children. Only Mario has let himself become a father, a brother to them. It will tear him to pieces when one does not come around again to the pit.

Minutes passing. The stopwatch going around.

Morris coming by on schedule. A space of time.

But not Brusetti. Where is Brusetti? Is that him, over there where the flames devour good metal?

"What do you think?" Mario asked.

"Ah! What can one tell from the loudspeaker, and the gravel in the mouth of that Frenchman? But it does not look good."

Mario began to dance on one foot and then the other. Short, tight movements, the dance of nerves and tension and fear.

"We saw only the flames, Mario. It does not mean we saw the impact. Perhaps he was able to get out before the fuel exploded .... No, no—it is someone else. Here comes Brusetti. You over there! Wave him in!"

Brusetti was driving like a drunken man, weaving slowly down past the grandstand.

Brusetti's car approached, dangerously close to the stream of cars racing by him. The car wobbled and surged, and the driver's head was bent over the wheel as if he were asleep or dead, or perhaps trying to hide from the thing about him.

"Mario, get him out of that car, quick!"

Brusetti nearly overshot the pit before the car lurched to a stop and Mario helped him out.

Brusetti looked for a moment with tortured eyes at the pillar of flame across the course. He turned away with a jerk and looked at Mario. Corsatti heard the twisting words before Brusetti tore away and headed for the rear of the pit to lie down on a bench and retch at his vacant insides.

"Right in front of me—I saw it. I could feel the heat hitting me in the dark. God, I could see that terrible Frenchman sitting in what was left, his eyes were open. I swear they were open and the flames were reaching for them ..."

Corsatti shut his ears to it, and when Mario came back over he took a deep breath.

"Brocco needs more time. He is too tired. Let Janis go in for a while."

"You think he is ready?"

"Ready enough for this. There is not too much to worry about. He has at least raced in this car before.... You! Are you asleep on your feet? Hose that stink off, be fast with those tires! Where do you think you are? See to him, Mario, or he will be making *pasto* again in the house of his cousin. Tell Janis, so that he will be ready when those fools are finished with the car."

He watched Mario tell him and the sudden explosion of excitement in Janis' face. The frenzied reaching for helmet, and the leap to the car, and then the brief, unendurable wait during the last few seconds before he was off.

"He is happy. Too happy," Mario muttered.

"Perhaps. But I think he will calm down. He will more than likely scare himself a time or two, but we will relieve him soon."

Mario continued to watch the tail lights worriedly as they grew smaller and vanished around the first turn.

"It is not as tragic as that, Mario. He is good enough to hold Brusetti's position without danger."

"I know he is good. It is his enthusiasm that gives me cause for alarm."

"Yes, he is good. Janis will be interesting to watch next season. But do not forget. This is his first taste of professional driving. You may be assured that his enthusiasm will cool, and he will become concerned only with keeping whole this first time. Now, as before, my friend, no man drives until I know he is ready."

Mario relaxed.

"It was like seeing an old friend off on a long voyage. The first departure is always the hardest and the saddest."

"Mercedes is calling Schiller in, to the pit. Call Morris in now while the time is good."

Mario signaled with the board. Morris came in for tires and fuel at the same time as Schiller. Taglio relieved him. The exchange was silent, the silence of tiredness rather than language since Morris spoke Italian, and partly because Taglio had little use for foreigners in general.

Morris stretched out on the bench, and found fitful sleep almost immediately, in spite of the groaning and retching of Brusetti nearby.

Minutes passed. The Germans flashed by in white blurs of speed. A short interval, and then Taglio was pursuing them hotly. At that point, Mario angrily held up the blackboard. Ever alert, he had seen it as Taglio entered the straight—Martin Janis on Taglio's tail and not where he was supposed to be.

Corsatti caught a brief glimpse of Martin's head, the white helmet bent low behind the shallow wind-screen, the car moving swiftly without hesitation or wasted motion as it entered the turn at the end of the straight. No evidence of nerves. He would be all right and probably better than Brusetti was before the Talbot spun out.

Corsatti sat down, finally. The hour was late. The first sun was touching the horizon and he was tired. The number of cars in the race had thinned considerably—the toll of time and distance, the price of strain and frayed nerves, of mechanical failure and bad judgment. Mercedes still led by a comfortable margin. Christ, those cars were good. Maybe not so good in the turns, but by God, watch them make up for it in the straights.... Here comes the second-place Mercedes, and Taglio is gaining on him for once.

SPEED DEMON

Corsatti looked again. Not Taglio. He saw the bent head over the wheel, the purposeful and slightly exaggerated bend of shoulders. It was Martin Janis moving up rapidly. He must have passed Taglio in the back stretches.

Mario had noticed it sooner and had already waved another slow-down with the blackboard.

"He ignores the board again! Black flag?" he asked.

"No. Not yet," Corsatti almost whispered.

"But he is ignoring instructions."

"I know, he's tossed my planning to the devil. But I am more interested in the manner of his driving. Let him go for a while and see what he does with it. If he begins to show signs of trying too hard, use the board on him again. Very interesting…"

"It does not seem to be a strain for him," Mario admitted.

The second-place Mercedes, in on the last two or three laps, was still there as Mart passed again. They noticed him pick up speed.

"He has seen the delay in the Mercedes pit," Mario observed.

The white car stayed there for the time of another lap with mechanics swarming over it frantically. It pulled into the race again just after Mart went by.

Corsatti watched, interested, fascinated and curious to see what the boy would do, watching for the first signs of strain with the order for the black flag just behind his teeth. His strategy was gone now. It was a gamble, what would happen. An interesting gamble….

"I just heard that Hoff lost second place with his pit stop," Mario told him.

"I figured as much. That means we might come out of this with a second place if Janis and Brocco can hold that spot and keep Hoff from passing them. What kind of margin do we hold?"

"It was only about three miles, but maybe it is better we stop him."

"He has not shown signs of endangering himself, and the car seems all right. Second place is good. Very good."

"But he believes a driver going on sheer nerve could defeat the Germans with a slower car. With only one car in front of him, he will try to overtake Schiller—I'm sure he will. He'll lose his head and drive with too much confidence. He'll move beyond the limits of the car and himself. He has not had that kind of experience—he won't be satisfied to stay where he is."

"Why did you not tell me of this before?"

"Who would know that he would try this? He said he would take it slow. I knew of his great impatience, but I did not think he would be so foolish. He drives well, that one, better than a man should be expected to so soon. But no one could keep that car out in front of the Germans—no one! But what is this to a hotheaded child who thinks he can smell victory? Believe me, I know this boy."

Corsatti bit his lip. He tried to keep his voice calm.

"Very well. Have them flag him in next time around."

But Martin Janis did not come around again.

The Mercedes ... and then what was again the second-place Mercedes, with Taglio drumming along behind.

Taglio signaled a spin-out and that Janis appeared to be okay. The loudspeaker blared a moment later, and they could hear enough to confirm Taglio's signal. Janis had spun out. The car was in bad shape, but Janis appeared to be only unconscious. An ambulance had removed him to the rear area.

"I was afraid of this," Mario said. "The young idiot."

"Perhaps if I were closer to him, I would have known."

"Do not blame yourself. Martin is not like any other driver we have had on the team. He and the girl asked me once to tell them what kind of a man a driver is. They wanted to know. I begin to believe it is Martin Janis we do not know."

"Well, when you can talk to him, you may inform him that he has been suspended from all driving for a month. Perhaps this will teach him to be more patient, and to obey instructions after this."

Corsatti sat down and closed his eyes.

For a moment, a Corsatti had threatened Mercedes seriously. For a while, a driver had driven with a great intent and a rare imagination, a will that moved Corsatti's mileage past the Germans' second best and almost broke into the open. It was impossible, of course, to keep ahead—but still, for a moment it was almost like someone else behind the wheel. With a sudden display of skill, it almost seemed a return to a time when there was a greater driver than had ever been seen .... But how was that possible? Perhaps it was all an illusion, a mistake—just a young man driving beyond expectation, but only for a little while. There was bravery there, and daring, but what of the times to come in a formula-one racing machine?

For now, the moment, it did not matter.

Corsatti would not win that day. Winning would be more than luck, now. Corsatti had not won in some time, and probably wouldn't for a while, at least until the new engines were available.

But Martin Janis was alive. That was the important thing.

CHAPTER FIFTEEN

ANNA PAVANNE sat on the edge of the bed in her hotel room and smoked a cigarette. She watched Martin's face which, except for the long, dark bruise just above his eyebrows, seemed to be in the repose of normal sleep. The doctor had left a few minutes before. He had examined Martin and found nothing wrong that two or three days of rest would not fix. The crash helmet Martin had worn during the race, plus the restraint of his safety belt and the extreme rigidity of the car itself, had kept the shock to a minimum. He had been fortunate, considering the speed. And now, Mario Felice and Robert Morris were there, the race being over, and waiting. Anna saw Martin's eyelids flutter and then his eyes trying to focus on the ceiling light.

"It is about time, my friend," Mario said.

"My head!" Mart groaned, and winced.

Mario grunted unsympathetically.

"You gave it quite a rap," Morris said.

"What in hell happened?"

"You were trying to do too much," Mario gestured angrily. "I warned you. But perhaps you are the reincarnation of Nuvolari."

"You know me better than that, Mario."

"I thought I did. It is bad enough that we lose the race. The Germans win again. That has become usual. But you become the great driver, the one who knows everything. Corsatti puts all his experience and judgment into planning a team strategy. He takes the course into consideration and the cars we are running, thinks about our lap times in practice and about the German lap times.

He applies all of this and decides where each Corsatti should try and hold a position. This is team racing. But of course, Martin Janis knows a better way. He thinks things are moving slow and makes his own attack on Mercedes. As a result, Corsatti loses a few million lire of automobile and almost loses a driver. It also cost us a possible second place. Hoff's car retired again. Taglio broke an axle toward the end. And where was our reserve car?"

"I suppose I have been canned."

"He means dismissed from the team," Anna explained.

"Hah! For your own good, and for the sake of the sweet girl you sent away last night—as a courtesy to this gracious woman who clutters up her room with you, you should be put on the first boat. But you are still with us. You have been suspended from driving for a month, but you are still with us. *Buona notte,* Robert." He frowned at Mart and left.

"Suspended! Well, seems as if I've been a naughty boy."

"I would say so," Morris agreed with him.

"I was only trying to pull a win out of the hat for them."

"At the expense of team strategy."

"Damn the strategy! No strategy is going to beat Mercedes. Look at it. Mercedes has both endurance and speed. Corsatti has endurance but not as much speed. What good does it do to try to plant someone behind Mercedes? We haven't got the power to get behind them with an effective harassing action and make them blow up."

"They may not blow up, but they might make a mistake."

"Schiller make a mistake? Who are you trying to kid?"

"None of us is infallible."

"The only thing to do is to get out in front of them in any possible way and stay there. Maybe we tear the wheels off. They'll avoid taching red, and maybe ours will blow up being there too long. But maybe it *won't* happen! I think it's better than just sitting behind them and watching them get farther and farther away."

"You're impatient, and so am I. But—look, chap, you should be resting, not arguing. We'll see you tomorrow. And I want to thank you, Miss Pavanne, for your room and trouble. Good night."

Morris left and Anna came around and sat on the bed. She lit another cigarette and smiled at him.

"You haven't had much to say," Mart told her.

"I've just been listening to you. I think you're right."

"You're damn right I'm right. But it doesn't look like anyone agrees with us."

"I wouldn't say that, Martin."

Mart lay back in bed and closed his eyes. "What would you say?"

"While I was out at the course, and later while you were here and your friends were here to watch over you, I moved around listening to people talk. Around the course, at the different cafes and bars, wherever the spectators gather—I asked questions of people who had seen this and heard that during the race."

"So? What are they saying? What's the matter with that crazy American?"

Anna smiled.

"Yes, they think you are crazy. But they were sitting up and taking notice, too. The talk was all about the remarkable things you were doing with a slower car. The Corsatti is no match for Mercedes in speed, but still, the American was catching the famous Schiller. This was exciting. This was a great thing to them. Your name is on the lips of every spectator there. They don't know it wasn't part of Corsatti's strategy. All they know is that they saw the beginnings of a great new driver. But it doesn't matter."

"Why not?"

"The opportunity will not come again. Corsatti has suspended you for thirty days. He will make sure you obey orders next time you drive or you will not drive. He will keep you on the sidelines until you do obey, or until you leave him. But it is senseless to talk about this now. Morris was right. You should be resting."

Mart sat up angrily. He looked as if he wanted to lash out at something, to hurt something. He still believed he was right, and Anna smiled. He was beginning to understand.

"Anna."

"Yes?"

He hesitated, but she saw it coming with no surprise. Anna had been certain that it would happen that night. The suspension of his driving had clinched that.

"Does the offer still go? The car of my own, and you and me?"

Anna smiled. "What about Charlotte?"

"She's headed for home."

"Are you sorry?"

"She was a nice kid, but—no, I'm not sorry. She doesn't belong in any of this. That was all a mistake. The whole thing has been a big mistake. I'm tired of it. Those people you talked to—they really thought I—I was like you said?"

"They saw the beginnings of a great driver. One could be wrong. Two could be wrong. But not all of them."

"I really got the rave, huh?"

"Like you used to in your own country. Only it means more here, Martin."

Mart nodded, and there was a gleam in his eyes.

"Well, how about it, Anna? Does your offer still hold?"

Anna smiled and turned out the light. Within moments she was beside him, enfolding him with her body.

"Just hold me, Martin. Until you are feeling better, just hold me and go to sleep. This is my answer."

Martin and Anna reached Liverpool less than two weeks before the British Grand Prix at Aintree. There, Anna made the arrangements to have delivered a three-litre Ferrari for daily use and future sports car events. And within four days after their arrival, they took delivery on a new type formula-one Maserati which she had ordered flown up just before leaving France.

It took money, a lot of money, and the idea of buying both cars, not to mention the idea of flying one up from Italy, astounded him. Briefly, he had wondered how much Anna had really extracted from Ramsey Barkdale. But he did not worry about it. It was what Anna wanted to do, and the Maserati was his choice. He was grateful to Anna—and he loved her. He had been a fool not to go along with her ideas before. The reactions she had found at Rheims seemed to bear that out. There was even a small paragraph in one of the French papers noting that the young American had shown a skill and daring reminiscent of other times. It boosted him inside, and he was free from the impatience, the feeling of being tied down, the waiting at Corsatti's.

With time growing dangerously short, he began practice feverishly.

The new Maserati was a shade faster than the Corsatti. It had a new five-speed gearbox and a new cylinder head, and a new type of carburetion. Disc brakes allowed it to go farther into the corners. The other Maseratis had not done so well that season, and indeed, Mercedes was still superior. But this new model held a promise. If it was driven right—He remembered Morris' comment about Mercedes suspension being touchy, and how they cut power at the turns a little sooner than usual. That's where the new Maserati would have the advantage. It had a promise. If it was driven right....

And he started practice a different sort of man.

No matter how disappointing the time with Corsatti had been, and no matter how unpleasant leaving them had been, he had to admit he had learned there. He had come from the United States with untrained enthusiasms, and a skill which was at once admirable and rare. But because of the wild enthusiasms, the skill had not been channeling in the right direction.

The business of driving a sports car in a Sunday afternoon race was a science and a skill of the few, and nothing to be taken up lightly by just anyone who acquired the notion. But even so, Grand Prix driving was a far more serious thing—a profession more than a sport, a need more than a pleasure for those who drove, as if the rest of the world were a disease of clumsiness and slow motion, against whose spastic encroachment the only defense was speed and agility. Their daring was tempered by respect, their bravado quieted by knowing and fear, but they kept moving, kept racing, livid with the hunger that traced through their beings like a vivid blue beam of electricity. There was no resting.

Martin Janis had increased his knowledge of motors, and soaked up the atmosphere of racing, and gone his practice rounds, and had driven in a race. It was not what could be called the first race. The first, the one to paste in scrapbooks, to remember in later years and a hundred thousand miles and countless turns away, was yes to come. But it was coming, only a few days away now, and he was entering it for himself and not as a reserve driver. Entering it at the beginning, and luck willing, he would drive through to the finish.

But he had driven in a race, and it had taken some of the steam away, some of the impatience, the edge off the painful hunger of the starved. And in the brief instant when the Gran Sport broke loose from the pavement in France, and slid wildly off the road to crash, he learned something. Professional racing in Europe was a far faster and deadlier thing than even his expectations. The fear he had felt at times, the worry that comes with waiting—as he'd known in races at home—was now in the background constantly. It was something sitting on his shoulders, and with it came a new respect. And with the respect, a new ambition to do better than before.

It was a more sober, a quieter, and in some ways, an older Mart Janis who rolled out for practice each morning.

He drove faster, but steadier. He cornered as fast as before, but with smoothness rather than abandon. He kept his exultancy a thing burning inside, channeling it to honing his skill down closer to the knife-edged perfection every driver seeks, rather than running down the ribbon of pavement like a shout in the wind in the wildness of summer.

Martin Janis was almost impassive on the surface, swooping down Sefton straight, feeling the wind burn across his face, hearing the high song of the motor. He was a happy man, a more serious man, knowing he was good and yet knowing there was much to learn. What kind of man and where did the craving begin—these things he did not know, and he didn't care. The questions were gone. Whatever kind of man he neded to be, he was, and he was just beginning. He had cars. Anna had seen to that, and he had a mechanic. A thin, stringy fellow named Gaetano Bertoli. Anna had known him in Rome. A wire brought him here as if it were a queen's summons to duty, and there were two more coming in time for the race. Anna had seen to the whole thing...

A blur of red passed him coming out of Bechers Bend and showered him with fumes and noise. He would have known the car and the helmet, the set of the shoulders anywhere. Benito Taglio, out for a practice run too.

Mart glanced at his watch, thinking he had made some kind of mistake. He had had the track mostly to himself in the mornings, most of the other outfits coming out later. Taglio must have spotted him earlier.

Taglio had passed too close, with the insolence of the artist, the egotism of the master, and the hatred of a past champion for the insignificant and clumsy novices. Sure, Mart thought, that was his game. He wouldn't like the novice moving out of his camp, away from the waiting that was fitting for an apprentice and into an independent role. So heckle the novice, make him nervous.

Mart grinned a little and picked up speed and waited for Taglio to make the lap and come up from behind again. He wasn't angry because of Taglio's attitude, nor was he remembering the insult paid to him at the birthday party or the incidents on the track at Turin and Rheims. But he had never had a real duel with Taglio, only the latter's efforts to stop him. Skill for skill, how good was Taglio? Taglio, who had won many races, how good was he, and how well would someone like Martin Janis do against him in a small skirmish?

Mart let his speed pick up gradually and almost imperceptibly, waiting for Taglio to overtake him and pass And when the Italian went past screaming at Village Corner, Mart floored the throttle and kept with him, following him around the course.

He could see Taglio throw his head back and laugh—laugh at the young American's impertinence.

Mart took on more speed and kept with him. Sliding through Bechers Bend, down the Railway straight, and past Melling Crossing and through Tatts Corner. He began to feel good inside. Taglio was not pulling away anymore.

They went around for five laps in that fashion, Taglio almost all out on the course and trying to shake him with full power in the turns. Mart began to grin.

There was power enough left over in the new Maserati to pass. What would Taglio say to that? Mart pulled up closer and the Italian grinned, the expression hard and white in his face.

Mart drew closer and drifted through the jig just past Melling Crossing right on Taglio's tail, and again through the last turn. Then, as the straight opened up before them, he started to pass. But Taglio had anticipated the move and let his car out all the way. They shrieked up the straight, neck and neck. There was no time to pass yet. Taglio shouted curses at him as they sped along, his face livid with hate. Mart almost hated back, but enjoyed himself too intensely to do more than grin.

Down through Waterway Corner, another straight. The Anchor Crossing turn began to loom up in the windscreen and Mart began to wonder what Taglio would do if really pushed into a corner. Who would break first? Probably himself, Mart thought. Taglio was too smart. The young American was too new and maybe too apprehensive about risking anything after that spin-out at Rheims. That's what Taglio would be thinking, and he was right.

Mart watched the turn coming closer and closer. Taglio played it as if it wasn't there; he wasn't backing off yet, and he was smiling in anticipation of seeing the American slow down to let him through. It was smeared all over Taglio's face, and Mart began to feel anger in those last seconds. He tried to reason it out and take his foot off the pedal or use his extra power to pull past, but the smile on Taglio's face kept him from doing it.

He held it there, watching it happen, a tightness beginning to well up in his insides, a coil tightening down to the hard knot near breaking point. His foot was like lead, and his arms immovable rods extending from the shoulders to an immovable and useless wheel, and the engine screamed on without losing one beat of its tempo, as if freed of the control from the cockpit and free to whistle unchecked down to its own destruction.

Out of the corner of his eye, he saw the smile on Taglio's face begin to fade, the lips straightening out to a painful grimace, and then, the red of his car beginning to move back, to slow.

Mart felt savage pleasure returning the use of his limbs and letting him stamp the brakes in time to make a hard, howling drift through Anchor Crossing ahead of Taglio.

Martin made one more lap, slowing down, watching Taglio in his rearview mirror until he pulled in and stopped. He lit a cigarette, watching the studied and careful laps the other made.

"That hurt more than the punch in the nose you gave him," he muttered to himself, "or getting past him at Rheims. He won't forget it."

He saw Anna and the mechanic coming in then. He climbed out of the Maserati and threw his helmet in the seat. Anna waved and as she did, he caught a glint of light, and above, in the grandstand's shadow, sitting high in the bleachers, he saw something he hadn't noticed before. Corsatti, wrapped in his overcoat, with the binoculars draped around his neck.

CHAPTER SIXTEEN

THE shadows were cold, high in the grandstand, cold in the English air up there under the roof's overhang, sitting on those hard boards. But from there, the spectator could see well and far, and remain unnoticed. There, the bulky figure in the overcoat with the cigar jutting from a massive face would not disturb or inhibit or draw away from the concentration needed by the young man below in the fast red car.

Mart Janis had already started his practice run when Corsatti sat down in the shadows of the heights to watch, the engine whining crisply in the sharp, clear sunlight, the car a blur of red catching the sun and becoming an impossibly brilliant jewel.

Corsatti watched the car make the laps with precision.

The driver was the boy who impulsively and recklessly challenged the racing white of Germany and lost because of the recklessness and because the machine could not give the speed he had asked of it.

Martin Janis had given a display of remarkable driving. It could not be unexpected, with his performance in American sports car races. Janis was good in them, and the fact was important.

But the big test was the way he handled the racing machine, this new Maserati.

It was true, the final truth would come only when Janis took the racer and drove against a dozen, fifteen or twenty other men, all bent to the same task, of getting up front as fast as possible after the green flag, of moving into the lead and staying there, and unless directed otherwise in the interests of strategy, reaching by all his art and skill the checkered flag before anyone else.

The track is a crowded affair and not the simplicity of a calm practice session by one's self or with the members of one's own team.

But there are things that can be learned by observing practice.

Corsatti's eyes followed Janis around the track, and the motion was like painting a picture or drawing a diagram. The speed in the straightaways, the attitude of the car entering the turns, the recovery and acceleration—all of these spoke to the practiced eye.

Corsatti smoked with some relief. Janis was no longer with them, but he liked Janis—and unhappily, he felt concern for all of them. All of them, no matter the marque they drove under. There was still worry with him, but not as much as there had been when Janis first left.

Martin Janis was a changed man. His handling of the racer was different, the practice different than it had been back in Turin.

Here in the English air, the crash behind him, there was patience, method and precision. More speed now too, both in the straights and turns, though it seemed slower because it was smoother. Speed was something worked up to as the individual personality of the car was learned.

Around and around, like clockwork, accelerating in the straights and slowing a little but not too much, shifting, power-steering with the rear wheels mildly in the turns, accelerating out again, over and over with no break in the rhythm. Learning ... learning every imperfection and perfidy of the concrete ribbon, feeling every subtle shift of weight on the whels, learning exactly what each part of the car was doing, with exactness, and then increasing the speed a notch and repeating endlessly. This was good practice, the mark of a good driver, and insurance for the future.

But still—Corsatti sadly lowered his glasses. He wished he could be sure. He wished Janis was still with them, just so he could be sure before the boy was turned loose in a race. The Maserati was a good car. A very good car, but it did not inspire the same confidence in the way of suspension and balance as the Corsatti did. He was not sure or completely confident of any car, but the Corsatti was a known element. More than anything else, Mario would be there to see to the car, if Janis had stayed with them.

But he had not stayed. How would it go for him alone, then? How would he do?

It still remained for a full scale Grand Prix to tell the full story, to tell of promise and possibility, to speak of courage and strength.

But there was one comfort. Martin had learned a lesson. The spin-out at Rheims had taught him a good lesson.

The girl who had left would have been glad of that. Maybe this new one, this Italian girl—Mario had talked to the mechanic Bertoli, and Bertoli had said a lot of things. She sounds hard and cruel and like the kind who would not flutter and weep at the edge of a course with the cars making hell in the wind. Maybe this was the kind of woman a driver needed. And yet, was it?

Women.... Women and racing never really mixed. A man needed a woman, and perhaps when you know of the stresses upon a racing driver and the briefness of his life, perhaps they need a woman a little more. But if it went too far—if it became wife and children to think about, during the racing the bones became jelly, the mind not as quick, the hand less firm on the wheel.

Now, the redheaded one. What was her name? She had not been Janis' wife. There had been no children. The girl loved him, true, but he had not really loved her, or if he did he had not seemed to realize it, and it was a free thing like the wind blowing between two trees. This was all right for Janis. This had been good.

But for the girl—for any girl like that—she still must watch him, or if she is not strong enough, sit in her room or somewhere away from the race and think about what could be happening, wondering if she will see him when it is over and if he will walk in the door or whether she will find herself seeing what is left of him in a hospital, or perhaps, being asked to help bury him.

It would not have been good for that redhead.

There would have been nothing else for her but to love this man with his car, to be satisfied to be a part of a convenient background, to have him only for the brief moments of night when he perhaps tired of talking of racing and cars.

It was best that she had gone.

So, in the end, perhaps Anna Pavanne was the right kind ....

There was a second glint of light in the sun.

Corsatti focused his glasses on the car entering the track. Taglio. Why was he so early? Must check with Mario to see if there has been a change in practice schedules.

Poor old Taglio. Corsatti lowered the glasses. Not many races left for him.

Oh, Taglio could be depended on to turn in a dazzling performance, and the fact that the Scuderia had not done better than second for a long time, with the exception of the win at the Mille Miglia, was not Taglio's fault. Mercedes had too much speed.

But Taglio—there were suggestions here and there—nothing more than a tremble to the fingers that was not there before, or a cutting off for a turn a fraction sooner than before, a quicker temper, a little more boasting, perhaps too much drinking at times.

These were signs. His time was not far away. The time to quit before it got him and broke him.

Taglio moved the car out into the middle of the track and boomed mightily up the straight.

The car picked up speed and rocketed down to the turn and drifted beautifully through and out again, picking up more speed. He was going much more than Janis, swooping around and coming from behind. Corsatti rose to his feet, a shout caught in his throat. He was coming too close to the boy. Too damn close.

Taglio blurred past Janis, close enough to make the Maserati bobble for an instant.

Corsatti sat down. It was useless to try and get down out of the grandstand in time to stop them. Besides, Janis was now warned, and no independent ever risked his car unnecessarily.

Taglio never did like the boy—a foreigner, a novice who did not behave in the accepted manner of novices. The boy was good. That was what rankled Taglio the most, perhaps. Taglio had little use for those who had not been proven, those just beginning, their whole career before them, the envy of those who could not begin all over again. It came to all of them sooner or later if they lived long enough to see it. But to see one who was good from the beginning—it could make a man more than envious. It was like the hot red lash of a knife blade across the face.

Janis is picking up speed ever so slightly .... What is he up to?

Taglio, coming around again, as before.

Taglio passed close, and Janis accelerated to stay on his tail.

Corsatti chewed his cigar, feeling temper inside begin to mount. The idiots! The crazy childish idiots! The track was no place for these donkey antics!

He watched Taglio lead the boy around the course, fast. But Janis hung on, smoothly; again that lack of effort as if he and the car were one single and expert execution of design and intent.

Faster and faster. No mercy. The master and the novice.

Corsatti raised his glasses and watched as they passed below in front of the grandstand.

He caught Janis' face briefly. There was no anger there. Only curiosity—the face of a man engrossed in an experiment.

Janis had taken the bait thrown to him by Taglio, but there was no anger, only the challenge and the irresistable curiosity to find a comparison. The master and the novice.

Janis was too close on Taglio's tail if he planned to stay there...but no, he was going to try and pass. He saw Martin make the move, but Taglio moved up with him. He watched them rocketing down to Anchor Crossing and the test became obvious: which one was going to hit the brakes first? The choice had to be made quick, now, if ever.

Corsatti stood up again and watched. What were those idiots waiting for? By Christ, if they crash—if one of them gets hurt or killed...?

At seemingly the last possible instant, in the last available inch before disaster, the Corsatti slowed and the Maserati fought through the turn and ripped up the straight.

Corsatti saw Taglio's shoulders slumping, the bitterness of his jaw, and an angry continuance around the track. And at that moment, Anna Pavanne walked in then. Anna and the mechanic Bertoli.

Martin Janis was pulling off and stopping now, and lighting a cigarette, watching Taglio without smiling, and when the woman waved, glancing up toward the grandstand.

The hand holding the cigarette stopped abruptly in its travel to his mouth, and the eyes squinted against the light.

All right, thought Corsatti, I've been discovered, Martin Janis. I have been watching you. Do not let it disturb you.

I am like a father watching a wayward son, wishing I could take you away from cars for a while and let you cook in your own misery for taking chances like that.

Martin walked toward the woman and the mechanic saw to the Maserati when they had left, and Taglio drowned the pain and butchered pride in heavy practice.

I would like to have you back, Martin Janis, so that I might be more sure of you—you, the child in this game on whose person the word novice seems not to fit. You, for whom driving seems to be as natural as breathing. But no, you haven't convinced me yet. The real test is yet to come. But by my Christ, you have something that has no right to be there so soon .....

Corsatti began walking down slowly to the sunshine and toward an exit gate, with a cigar in his mouth that had long since died.

CHAPTER SEVENTEEN

Martin Janis lowered his goggles and huddled in the Maserati against a strong, rain-filled wind. The British Grand Prix at Aintree was about to begin, and his Maserati, by virtue of an eighty-five mile an hour average lap speed, was not too far from the front cars in the starting positions. He grinned. He was among familiar faces. Ahead of him on the right, Benito Taglio. Directly ahead, Robert Morris. And behind, a couple of cars, Brusetti and Brocco, whom he couldn't see. Like old home week, he thought.

Morris was quiet and calm as usual, and Taglio's head had a too-proud lift to it. Brusetti seemed nervous, as if he were still tense from the crash he had witnessed at Rheims. Or perhaps it was the weather.

Ninety laps of a three-mile circuit ahead, and rain was slicking down the pavement and a strong wind was blowing. It wasn't good. Coming down the straights at speed in a strong wind was akin to skimming against a brick wall all the way.

Mart glanced to his right to the pit area and saw Anna and the three mechanics—Gaetano Bertoli, Angelo Gozzoli, and Benozzo Piambo—who made up his crew. Anna seemed unconcerned about the weather or anything as she stood there with a clipboard and a stopwatch. She would keep track of his lap times, and the positions of the cars he would be immediately concerned with, and relay the information to him by means of the small blackboard. There was no other arrangement, no special strategy she needed to cue him on. He was out to win, and he simply planned to keep as close to the front as he could, and when the last few laps were reached, go like hell for the first place. If the car wouldn't take it, then that was the gamble they took. They were not a team.

He smiled at her and returned his attention to the man with the green flag. Anna was quite a gal, he thought. He thought of Charlotte, and the idea amused him. Charlotte would never be able to stand there in the pit with a stopwatch and make sense of anything. She would be sitting back out of the way with a blanket wrapped around her, looking pale and shaken before anything had even happened, like a frightened child. Anna stood erect, her color good and glowing even in that cold, and she was steady, her hands quiet and efficient.

The flagman was raising the green flag then, and the roar of engines rose until it was shimmering like one sustained explosion. Then the flag snapped down and there was no time for thinking. He heard the tires of the front cars screaming under tremendous acceleration, and his own squeak a little as the Maserati shot into motion. He had no room for accelerating very hard yet, nor did the others around him. It was too crowded, and would remain so for pretty much of the first lap.

After the first lap was over, and the course began to thin out, Mart began to gradually move up.

Damn rain, he thought as he passed three slower cars, damn the rain. Hard to see. Everything was swimming. Drops of water hit like bullets at that speed, coming up like a brown fan from the road whenever he got close to another car. He stayed in that spot through the second lap around, feeling it out as if he had not driven the course before.

Then again, moving up. Easy—no wild stuff like last time—particularly in this rain. You're Janis, first time out, not Nuvolari. Easy....

He opened his mouth and let some of the rain sting through like cold hard pellets against the dryness of it.

A Ferrari zoomed up on his tail and it looked as if the driver was going to ride it right into his cockpit before he pulled out and shot past with a new, terrifying roar. His hands shook a little. This wasn't like practice. Well, calm down, he told himself. Concentrate on the Ferrari that just passed. Go on, catch him and pass him—there's room—it's the Railway Straight.... You chicken?

He grimaced, remembering how he'd called someone else chicken a long time before. Grimly, he moved up on the Ferrari and passed him and moved back into the position.

Langlois was next in the blue Talbot. Mart hung on his tail as they shot past the canal with the rain pebbling its surface.

He determined not to worry at this point. Not to try to pass him along here. To wait till he hit the nice long Railway again. Time to get him and pass before that little jig that comes just after the course swings around Melling Crossing and gets involved at Tatts Corner. So down Sefton, through Cottage and Country, and out of Village. He was careful on the straight going into Bechers. It was deceptive. Long enough to build up speed and think you can keep most of it through Bechers, but not in this rain. Now it was the Railway again. Now ....

He stabbed the throttle and heard the wheels chirp and he left the Talbot in a fan of brown spray and took out after a blur of red which was one of the Corsattis in front of him. Catch it, he figured, and he would hold it for a while. He'd be close enough to just hold for a while and let the laps pass. Hold it until the final sprint.

He felt speed building rapidly, was vaguely aware of the tach needle climbing in a swift arc to the red. He was too preoccupied with the sweep of road and the lightness of the wheels on the wet surface to see the needle drop a fraction and try to rise again. But he heard the interruption in the scream of the engine, heard it grow worse swiftly, until at Melling the engine began to cough and sputter and surge. The fuel not getting through, but angrily he fought through Tatts Corner and limped down the straight and into the pits.

The mechanics had heard it and knew what it was before the car had stopped, and immediately had the hood off.

Anna shot a quick question and the mechanic muttered something.

"Cracked fuel line," she said. "How do you feel?"

"Disgusted!"

"You're doing fine, Martin. Plenty of time to catch up."

Bertoli had the fuel line replacement in and the hood back in place then, and Anna stepped back with a nod.

Mart rammed back into the course. He had it to do all over again.

Catch the Ferrari, the Talbot, try to move up, and then catch the Corsatti he had seen. His heart was pounding a little, legs beginning to tremble, especially the right holding the throttle down. But that would go away in a minute.

The time in the pit had been short. The mechanics had been quick. He couldn't help but think of them. The drivers receive the acclaim, the cheers, but how many races are won in the pits by quick and nimble hands?

He caught the Ferrari two laps later, and caught up with the Talbot just in time to see him spin out at Anchor Crossing. A Corsatti lay ahead, not moving too fast. It didn't take much to catch him. Brocco, his face a calm mask of nothing, stared stolidly ahead, and as they came out of Bechers Mart passed him with a wave. Before him now, another Ferrari, then a Lancia and then Morris ahead. Mart poured it on even harder until he also caught the Englishman and passed.

He felt tension building now. Moving too fast. The surface of the road felt like glass, or glare ice. He decided to hold her here for a while. Don't drive like Taylor did that time at Pebble, he told himself. Easy ... easy. He skidded at little at Tatts Corner and sweat broke out at the backs of his legs and under the goggles and where his back was jammed against the seat. Morris was in back of him, Taglio ahead. That meant the Germans were just beyond. Hold it there. Let the laps pass. There is time now, plenty of time. Just hold it.

Laps passed. The driving was something less than automatic with the wind and rain to fight every yard. The Maserati was good in the rain, better than that big Ferrari back there. Took a real driver to handle that Ferrari in the rain. Yes, the Maserati was good, but *good* is only relative. The pavement still felt like glare ice. There is a getting used to it, but no finding of ease with it. There weren't many laps left. Only a small part of the 270 miles remained. But the small part ahead was bigger than the whole.

Down the Railway, moving up a fraction now until he could see the rain whipping from Taglio's dirt-streaked helmet. He held and waited for a chance to pass. Taglio's speed increased to off-set his advance—just a fraction. Taglio was smart. A fraction is never small in racing; it can be measured in time on stopwatches. It can be heard clearly by those who stand where the cars pass. Sometimes it can be as unsurmountable as the last three hundred feet of a mountain's summit, as unreachable as the last tenth of a second protecting a world record in a foot race—one spark beyond whatever it is inside a man that measures out what he can or cannot do.

Taglio had to slow down. The turns would make him do that, and when they did, the disc brakes of the Maserati provided an advantage. Mart waited, and there was a gradual slowing near Melling Crossing, and again at Tatt's Corner, the Maserati going deeper before cutting power. He could hear Taglio's motor before, but now he could make out the tires singing on the wet surface. Taglio glanced quickly over his shoulder in the acceleration out of the turn into the start-finish straight. There was anger in his face.

Mart started to pass, but Taglio blocked him. It looked accidental, like the fishtailing that can come under acceleration on

wet pavement. But it wasn't an accident. Not with anger showing there. Taglio had done a dangerous thing. There wasn't much
room for anything but straight, businesslike driving in weather
like that. Mart tried to hold back anger. It wasn't likely it would
happen again. Taglio had too much to risk. He was point driver
for Corsatti now. He was close to the Germans and Corsatti
himself was watching. Taglio could not throw all that away with
anger and a reckless move.

There was still time. Martin moved up again and edged
closer to Taglio. Taglio looked frozen to the wheel with anger and
tension, but made no move this time, and Martin passed. Past
Taglio and down past the pits with Anna signaling twenty laps to
go. Twenty laps, sixty miles to catch and pass the Germans.

Mercedes. This was the master. This was the team that
arrived on the scene with their cars, truckloads of spare parts,
an army of men to prepare every last detail. The masters, and *he*
was challenging them now. Not the experts, his ex-companions
Morris and Brocco and Taglio, but Martin Janis.

What would Corsatti think of this? And Mario? Their former
apprentice challenging the great Star of Germany all by himself.

Taglio was pressing him. Mart could barely make him out in
the rearview mirror, all gunked up with rain. He made a quick
swipe at it with his hand. Yes, Taglio was pressing.

Mart pushed down with his shaking foot and pulled away.
He held him off for four laps, and Taglio could not pass, but he
held there like a leech, pressing, making him keep his speed high.
It was too fast now. Too damn fast. He couldn't keep it there in
the rain. But he did, through Anchor, and before he could really
get set for them, Cottage and quickly again, Country and Village
with Taglio hanging on. He skidded at Village and almost lost it.
Goddamn it, he thought, trying to brush the film of water and oil
off his goggles, Taglio's too close, trying to burn you up.

Easy! Calm down, you're doing fine. Just take it easy. Don't
botch things now.

He tried to ignore Taglio, and added a fraction of speed in hopes of shaking him. The three Mercedes jobs were just ahead. He could see the third one clearly. Strangely, it was not a welcome sight; it was almost frightening in its symmetry. But still, there was no time to waste. No more biding of time. Not many laps left. Move up, closer, until the great silver car was just yards ahead. The Maserati *could* catch them, if driven right, if he used the turns to advantage. If driven right, and he was doing it. He kept inching up.

Taglio was close on his tail, the Mercedes just ahead. No room for mistakes now. No slackening off. It couldn't matter that the road was like glare ice at that speed, or that the rain cutting across his face broke visibility into small fragments, or that tension took each and every movement and encased it in hot tin.

His heart was pounding harder, and his leg shook on the pedal and he felt sweat pouring out. Down the short Sefton Straight in to Cottage Corner, and then almost instantly, Country Corner, Village, and the short straight into Bechers. He roared powering it hard through Bechers, but Bechers was deceptive in the rain. It would've been all right if he could have slowed a little more there, but Taglio was pressing with all the skill and anger he could muster.

The sprint was on, the sprint through the last laps, and he was almost losing it in that turn. Taglio's engine roared at the back of his skull, pushing, pushing, keeping it hot, trying to make him rattle. Mart's arms trembled almost uncontrollably, and when Bechers was finished with and the Railway stretched ahead, the Corsatti took over, and that instant took care of it.

With the muddy rain smashing against his goggles and face and the sound tearing at his ears, and the terrific pace, he knew he couldn't do more. He was frozen and tight, wanting to catch Taglio and the Germans again, but was unable to move his foot down to get the speed that was there. The whole crazy thing seemed to collapse and there was too much rain beating down and too much of everything. His foot came up off the throttle, and he wanted to scream as if the rain were tearing holes in him, as if it were drowning him as it rolled over his face and mingled with sudden hot tears.

He did not see the cars swooping down on him, but he heard the terrifying agony of their tires as they tried to avoid him, and there was the wind and gusts of their passing and he saw them vanishing ahead in the spray—Corsattis, Ferraris, the Talbot, all making the last minute bids to place closer to the front and he could not hold them from it. He could only pull to the side with his heart in his throat to go wobbling down the edge of the start-finish straight and pull into the pit before the race had finished.

Anna came over to speak to him, but Mart brushed her aside. "Skip it, Anna. Just skip it."

He went to the rear and found the Ferrari coupé. He looked at it for a moment, and then got in—no use waiting to try and find a taxi. Drive the damn thing and get out of here. Scram, you and your cowardice.

Mart drove quietly into Liverpool, parked the Ferrari in front of the first pub he saw and went inside. He ordered Scotch with ice and sat down with it in a corner. He drank half of it quickly and looked at himself. He had never thought he would ever turn to jelly in a race. But he had. Sure, there were moments of fright in every race, but after they happened, they were done with. You didn't stay scared, not scared like this, not unless—

He brushed off the attempts of a cockney gentleman to engage him in conversation about his strange attire, the white coveralls that were still wet from rain and stinking with fuel.

He didn't want to talk. All seemed to be ended now, not by his own choice, but by something he could not believe but could feel trembling in his body. Fear. A lasting fear. And no one could drive if that was there. What good would a man be?

You're finished, he said to himself. Face it.

Go back and race at Pebble Beach and those places. Go and get your job back at the box factory.

These are gods driving in the Grand Prix and you're just Martin Janis, a mortal from California. You won a few races— child's play compared to what this has been.

He let the drink turn to water, and rested his head on his arms, closing his eyes. You won, Taglio, he thought. You proved your point....

"Martin."

He straightened up, frowning, to see Anna.

"What happened, Martin? The Maserati was all right."

"What do you think?"

"I know what it looked like, but I cannot believe that of you."

"Go ahead and believe it. Taglio got the best of me. I chickened out! I'm a coward and you've wasted a lot of money—"

"I don't believe that. Something happened out there and you aren't telling me what it is."

She smiled and took his hand, but he jerked it away.

"I told you what happened. Now damn it, leave me alone!"

"But Martin ..."

"Look!" He lifted one hand in front of her and let her see it tremble. "See that? Look at my face and tell me what you see! The car is all right. Okay, what else is there? Didn't see any black flag waving me in did you? Taglio kept me in a league where I didn't belong. It was too much for me. I cried out there ..."

Anna looked at him for a long time.

"I'm sorry, Martin."

He shrugged. "I'm sorry too—shouldn't have yelled at you like that. I feel like a string about to break.... It won't happen again."

"You're through with professional racing."

"Looks that way. Hell—look, we can take the Ferrari over to the States and do a few around the country. Like we used to."

Anna shook her head. A curious expression crossed her features.

"Amateur races are not enough. And let's do it quietly. If you'll give me the key to the Ferrari, I'll say good-bye now, Martin."

"Good-bye...?" He heard her say it, was numbed by it, and yet inside he was not really surprised. He had lost a race, hadn't he? He had had a chance to win a race and quit, hadn't he?

"I wanted a winner and a man, Martin. A champion—not a coward and a quitter." Her mouth twisted with sudden disgust. "Not a miserable, creeping insect of a man!"

"But—" Martin said, and then stopped. What was the use? There was nothing to be said. He pulled the key out of his pocket and slid it across the table.

"Go find yourself a champion."

"I will."

Anna stood up and walked out of the pub.

Mart called for another drink and tried not to think of Anna being gone. She had never loved him, he realized now. She had seen only a potential driver—a possible champion, glory to share. That was all. He had known that since the Pebble Beach race, he thought. Sure, and he had to go back to her anyway—accept her offer and lose himself with her again like a damn fool who forgot the rules. There was nobody to blame but Martin Janis.... Well, he was better off with her gone. Sure, he thought, go back to the States now and drive sports cars for fun. Didn't really want to drive these Grand Prix devils.... He shook his head and tossed off the drink. It wasn't true. He wanted to, but he was scared of them. He was a coward. And no matter what, he still loved her.

"Bring the whole bottle over."

Mart stiffened at the voice and looked up.

"Hello, Martin." Mario Felice looked down at him. "It wasn't hard to find you. I only had to follow the vampire."

The bartender brought the bottle over.

"A man needs more than one drink to cure what you've got."

"What do you want, Mario?"

"I just came to cheer you up." Mario paid the bartender.

"Just like a goddamned good fairy! Well, I don't need cheering up! When I finish here I'm grabbing a boat for home. So go on back and putter with your goddamned motors. I'm through with it."

Mario chuckled and sniffed at the bottle disapprovingly.

"This has no soul to it. You should drink fine Italian wine, my friend."

"You think something is awfully amusing?"

"Yes, I do."

"I don't see anything funny. So shove off and leave me alone."

"I believe that in your country they call it buck fever."

"Buck fever!" Mart stared at him incredulously. "You're crazy!"

Mario shook his head.

"I have seen it many times. Too many times to let a promising young driver let himself be transported to the middle of the Atlantic before he discovers it for himself. So inconvenient, the ocean ..."

"I still say you're crazy."

"I was in this profession before you were born, Martin."

"So? What do you want me to do about it? You didn't see how Taglio tore me to pieces out there."

"I know what Taglio did, but that had nothing to do with it."

"No?"

"Of course not. It would have happened whether Taglio was there or not. It began to happen to you before the race even began. You are new to the game. You take your car and drive well, and you move up toward the leaders. And what do you find there? A pace that is the devil himself to hold. And you find there the finest drivers in Europe, and you ask yourself what right you have to be there—you, Martin Janis, like a child among adults in an adult's game suddenly telling himself he is not big enough.

"It was not Taglio, my friend, but the total, the whole thing. It happens to a lot of drivers. They never seem to be aware that this is what is happening, but that is the truth of it. Buck fever. Now I want you to have two or three drinks. Get drunk if you like. Then come back to Corsatti."

"Come back and be a novice for old Corsatti, huh? Pretend that I'm going to be something? The old apprentice gag ... dreams of glory ... every dog with his day?"

"Call it what you like, my friend," Mario shrugged.

Mart stared at the old Italian.

CHAPTER EIGHTEEN

MARTIN JANIS listened to the rattling rhythm of the rails and the penny-whistle shriek of the train and felt the gentle swaying motion of the coach. He watched the darkness beyond the window, catching a glimpse now and then of some light far away, or the dizzy scurry of lights and faces and dark, huddled shapes as they rushed through a station somewhere in France. He had lost track of the unpronounceable names of towns they passed through. It didn't matter. Tomorrow would find Germany outside the window. Germany and the setting up of quarters and headquarters and practice.

"You've been rather quiet," Morris said.

Martin nodded. "Just thinking about Aintree."

"You aren't still worrying about that, are you?"

"No. I figure that part of it's done with. You know. Kind of like a vaccination. Get buck fever once and it doesn't happen again. It was a new experience, being close to the Germans. I'd been there before, at Rheims, but nobody was pushing me there. And at Rheims, it was sports cars at least. But Aintree, just the thought of it. Taglio pushing, the rain coming down and everything being so slick. Like Mario told me. A kid in where the grownups were playing games. I can see what he meant now. Well, it taught me a lot, and that would fry Taglio if he knew. I figure I'll be able to really go out and drive now, and not run home to mama like he'd like me to do. Speaking of Taglio, where is laughing boy? I haven't seen him since we left England."

"I thought you knew," Morris frowned a little.

"Knew what?"

"He's going by plane. He's with someone…"

"What are you hinting at?"

"Dear me, chap, I would've expected to be the last to know about it, but not you of all people. It's Miss Pavanne. She's with Taglio. They seem a bit cozy…. I say, you didn't know?"

"No."

"I'm dreadfully sorry."

"Don't be. She's trying to collect a champion."

"I beg your pardon?"

"She thought I was champion material. That was her only interest in me. I suffered the usual spurned-male doldrums, but strangely enough I don't feel too bad about it now. I'm better off without her."

"I would say so. When she saw you get rattled at Aintree, she thought that was the end of your driving, eh? I think she made a mistake there. And she expects Taglio to turn into a champion?"

"Not too bad a choice. Taglio was champ once, you know."

"Yes, but my dear fellow, Taglio is getting a little old for racing. He's a tremendous fellow, but—well, you know it and I know it. He's going downhill. She knows enough about the business to see that, doesn't she?"

"She's been hanging around races all her life."

"Then it doesn't make sense. I don't like the look of it."

"What?"

"Something's rotten here. Did she really lose her temper after the Aintree thing?"

"No. She took it rather quietly. She usually has quite a temper."

"I don't like the look of it at all."

"Why? I'm rid of her, and I'm better off."

"These young, spirited Italian women—when they become angry about something, they don't hold it in. I know. Bit of trouble with one myself once—wonderful creatures, like young golden animals .... However, you say Anna was quiet. I think she plans to cause trouble for you."

"I just told you, she wasn't really interested in me."

"It seems obvious that you did mean more than that to her. Why else would she join a man who had already passed his best years?"

"You mean to sic Taglio on me? You're imagining things! You Limeys and your mysteries and ghost stories!"

Morris laughed quietly. "Yes, it is a night for it, isn't it? We might be speeding through the darkness on the Orient Express for a secret rendezvous in Switzerland, and Anna is the dark woman with the long cigarette whose real name is Sonia! But seriously, I would watch out, you know."

"Nah! Look, maybe she is wrong, but maybe she *does* think Taglio can be top dog. On the other hand, maybe *we're* wrong about Taglio. Maybe he will be champ one of these days, with that new engine to help him out. There have been older men than him racing."

Morris shrugged and then shook his head. "Maybe so, but ..."

The door to the compartment opened and Mario looked in.

"Martin, Corsatti wishes to speak with you in his compartment."

"What about?"

"I think that is up to him to tell you."

Mario smiled and Mart followed him into the passageway and down the lurching length of the car.

They stopped outside of a compartment and Mario nodded.

"What's it all about? A lecture for bad boys?"

"I told you there would be none of that. Now go on in."

Mart nodded, wondering, and rapped on the door.

"Come in," a voice called out.

Martin stepped in. The shades were drawn, and Corsatti, for once minus his overcoat and hat, sat studying a sheaf of papers. He indicated a seat, and kept on reading.

Martin sat down, and waited, studying the somber and massive face with its twisting of sadness and the penetrating eyes. He had not seen Corsatti this close for as long a length of time before, nor had a chance to study the man as thoroughly.

A couple of minutes later, Corsatti shoved the papers into a brief case and looked up.

"Good evening, Mr. Janis," he said with very little accent, his words curiously tight, as if he found it hard to breathe.

Mart nodded. "Mr. Corsatti."

"I did not bring you here to discuss your brief adventure with the Maserati. I do not intend to talk about that at all. It is not important. I seldom talk to my drivers. I very often do not even observe the common rules of courtesy. No doubt you know my reasons, and that therefore this meeting must be of importance."

"I gathered that it was."

Corsatti lit a cigar and blew smoke toward the ceiling.

"Very well. Then we can get down to the business at hand without the false impression that Corsatti has changed the rules and that you may fawn like a puppy in the warmth of a new friendship."

"Now wait a minute!" Mart jumped to his feet.

"Mr. Janis," his voice rolled on with the force of a juggernaut, "I asked you here to tell you that you are a member of the team and no longer a reserve. You will start in Germany."

Mart froze and stared at the big man. His mouth hung open, still forming a word that had never had a chance to come. His anger crumbled away, and he had forgotten to breathe.

"That is all, Mr. Janis. You may go now."

Corsatti turned and reached for his brief case again.

"The German Grand Prix..."

Corsatti looked up, the color in his face deepening. "Mr. Janis, we have finished talking."

Mart felt the words like a slap. "Now just a minute ..."

"I have given you as much time as I am going to give you. The only reason I told you instead of having Mario tell you, is that the occasion seemed to demand it. Do not make me regret it."

"Yeah? Well whether you like it or not, there's more to be said here."

"Whether I like it or not? Perhaps you forget who is in charge?"

Mart shook his head and his voice became quiet.

"I haven't forgotten anything. After Mario told me about you and I began to understand, I didn't try to break in on your privacy. I've minded my own business."

"Thank you!" Corsatti said it impatiently.

"Let me finish. I didn't ask to come here tonight. You asked me. I can't help it if your son was killed in Belgium. I can't help it if all drivers remind you of your son in some way. I sat around sweating out a long training, accepting little tidbits of driving, expecting to be a long time in getting to where I want to go—to be a team driver for Corsatti. I don't consider myself anything special. Oh, sure, I got a word of praise here and there, Mario says things to give me hope, but that was his only reason, to help me work harder. Those things don't fool me. Working up to be a pro doesn't happen overnight. I've been cocky enough at times to think so. Sure. I got sore when you suspended me and ran out on this outfit to try and be one overnight, because some gal twisted my ego all out of shape. All right, I learned a lesson driving at Aintree, but not all the lessons. I didn't even scratch the surface, and all of a sudden, without even bawling me out for running out on you, you drop this in my lap and I'm just supposed to accept it without a word."

"Perhaps you do not want to drive at the Nurburgring?"

"Yes. I want to drive there. But I'm scared too. Funny, isn't it? Wanting to drive so bad I can taste it, and being scared enough to shake in my boots thinking about it. Do I have to go sit in my car at the starting line on the Nurburgring and wonder how I got there so soon and wonder if I'm ready? Is that the way you told your son?"

"My son became a team driver more gradually."

"Then it seems like there's even more reason to tell me why."

Corsatti looked away and smoked thoughtfully, staring at the wall, saying nothing, and somehow not seeming as gross in stature.

"You are thinking of your spin-out at Rheims, and how you lost your nerve at Aintree, and that from those two performances it is obvious that you are not ready yet. Let me say that all drivers spin out now and then. Drivers are not perfect, and most of them have suffered what you suffered at Aintree. Call it a baptism of fire or call it a good lesson and the time of growing up. Call it what you like, but you needed it, and don't look at it as Taglio's doing and don't come in here and question my judgment. If it will make you feel better, I repeat what you have doubtless heard many times around the shop in Turin. No man drives for Corsatti until he is ready to drive."

Mart sat down and frowned. "So all at once I'm driving in the German Grand Prix. One of the toughest races in the world. Not one of the quieter races. From practice and a few laps in two races, you've decided I'm ready."

Corsatti angrily stood up and raised the shade of the compartment and stared at the blackness and the little lights flashing by in the distance.

"All right! Very well. I will tell you why." His voice was almost high-pitched and agonized. "Then you will leave."

"Yes. That's all I wanted. After that, I won't bother you anymore." He wasn't angry anymore. He felt sorry for the man now.

Corsatti stood looking out the window for a long time. When he sat down again, he was more calm.

"Now and then, we get a driver who possesses remarkable talent. By *we,* I mean the racing profession as a whole. The talent is unexpected and unusual, and of a nature that makes our usual training time unnecessarily long. Except for the study of motors, you did not really need all that practice. This has never happened to us at Corsatti, until now. You are such a man, Mr. Janis. From a little driving how do I know so much? I have been in the profession long enough to have seen it happen in other teams two or three times."

He paused, seemed to be considering something, before he went on. "Sometimes a talent like this is years in coming. Sometimes it is there from the beginning. But in either case it is as a diamond among glass. There is no mistaking the brilliance, and I can only apologize for not taking you out of the practice status earlier. But it was something we could not determine until you had actually raced. However, to go on, I do not feel that it is irrational to predict that in three or four years, with that many seasons to round off your experience, you could perhaps be the greatest driver the world has ever seen—or at least as good as one other. Your Anne Pavanne was not wrong in her appraisal."

Martin shook his head and tried to swallow what he had heard. He didn't know what to say and so he blurted, "I suppose I'm expected to say something real catchy here."

"Mr. Janis, as long as we have gone this far, I have one more thing to say. I fully believe that talent and being psychologically prepared are two entirely separate things."

"I don't understand."

"I feel you are ready to drive at the Ring, and to drive well. But if you are nervous about it, if you would rather drive in a few smaller races first in order to accustom yourself to your new role, you are not required to drive at the Ring. It is your choice."

Martin Janis stared at the toes of his shoes and tried to think clearly over the excitement he felt. He was afraid of the Ring. He was afraid of all the courses. He knew that was normal. If there were no fear in the men who committed self and car to the high altar of racing, they would be dead or crippled in short order. He was afraid of the Ring, and knew there was more to fear there than there had been at Aintree. But even knowing now—buck fever once, like a vaccination wasn't it?—he wanted to drive it, and he wanted to win, to lap the course in a time of ten minutes, down among the times of the champions, the immortals. Maybe not this time, or the next ... but he wanted to begin.

"Perhaps only a few laps, just for the taste?" Corsatti suggested.

"I'll drive it. The whole distance. I'm sure I won't get rattled this time. I could never be happy sitting it out. If the pit tells me to go the limit, I think I can go the limit."

A faint smile flickered for an instant in Corsatti's huge face.

"Good night, Mr. Janis. Oh, before you go. You might be glad to know that the new engines and brakes will be installed for the race. They were flown in from Turin yesterday. They will give us a good chance of catching Mercedes."

Mart grinned and nodded his good night, and left.

He walked slowly down the passageway, moving the distance with the lurching of the train. He paused by an open window and sucked in deep breaths of cool air, and stood watching France rushing by in the darkness. Ahead was Germany, the Eifel mountains of Germany where a concrete ribbon writhed dangerously over one of the most fantastic bits of racing ground existing. The Ring! And he was going to drive it. Not as a novice, not as the novice he had considered himself, but as a regular member.

He looked at his hands, his arms, ran his fingers over his face, feeling strange and yet the same. An unusual talent—Anna had said it many times, but it hadn't really meant anything hearing it from her. He could see that now; it had been something to touch his vanity, the words of a woman. But coming from Corsatti, all at once.... Where had it begun, and where was the dividing line? Surely there had to be a shout and a cry somewhere to mark his entry into this special world to combat the gods and make a place for himself in their midst, among the flashing wheels and terrible slicing sounds of engines, a Gotterdammerung....

Martin walked slowly back until he came to Mario's compartment. He went in and sat down. Mario watched him with a quiet smile.

"You knew, didn't you?"

"Yes," Mario said. "I knew."

"I can hardly believe it."

"I am happy for you, my friend. Now that you have arrived, what about Anna?"

"What about her?"

"Are you going to show her the difference between buck fever and cowardice?"

"Why?"

"She is a beautiful woman, Martin," Mario went on. "She will not come back of her own accord. You must go after her if—"

"I don't want her back."

Mart looked out the window and realized he could have her back now if he wanted. But he didn't. It wasn't pride, the usual thing that comes with a quarrel. He didn't care anymore. There had been days of hurt and ache and loneliness. But somewhere back on the line it had stopped. He didn't want her, and he didn't know why.

"That is what I hoped you would say."

"What's on your mind, Mario? First we talk about my good luck. That's all I could want to talk about for days to come, and now you're talking about women."

"You heard about the new motors being sent up here?"

"Yes. What about it?"

"In the letter Miss Baroni sent me informing me of the shipment, she said something else. She saw Charlotte in Turin. This was just three days ago, Martin. It means Charlotte has not gone home."

Mart felt a momentary excitement, but he concealed it. Charlotte hadn't gone home? What was the matter with her? Hanging around in a strange country by herself. She was too nice a kid, too sweet. But it was her business.

"I'm getting old. Martin. I do not have much interest in women anymore. But I know the difference between good and bad, and I know a few other things too, about you, whether you know it yourself or not."

Mart hardly listened to him.

Mario pulled out an envelope and handed it to him.

"Don't open it now. I want you to think about it. There's time. It'll be a few days before practice can begin with the new engines to install. The envelope's contents will be self-explanatory. Now you better turn in."

Mart nodded and stood up. "You too. You're talking kind of crazy."

"Maybe, maybe not." Mario smiled quietly.

Mart went back to his own compartment. Morris had already turned in and was snoring fitfully. He had left the lights on.

Mart sat down and looked at the envelope. The old man had ben mysterious about it. He ripped it open, and found plane tickets. A round-trip ticket to Turin in his name, and a one-way ticket from Turin to Germany made out to Charlotte Greyne.

Mart threw open the door and ran down the passageway and burst into Mario's compartment again.

"Now I know you're crazy. Why should I go chasing off to Turin because she didn't have the good sense to go home?"

"Why? You are in love with her, and she is in love with you. It's as plain as the shock from a sparking plug. Although it would seem some people don't see it at all—especially one rather stupid driver I know."

"Me in love with her? She's just a kid. You're nuts!"

"I may be nuts, as you say, for even trying to get that nice girl involved with a man like you again. But I know what I am talking about, even if I am just an old mechanic. I have eyes. I have ears. I see and hear you together many times in a few months. And I know one thing. The thing between you and Charlotte, the way you talk to each other, the way you look at each other—it is too much like music to be anything else. If you do not know this, then I am very sorry for you."

"Now look, Mario—"

"Go, get out of here! I am an old man and I need my sleep."

"I—" Mart took one last look and left. He stomped back down the passageway to his own compartment and turned in.

Charlotte! Strangely, the thought was exciting. She was a sweet kid, nice as they come—but in love with her? If that had been the case, he would have been in love a thousand times already. There were a lot of nice kids in the world.

And Anna? What of her? She was exciting, and interesting, but not *nice* in the usual sense of the word. What then? Was his attraction to her purely physical? He lit a cigarette and smoked for a while. Maybe it was only an infatuation, maybe it was only acting like a kid because it seemed smart to have affairs. Exciting because it was another man's wife, and because she had money, and because she was truthfully aristocratic, and how often was there a shack-up like that? Maybe it was the praise she kept heaping on him. Sure, something crazy like that. She wanted him to satisfy her ego, and he wanted to hear her praise for his own. Crazy, stupid, kid stuff, but... He didn't know and it didn't matter now.

He rolled over and tried to go to sleep.

But he couldn't. Since Mario had opened his big mouth, all he could see was Charlotte's face there in the dark.

Charlotte? Maybe Mario was right. Maybe that explained a lot of things. Maybe he had only been kidding himself, thinking he didn't care where she was or where she went, what she did. He was too wrapped up in cars and his own ego to see it. Maybe that was it?

Maybe Mario was right.

He thought of her smiling face and her wonderful body, and her soft voice came to him, not with all the demands and greed and egotism of a woman who wanted a champion, but just a girl who wanted him and cared, and was frightened. Maybe that was the difference.

He thought of her smiling face, and the rattling of the train began to subside, and the swaying became softer and remote. He saw her face, and blending with it, the bridges of the Nurburgring—the two encountered coming down from the Schwalbenschwanz and Galgenkopf, two of them, seemingly standing under an unnaturally blue sky, blue as if the Ring existed only in an immense twilight. A strange twilight, strange like the bridges, and the words of Robert Morris repeating themselves to him: *A lot of us are afraid of the bridges.* The camelbacks with the pavement coming up to meet them. We all have our private frightening places....

A trickle of sweat formed and rolled off his temple, and Martin was sleeping restlessly.

CHAPTER NINETEEN

M ARTIN JANIS got out of the taxi in front of the Hotel Parigi in Turin and paid the driver. He walked into the hotel and rang for the desk clerk. It was mid-morning, and he had stepped off the plane from Germany only fifteen minutes before. It seemed strange, seeing the small hotel again.

The clerk Piero came through a curtained doorway from a room in back and smiled his welcome.

"Is the girl still here?"

"She is . . . out." Piero struggled for the words.

He walked up the stairs to the room, and he found it darkened when he stepped in. Next door the phonograph was going again, *Death and Transfiguration,* coming into the darkness and musty air. Mart threw the shutters open and let the light come in.

Nothing had changed. He sat down on the bed. The room was neat and tidy, as it always was. Even his own things, the few possessions he had kept there, were still there in the same places. He lay back on the bed and closed his eyes.

If it had been Anna's room, there would have the scent of perfume, and with Anna in the room, the rustle of silks and a beautiful, accented voice—the feeling of something almost imperious. Anna was a woman who could hold her own anywhere in the world, something beautiful and perfect, like some of the statues that stood in the gardens and parks of Turin.

But this was Charlotte's room. There was only cleanness here Cleanness and a scrubbed feeling, a bit of childish attempt at decoration here and there, and with Charlotte in the room, a small voice—a plain, small, unaffected little voice that could be heard in any coffee shop, at any dance, or along the streets of any small town he had ever been in back in the States.

Odd, that it took Mario to see the whole thing as it really was, and never himself. Sure, he'd been too wrapped up in racing and cars. There was an old joke running around in sports car circles about sports car widows—the gals who good-naturedly or otherwise had to play second fiddle to a car.

Anna would never have been a sports car widow. Anna had taken command of everything ever since he had known her, had overpowered everything he had ever felt. She understood all about him and cars—maybe knew too much about both. Maybe that was it. Maybe that was why he never really knew how he felt. There just hadn't been a chance.

The door opened and he sat up.

She almost dropped the groceries she was carrying and started to run out again.

"No, wait!"

Charlotte was white-faced and troubled. She looked more like a lost child than ever.

"What do you want?" She wouldn't look at him.

"You. I flew all the way from Germany. The least you can do is talk to me."

"What is there to say?" She put the groceries down and stared out the window unhappily.

He went over and stood in back of her.

"I don't want to make a lot of excuses for what happened. I really don't have any. But, Charlotte—I was getting pretty short-tempered about waiting for a chance to drive. And when we started going around about that Englishman who was killed—well, my temper went, that's all. It's not a matter of being cold-blooded .... Look at me and what do you see? I'm just a kid, Charlotte. I—I talk big and I try to be real calm about these things, but I'm just a kid and I feel sometimes like I'm hanging up in the big sky with nothing to keep me from falling. I'm scared and I feel like I want to find my mother's skirts and hide in them so that I can cry and nobody would know about it."

He hesitated a moment. "But I don't cry. I hold myself tight and tell myself I've got to learn to accept things as they should be accepted. Like death in racing. It's too bad, but you don't go to pieces or wear black when it happens. None of us on the team even knew him. You can't make it a personal thing every time a driver skids out of the picture. If we did, we would all go crazy thinking about it—maybe the guy had a wife and kids, or a girl like you, or maybe his mother raised white roses outside of London—and we'd get to wondering if next time it might be us taking that long skid and what would happen to the wife and kids, the girl like you, the mother ... it would tear us into a thousand tiny pieces to think about it. Can you understand that, Charlotte?"

She said nothing. Her face worked a little as she tried to keep from crying.

"I thought we could try again—maybe take some time away from racing and anything connected with it. I have a couple of days before I have to start practice. We could go down to the coast for a day or two—just the two of us. A little breather. We haven't had one since the trip over on the boat."

"Pretty sure of me, aren't you?" she said.

"No." He shook his head. "I just need you."

"What about Anna?"

She's—"

"I read about it," she interrupted. "In one of the London papers we get here. Anna Pavanne and her driver—the cars she bought him, about the intention to enter at Aintree. Aren't you afraid she'll take your cars away from you?"

He turned her around so that she would have to look at him.

"I'm back with Corsatti now. That business with Anna is all over. Get that straight now. *It's over.* Understand? I goofed at

Aintree. Lost my nerve, and when that happened, lost Anna and the cars. And the funny thing about it was that it didn't matter to me. I saw what she was. I knew it before, but I guess it sank in good this time, and it took Mario to knock some sense into me about the rest of it—about you. Charlotte, I've been really stupid, walking around with my head in a sack or something. I've been in love with you all the time. I know I've never said it before— you asked me before and I could never answer. I can now. I love you...."

She looked at him for a moment and then the crying came. She fell forward into his arms.

"Don't leave me again," he said. "Not ever again."

"I won't! I won't, darling."

She kissed him feverishly, washing his cheek with her tears.

In a little while, they walked downstairs and caught a taxi and rode out to the Corsatti plant and found a car to use.

"Why don't you let me drive, Mart? You look pretty tired."

"Think you can? The coast is a good sixty or seventy miles."

"Sure, unless you want to go back to the hotel and rest first."

"No. I want to start now. I don't want to see Turin for a while, or hear that old lady playing that record. Come on, I can sleep in the car all right."

They filled the tank and stared out, back through Turin and out into the countryside again, driving down pleasant mountain roads and through quiet valleys and sleeping villages.

"Well ..." Charlotte laughed at the leisurely pace. "This is one way to go for a peaceful drive. With me driving these things."

Mart made a face of mock disgust and slid down in the seat until his feet were against the firewall.

It was late afternoon when Martin woke again. He saw the sky above him and the motor was silent. He sat up to find himself parked at the shore with a bunch of packages in his lap and blankets draped over his feet.

"Hey, where are we?"

"A few miles south of Genoa. I got to thinking while you were asleep. What's the point in fooling with a hotel? It'll be warm on the beach tonight. I bought some sausage and bread, fruit, and a couple bottles of wine, and peanut butter, and blankets ..."

"Wait a minute. Peanut butter?"

"Isn't it wonderful? I didn't expect to see any. I've been wanting some peanut butter for so long."

"Peanut butter! Come to a new country with new foods to try, and you buy peanut butter."

"Stop it! Now don't you think it's a good idea? We can sleep under the stars tonight to the soft music of the Mediterranean ..."

"Your travelogue is likely to be upset by a few sand fleas."

He laughed at her pouting face and got out of the car. "Sure, it's fine with me."

"How about a swim?"

"Okay. Maybe it'll be good for the cobwebs."

She jumped out of the car, stripped out of her clothes before he could even get started, and was running out into the water. He watched her wonderful slimness, and soon followed her into the water. It was just cool enough to have a bite to it after the warmth of the day. He swam slowly and easily out toward the smiling face she turned to him from a hundred yards out. They seemed to float forever in a space where water and sky met in a glassy, imaginary horizon. There was no bottom there, no shore, just blue glass, and themselves meeting and embracing in careless gamboling ....

It was getting dark when they dressed again and built a fire from driftwood. They sat back to eat and open the wine.

Mart took a long swallow from the bottle and sighed.

"Feeling better?" she said.

"Much," he said. "I can feel the knots beginning to untie themselves. You've been kind of quiet though. And that peanut butter. You getting homesick?"

She shook her head.

"You know, it's always been *me*—how am I doing with with my driving, how I'm getting along toward that day when learning and practice give way to real driving and going after that prize money that will really let us live. I haven't stopped to ask how it was for you. Here I've hauled you off to a foreign country, dumped you into a dirty hotel and gone off to enjoy myself. I haven't thanked you for anything..."

"You don't thank people for sharing your life with you. I wouldn't have come with you, or loved you, or lived in that old hotel if I hadn't wanted to."

"You did all that even though I haven't offered to marry you. I never even told you I loved you until today."

"Do you really love me?"

"Yes."

"I like to hear you say it."

"I'll always say it now."

"But you don't know if it's enough for marriage. You wonder if marriage might not spoil it somehow."

"That isn't it. You know how I feel. Racing drivers and women. That's all right. But marriage—I have two tickets for the plane back to Germany. After this little holiday is over, I have to go back, to begin practice on the Nurburgring. I haven't mentioned it before. I promised that we wouldn't talk racing while we were here, but I'm no longer a reserve driver, Charlotte. I'll be driving the whole thing, the whole distance at the Nurburgring."

He saw the cloud come over her, and he took her in his arms.

"You see? It bothers you just to think about it. What would it be like if you were married to it? I have two plane tickets to

Germany. You don't have to come with me. You can wait for me to join you here. Why live with it if you don't have to?"

"I want to come with you. And I want to marry you."

"But damn it, what happens if I get killed?"

"Silly! Women marry airplane pilots and flagpole sitters. And the only difference between us and married people is that we don't have it legalized by a piece of paper. I know you."

"You're wrong. There's a big difference. Have you ever thought what it would be like to be a widow with kids? Damn it, at least with the way we have it now, if you get too much of racing and worrying, you can get up and leave. No strings attached."

"We aren't exactly strangers, Mart. We've been running that chance too. We aren't immune to having children ... No, I know you." She touched his cheek and smiled. "You're like the little boy in the field stealing ripe melons. They taste so much better than those found honestly in the supermarket. Therefore, when you take this young, unmarried girl into your room and take her clothes off and push her back into the darkness, the bed becomes a little sweeter."

"I've never been married. I wouldn't know."

She laughed at him and put her arms around him.

"Don't be angry. I'm only teasing. I understand what you feel and what you're trying to say. I don't agree, but it doesn't matter. I love you, and I'll stay with you as long as you want me. I'll watch you race and be proud of you and frightened for you. I'll be your confessional and your whipping post, your nurse and cook, and your warmth at night. And if there are any children, I'll give them your name and raise them proudly and happily.... And if—if you aren't there—I'll at least have a part of you I can live with always." She smiled to prove she wasn't feeling sad.

"You're just a kid ..."

He pulled her close and kissed her, trying not to see the little light of sadness behind her eyes.

The Mediterranean came softly, and the stars moved across the sky, and the fire died leaving a ghost of smoke to lose itself in the wind, and they moved gently with each other into the blankets until darkness and sleep began to touch them ... A moment in dreaming beyond the sounds of motors, beyond the landscapes that moved with paralyzing speed. There is no need for not thinking of it; for both of them, in their own way, it is there. Always there....

CHAPTER TWENTY

CHARLOTTE GREYNE sat on a box in the Corsatti pit and watched as Martin Janis, finished with practice for the day, brought his car in and turned it over to the mechanics. He stood there, looking for a minute back toward the mountains, toward the old castle of Nurburg and the high places that stood startlingly clear in that morning air.

He stood there like a man in love with something too big to put into words as he unstrapped his helmet absently.

'What do you think?" Mario asked him.

"Tremendous. You know, it doesn't matter how much you read or hear about this place. It doesn't really mean anything until you take a car over it."

"You will be all right on it?"

"Sure. A few days of practice and it will be a dream. Even those bridges aren't as bad as I figured."

"Do not treat them with too much confidence, my friend. Be careful with all of it. You have not touched the Ring with any real speed yet. Do not forget that your laps so far were around fourteen minutes. When the race comes, the good times will be down closer to ten."

"I know. This is just the first day of practice, Mario. It'll pick up when I get all those damn turns memorized."

"All right. And the new engine? How does it feel?"

"Well, like you said, I haven't touched any real speed yet, but I did open her up pretty good once after I left that second bridge.

It feels good. Lots of extra punch, and the brakes are great. I think we'll catch Mercedes this time."

"You are sure it runs all right?"

"Look, you old spaghetti eater, they were tested on the bench down in Turin. They were tested in a car on the track at Turin, and they were tested completely here while I was sitting on the beach for those two days. And you are the master mechanic who could overhaul an engine with a spoon. You're asking me if it runs all right?"

Mario laughed and shook his head. "And you, *stupido,* are the one who drives it. Now run along and see to your lady there. She has been waiting."

Charlotte stood up and Martin came over and they started walking toward the hotel.

"You can buy me some breakfast," she said to Mart.

"Breakfast! It's almost noon!"

"I wasn't hungry before. I had to come down and watch."

Mart's smile faded.

"What's that got to do with not eating breakfast?"

Charlotte tightened her grip on his arm and wished she had not mentioned it.

"Small case of butterflies, I guess. It's all right now."

"Butterflies. About what?"

She remembered how Robert Morris had talked about it at the Palazzo Turin, and how he described the bridges and private frightening places, and how Mart had dreamed about it, sweating and crying out in his sleep.

"This place. It's a little frightening. I can't forget what Robert said about it. You weren't exactly easy about it either."

Mart shook his head and took her into the dining room and they sat down at a table. Mart ordered only coffee, and Charlotte asked for toast and grapefruit.

"Look, honey, there's a world of difference in imagining a place to be a certain way and finding what it's really like. Sure, I was shaking in my boots with the way Morris was talking, and I built it up real big in my mind. But I've seen it now, and I've done quite a few laps on it this morning. And it's not half as bad as what I had pictured in my mind."

"And those two bridges?"

"Well, I won't pretend I'm pleased with them. But they're not so bad. Why worry about them? Practice hard, learn to take them, and then if they still seem bad, treat them accordingly."

Charlotte looked into her coffee and tried to shake it off.

A sharp, high-pitched whine filled the room and made the glasses on the table hum with vibration.

"That would be the Ferrari team warming up. You can spot that sound every time .... Oh oh! Don't look now, here comes one of the Borgia girls!"

Charlotte looked up in time to see Anna Pavanne leaving Taglio at the doorway and walking across the dining room floor towards their table. She was wearing a smile like a mask, but her eyes were hard and brilliant.

"Well, *buon giorno,* Martin. I had heard that you had come back to Corsatti. Benito told me on the plane trip from England."

Mart stirred his coffee and nodded. He said nothing. Charlotte watched his face, wondering if it bothered him to see her again. She *was* very beautiful.

"I'm very curious, Martin. You said you were a coward at Aintree and gave the distinct impression that you were through with driving. Tell me, does the great Corsatti have some sort of therapy for this sort of thing? Do you pretend that it isn't there and just drive anyway? Can cowards win races?"

Charlotte began to tremble. She felt anger building up. She watched the smiling face dig and probe at Mart, and it was like watching some evil animal.

"Why don't you leave him alone?" Her voice shook. "He isn't a coward and never was!"

"I wanted to hear it from his own lips." Anna's voice had the quality of cold metal. "I was willing to drop the whole matter when he told me in Liverpool that he was a coward. But when I heard that he had gone back to Corsatti, I suspected then that he had lied, only pretended to be a coward, to be rid of me. I wanted to hear him tell me—after all the things I've done for him. I'd like to hear it from the man who could be so ungrateful to the woman who gave him his start in racing, and later spent a considerable amount of money to provide him with cars. The woman who also put money in his pocket, and gave him a place to live and everything a man could want."

Charlotte stood up, but Martin put his hand on her arm.

"Never mind, honey. I'll tell her. And I guess she has a right to know. Anna, I made a bad mistake. And you're really pretty much of an expert on drivers and racing. You make a pretty good manager. That's why I'm surprised you didn't see the whole incident at Aintree for what it was. I thought I was behaving like a coward. I wasn't pretending. I was getting ready to pull the covers over my head until Mario set me straight again."

"Oh? Please go on, Martin."

"It's kind of funny, really. Old Mario spotted it for what it really was. I wasn't a coward after all."

"No?"

"Too bad, really. Maybe you should have been a little less hasty about taking the cars and running off. Mario informed me that I was the victim of a little old-fashioned buck fever."

Anna looked puzzled.

"Buck fever? A sickness? I do not know the word."

"Yeah, you might call it a sickness. Nothing serious. It happens just once, and then it's usually over. A man wants something real bad, like catching Mercedes. He gets into a spot where he can catch them. But all of a sudden it looks too big, too impossible, and he says to himself, what in hell am I doing here? He gets all shook up, rattled, and naturally botches the works. Buck fever. I understand most of us get it once."

"And it won't happen again?"

"I'm with Corsatti again. On the team, and not as a reserve."

Anna sat down, looking stunned. "Mart, I wish I had known."

Charlotte watched her with growing alarm. Watch out, Mart, she thought, don't let her do anything to us. She's clever and beautiful—too beautiful.

"Well, you ran off with the cars."

How can you say it that way, Mart, Charlotte thought. You almost sound sorry about it yourself. Please, Mart...

"I make mistakes now and then too, Martin. You must forgive me. But why didn't you tell me about it? It isn't too late."

"Now wait, Anna. What about Taglio?"

"Taglio is fine." Anna shrugged. "He is good. But sometimes I doubt he will ever be a champion again. I never feel the confidence in him that I felt in you, and what I feel now—now that you have pointed out my foolishness .... Martin, I still have the Maserati .... Why didn't you tell me about it?"

Charlotte felt sick as Mart smiled.

"I don't know, Anna. After Mario knocked some sense into me in that Liverpool bar, I don't know."

Anna smiled sadly and apologetically. "It isn't too late—if you can forgive me ...."

Mart shook his head. "I got to thinking about it on the train. Maybe I kind of grew up. Maybe it was just a childish infatuation. Call it what you want. I just don't want you anymore."

Anna's face went white and the mask-smile went hard.

"What?"

A screaming relief pushed Charlotte to her feet.

"You heard him!" She said it half-crying. "You heard what he said. Now go sink your teeth in someone else and leave us alone."

Anna recovered some of her composure and smiled acidly.

"Really, Martin, is sleeping with a child the best you can do?"

Charlotte said nothing. She couldn't speak. It was caught hard in her throat and she was trembling. She saw something hard and white move into Mart's face, and the smile growing in Anna's. Charlotte picked up the cup of coffee and, without thinking, dashed it into Anna's face.

Anna brought her hands up and started to scream, but strangled it back and stood there as calmly as she could. She picked up a napkin and wiped the hot liquid away with trembling hands.

"I'll go now, Martin. I'll not bother you anymore. Taglio is waiting for me. But let me congratulate you on your not being a reserve driver anymore. Only, it is unfortunate that it had to happen here. A man should not drive his first real race here at the Ring. It is a killer, Martin. Take it as a warning from one who knows. It is a killer . . . ."

She turned and walked away and Charlotte watched her go, remembering the tone of her voice more than the words she spoke.

She watched Mart grin and light up a cigarette.

"Well, that's that. We won't be bothered by her anymore."

Charlotte nodded, but she was not so sure.

She was scared . . . .

CHAPTER TWENTY-ONE

THE names stretched out before him like some twilight legend. Beyond the south turn and into the depth of the course—Quiddlebacher Höhe, Adenauer Forst, Wehrseifen, Breidschied, Karussel, Brünnchen, Schwalbenschwanz—those, and how many others of the strange, hard-to-remember names? He knew them by sight, knew their treachery, the surfaces and dizzying procession of turns and hills and drops into seeming space; he knew of these things rather than the names, burned on his brain forever from the hours of practice. Therefore he did not sit in the Corsatti at the start *und zeil* as a pure newcomer to the Nurburgring. But the other part of it was new. The feeling inside, the fact that he waited for a flag under the pressure of a safety belt, behind a rumbling engine rather than sitting in the pit, and the never to be forgotten thrill that was his now, his first race.

Pennants rippled in a bright blue wind, and the air was right for that sharp, fine-edged visibility. He could see the tarred seams in the pavement down to the beginning of the south turn, the rising of hill and mountain with every rock and tree vivid there like a stereopticon print. There couldn't be a better day. The wind was a little stiff and would be like a wall in the gusts nudging the car at speed, but still, he couldn't ask for a better day. What if it had been raining? The Ring would be more than fantastic, in the rain.

He glanced around at the other drivers of Scuderia Corsatti. Brusetti nodded, nervously, a little smile on his face. Mart grinned back, in surprise. Achille Brocco too. Brocco lifted his open-backed glove in a wave. Morris nodded in his usual friendly manner, touched perhaps with a little of the British stand-fast, hold-firm type of encouragement. And Taglio. With Taglio, the same glowering hate, but it didn't matter. Mart settled back feeling part of the team. They accepted him now. Even if Taglio did not, it was a beginning. Perhaps not a shouting friendship, but a beginning.

Mario came over and tugged at his safety belt.

"How do you feel, my friend?"

"Cowardly, but not ready to quit like I did at Aintree."

"I know. Even I, sitting in the pit where it is safe, feel fear at a time like this. Be careful, Martin. Do not try to win this one. Do your best, but do not risk yourself beyond good reason. There are many races yet, and time to win them. Today, drive for yourself, not for Morris or Taglio or Brusetti or Brocco, not even Corsatti. Drive for yourself. This is from beginning to end, God and engine willing. This will be new for you."

"I know, Mario."

New, he thought, wondering if Mario had something else in mind. The feeling of being here—yes, that was new, but not the actuality of it. How could it be new when you had hoped for it so long, when fact was an echo of dreams that had repeated and repeated themselves for so long.

"And this new engine. It is good, but you have not driven with it for as long as I would have liked. If you have doubts about being able to handle the extra power, do not try. This is not going to be like practice. It will be crowded."

"Don't worry. I don't expect to win the first time out. But I don't intend to start something I can't finish. I'll just do the best I can. But I'll tell you one thing. Maybe it won't be me, but one of the Corsattis is going to win today."

"You must not be overconfident."

"You're like a mother hen I once knew."

"Hah! I will say it again. If I am like a mother hen, you are still wet from the shell."

The cars' idling began to build up a low roll of thunder and the big starting clock's hand was jerking around to the mark. Mario stepped quickly back and out of the way.

Martin Janis concentrated on the man with the flag, feeling the sweatiness of his hands on the corded wheel.

He thought back to a time that seemed ages before, a time removed and in another dimension. California, Pebble Beach, the beautiful little sports cars lined up on the grid waiting for the flag. Here and now it was the same. The uneasiness of waiting, the thought that this was the same, but faster, harder, and infinitely more dangerous.

The idling thunder rose in volume and cascaded across his ears. He touched his own throttle and watched the tachometer needle swing up. One last wave at Charlotte, a nod for Mario, then a signal gun boomed and sent echos rolling through the Eifel mountains and the flag came flashing down.

Tires tore at the pavement and cried in agony.

Easy now. Stay with them, but don't crowd them. The start is always bunched up. A lap or two to thin it out before the driving begins to be really racing .... The south turn now, doubling back parallel to the start *und zeil.* Easy, there are a hundred and twenty major turns, and how many little ones? Fourteen miles to a lap, after the conversion from kilometers. Something like twelve bridges, but two that really matter, and a twelve-hundred-foot variation in altitude in that short distance. A killer, like Mario had said. Poor Mario; Corsatti considered him ready, but perhaps Mario did not, really. Like a mother hen, with his drivers, his chicks ....

The cars began to spread out, and the turns came like disturbed clockwork, many of them blind and all treacherous. Mart began to move up, smoothly, feeling good, passing the slow and the overly cautious, those who were saving their cars until the very last for the final sprint through hell. The wind burned over his face, touched with sun, and the stink of exhausts began to sear his lungs.

Another car was passed, and another. Climbing now—a glorified hill climb, that's what this part was. Through the Breidschied turn, and now over to the Karussel, with Brusetti in sight, not quite himself at the wheel, and now the trip down. Hell was below. Hell is the Wipperman and the Schwalbenschwanz. Hell is the entire thing. Past Brusetti—God, he looks tense. The Corsatti drifted smoothly and responded quickly to Mart's touch. He could feel every motion, every shift of balance on the seat of his pants. It felt right.

Now the bridges. Over the camelbacks, the wheels leaving the ground, and down again and again into the air with a sickening sensation. *Whoomph!* and a skid. It was close and a little sweat broke out and Martin grimaced.

He felt good, though, when he went through the only real straight in the Ring. Past the pits and the blackboard—lap time twelve-five; he was tenth. No instructions this time. It was his race. No instructions, either, for Corsatti, or Brocco, or Brusetti, Morris or Taglio. His race, to his own designs, and the new engine feeling fine, feeling strong.

Ferrari lay ahead. He drifted through the south turn and pass. There was a duel for three miles with an Alfa Romeo before the other's acceleration faded and the Corsatti edged ahead.

Unaccountably, he thought of Charlotte for a moment. He felt closer to her now and was more keenly aware of the things she felt. Perhaps it was because he was free of the grating, impatient, almost selfish months of apprenticeship.

Certainly, it had been selfish. Almost every waking thought and every hour of the day had been devoted to pushing him closer and closer to the realization of his dream. And now that the dream was here, he was like the small boy who rode the merry-go-round sadly because there was no way for the one who had come with him to share it.

A lap, another lap; disjointed thoughts blurred and lost themselves in the white-hot wash of speed. Still another lap, bringing time down, moving up slowly. Ninth place, eighth. The bridges were not as bad as he'd imagined, but bad enough. He could still feel the grip of tension, but controlled now. A swing through three hundred and eleven miles of hell. Relax, he told himself.

A flickering whiteness caught his eyes. The right rear tire; fabric was coming through and it was three fast miles yet to the pit. He eased off. No point in throwing everything away for one or two places. He could get that back later. He watched it with a near fascination and tried to keep the stresses off it in the turns. A tire like that could go any minute.

The Alfa shot past, and he limped through the last two turns and slowed into the straight. Just a few more yards.

He stopped and the crew leaped to the car.

"You have to watch your rubber!" Mario scolded. "This is too close!"

New tires, fuel, oil, water—all in seconds.

"You're doing good. Now go! Spit in your oil!"

Superstition. No good lucks. Insults and threats as he shot back into the race. Appeasement to the treacherous gods of racing. Leave nothing to the precision of your driving or the preparing of the car. Insult and threat, and a St. Christopher to protect....

He wondered if Charlotte was watching, or had gone back to the hotel. That would be better, not to watch, not to hear, but only to talk about it over a bottle of wine when it was finished and done with.

The fast laps rushed by in a dizzying whirl of sound and motion. He passed several cars, loving the hell of the course now except for the two bridges. They bothered him, and they were something which never became familiar. But at least they were where he could see thm and not part of a bad dream. They were there in the sober light of day.

He began to hit the stride he didn't dream possible for him. Ten point five minutes on that last lap, and better this time maybe. It felt better anyway, and he passed Brocco and Morris. Taglio was ahead now. Taglio and the Germans. What was holding Taglio back? The cars could do it now, and Taglio was the old master—Il Maestro of the Corsatti team. Why didn't he make the move?

He moved up on Taglio's tail and stayed close enough to see the seams in his helmet, his goggled eyes peering at him spasmodically in the rearview mirrors perched on either side of the wind-screen. Taglio was moving more swiftly now, pulling away for a moment and closing the gap between him and the Germans, slowing less in the inferno of turns.

Mart moved up with him and looked for a chance to pass. This close to the racing white of Germany he must use caution, but if this close with no unbearable strain, why not? It would be a start toward the top—to be one of these helmeted gods.

Mart moved in to pass. But in one swift motion, Taglio swerved to block him. His real wheels caught loose gravel and shotgunned it over Mart's car, over the small wind-screen and stung and smashed like a hundred small bullets against his face.

Mart swung away and grinned. Old Taglio trying to scare him off again. Trying to make him lose his nerve and run away like he had at Aintree. Well, it wouldn't work that way this time. That was done with. He bored in again to pass and Taglio repeated the move. Their wheels screamed together and made blue smoke. Mart's car lurched and threatened to trip and he wrenched it away from there just in time, and as he did, he saw something horrible in Taglio's face. Taglio was trying to kill him.

Not just trying to scare him, to make him lose his nerve and his taste for the game; not the effort, as it was before, to run him off out of jealousy and pride, and the egotism of a driver who sees his own decline. Not that.

Benito Taglio was deliberately trying to kill. At that speed it could be nothing else. The thing in his face could be nothing else.

But why? Why risk everything—the career he was so proud of and which meant so much to him, and which would end if Corsatti found out about it. There were other drivers to see it, spectators avidly watching every move.

Why should he risk everything? What was twisting the little man so badly into this kind of insane move?

He couldn't help but remember Anna's words in the Sportshotel, on the first day of practice.

"But let me congratulate you on your not being a reserve driver anymore. Only, it is unfortunate that it had to happen here. A man should not drive his first real race here at the Ring. It is a killer, Martin."

She had gone then to join Taglio. He had seen them later, laughing and drinking, talking rapidly and quietly in Italian.

This race is a killer...yes. Mart had known that for a long time. But Anna evidently had not meant it in that way. It began to look as if Robert Morris had by some quirk of insight put his finger on something. The thing he had suspected on the train.

He moved up closer to Taglio again.

So that was it. Anna taking command again. Warping, twisting things to suit her own pleasures, her whims and desires and dislikes.

You poor fool of a Taglio, he thought. She hates me because I walked out on her—I came back to racing, but not to her or for her—so she twists you up, gets you drunk with her until you're all messed up and ready to do anything she says, even something like killing me.

Mart tried to move up again, but as before, Taglio blocked the way. Mart stayed close. Close enough to try and shout over the engines. He pointed ahead and waved at Taglio to put on speed.

"Mercedes! For Corsatti! Not Anna!"

For a moment, he couldn't be sure that Taglio heard or even understood. The motors were loud, and the wind, and the helmets made hearing hard. But the wave of his arm must have told

Taglio something, because the Italian shook his head and let his wheels swerve over against Martin's. That was his answer.

The tires screamed against each other. Angrily, Mart fought the lurch of his car and bored in against Taglio until Taglio's Corsatti began to weave dangerously. Taglio's face went white. Mart kept it up, taking the initiative now. Taglio fought it for a minute, screamed something and pulled away.

Not to admit defeat and let him by. Not in sudden agreement or sudden understanding of what Anna had done to him. It had been a scream of anger and fear ....

Taglio moved closer to Mercedes and then kept pace with them.

Mart moved up again. The Germans could be caught now. But Taglio's motions had become frantic, sloppy. Mart frowned and remembered seeing it before in what seemed a terribly long time ago—the erratic driving that comes beyond one's own limits, of driving beyond brain and reflexes. And Taglio was driving beyond his age. He had driven too many miles already—his body, brain, everything had been on tracks too long.

You're making him do it, Mart thought. Driving him too hard. You might've done that to Taylor, too... remember? If Taglio crashes, maybe it will be because you are pushing him too hard. But why doesn't he slow down and let me pass? Because it is hard to give ground to a newcomer when there was a time when you were *campionissimo*?

Mart eased off a little. There would be more time for passing him, better times down on the three-mile straight. Or perhaps Taglio would calm down later.

Before he could think about it, his slowing down became a useless gesture.

Taglio was spinning. Like the sharp and sudden beginning of a bad dream, Taglio was spinning, the car whipping rear first off the road and smashing end over end into a field, the body catapulting free like a white-clad doll to sprawl crumpled and still in the grass.

Mart touched the brake, hesitatingly, with his foot. He was the leading Corsatti now, the Germans were just ahead. There was no sign of the old buck fever. It could perhaps be a win for Corsatti—but Charlotte was in his mind. Charlotte saying cold and hard things, talking about a man named Taylor and something that had happened a long time ago. And Corsatti himself, the man who thought more of his drivers than winning the races that had to be won … the remarkable talent he had spoken of.

Talent! A talent for causing wrecks, it semed. Taylor had been wrecked, and he hadn't stopped. It was as if there had been shame in stopping, or even in being afraid.

He smashed his foot on the brake and screamed to a stop without letting the engine die, and removed the steering wheel. He climbed out and jumped across the road, back fifty yards to the wild skid marks, toward the sounds and stink of a burning car.

He saw Benito Taglio, quiet and unmoving, his body twisting at odd angles. Fear broke out in Mart with an icy sweat. Cold fear—afraid of what? He looked and seemed to know of what and why, not because he had known all along, and not because he had always remembered clearly. Time puts smoke across remembering and leaves a haze there. But Taglio sprawled there like that ….

The haze was gone and he knew of what and why. Like Tommy. Like his brother. There was no apple orchard here, no fallen apples and clotted earth. But the legs, the twisting of spine and neck, the paleness of skin wet with blood and shock—turn and run from it! You should never have stopped. You didn't want to see this, you never wanted to see this. Like Tommy all over again, the picture all over again, coming back. That's why you couldn't stop or think of stopping before. Run, you bastard, before you puke on the dead!

Something prevented him from moving, though. Taglio. He thought he heard a groan, thought he saw him move as the wrecked Corsatti exploded and turned the grass into a small ring of fire. Shaking, he kneeled down and lifted Taglio's head.

The Italian opened his eyes, stared at him with hatred and muttered something in Italian through a gurgling windpipe.

"Taglio … try and stay awake. It's going to be all right. There will be an ambulance soon. You'll be okay and driving again before you know it."

Taglio's eyes turned toward the road, and up the road to the car that sat idling at the edge, waiting there in the oily smoke of a burning wreck with the power of its engine and the strength of its untouched body. Then his eyes came back, quieter and without anger. They flickered for a moment and Mart knew the truth. It would be over shortly. Taglio weakly motioned for him to go back to the car.

"Don't worry about that. Plenty of time. Come on, you aren't going to conk out on me here, are you? What are those medical boys going to think if you don't help out a little when they put you on the stretcher? It's going to be okay."

He coughed in the thick, black smoke that rolled over them for an instant in the wind and listened to the cars roaring past. He remembered briefly that with each passing second, Mercedes was moving swiftly farther and farther away. But there were some things that could not be forgotten. Like Mario had said, there were other races, and time to win them.

"Taglio …" He bent his head closer and made the words slow and clear. "Taglio. Aintree … practice … *scusa*….. <a>nothing but luck! Understand? *Capisce?* Luck! And Anna—bad, Taglio, bad. Anna did it to me too. I *capisce* …"

Mart didn't know if the English was getting through to him for a moment, or if the Italian heard him at all above the roaring of cars and his own closeness to death, but his face relaxed and managed a grin, and Mart barely heard the tortured English, the repetition of what had been shouted so many times by Mario. Taglio raising one arm in a scoffing manner ....

"Spit in ... your oil ..."

The silence closed in then.

Martin pushed Taglio's eyes shut, looked around for a moment at the burning car, and then ran back up to the road. There was a lot of ground to cover, a lot of positions to regain, some real driving to do now. Mercedes was far away now, but still—. He was feeling released from something, feeling clean inside, free of something that had been there too long ....

Martin Janis drove like a machine, working his way up again gradually, methodically. He estimated that he had been out of the race for three or four minutes at the most, but it had been enough to worry Mario. He saw the mechanic's relieved face and signaled that he was all right and kept going.

The race became a succession of unending turns and unending time in which his consciousness was a balloon growing larger and larger with the fumes and noise and the wind of speed tearing at his skull. He began to feel reminders of the distance behind him, the distance greater than he had ever driven before, and the distance itself magnified by speed and treachery of road.

And the bridges. He began to worry about those bridges. Worry! He grinned. Morris was afraid of them too. Morris and all of them. We all have our private frightening places. Looks like I might as well join the crowd, he thought. He grinned again and shoved his worry away somewhere and tried to forget the strain, smiling in anticipation of what now lay ahead. He hadn't believed it when he saw it. It didn't seem possible that he had gained back a third of a lap. But there they were, with only a few seconds dividing them.

The racing white of Germany. He moved in closer. Herr Hoff—he saw the beefy frame bent over the wheel, his immaculate coveralls, the gleaming helmet, a reflection of his goggles in the rearview mirror.

Mart drew closer, drawing on a little of the extra power he had now. Hoff shifted over to prevent any attempt to pass. Down the Wipperman, and Mart moved to the right, and Hoff snicked back in front of him. To the left again, but Hoff did the same. To the right, to the left ... and now, Herr Hoff, he thought. Now! A quick stabbing movement to the right, but no following through.

Hoff swerved to the right and Mart drew abreast of the Mercedes. He grinned at the angry German and went on past, happy with the Corsatti's new song. It had been done. A Corsatti was at least the equal of a Mercedes, with power left. He wondered if the German had any left. He was bound to. But how much? Maybe the Corsatti could equal that too?

The Schwalbenschwanz now ... the bridges coming and his stomach twisting with the anticipation. Damn camelbacks—he wished they weren't there. Perhaps it was from being tired and tense now, but it felt as if he had dreamed about them too many times. And the dreams seemed strangely accurate now as he took them, and felt the soaring and the chirp of rubber and the little skid when it was over.

He streaked down through the last of the lap, the almost straight part, to the pits. The pit was advising, he was in third place, and to use caution. Ahead were Schiller and Bernd Heldmann.

Mart held it in the south turn, kept Hoff from coming up. And watching Heldmann for a way to pass. The tension was bad now; he'd come a long way and didn't want to lose it now. Bre idschied ... Karussel ... Wipperman. He could feel the bridges. Everything else was all right except for tired muscles and brain, but he could feel the bridges coming well in advance, feeling as if he were scrabbling at loose pebbles and rocks at the edge of a precipice. Not falling yet, but sliding. Sliding down toward the emptiness and space ....

But to slow down was to be passed, and he couldn't keep slowing down each time he came to the bridges. He knew what it was like to be pushed now. Sweat ran from the backs of his knees and he was holding his breath. His knuckles were near bursting from gripping the wheel. The car soared . . . and then again. *Whoomph!* . . . a skid, a frenzied correction, and careening down the shoulder, the center again.

He felt sick inside. Weak. But closer to Schiller and Heldmann. He shook his head and kept his speed.

You've got to learn, he thought. Go in straight, keep the wheels straight when she goes up, and come down with them straight. Got to remember that. Keep everything straight and it will be all right. The car will take care of the rest. There were maybe a hundred miles to go, more or less—he had lost track. But so little. So little. He kept thinking that, but the growing weariness in him kept saying so much . . . so much . . . so far!

His hands tightened. The image of Hoff in back of him and the bulleting white of Heldmann and Schiller ahead, and he was moving closer now. Got to take them, he told himself. Power enough now.

If you have any doubts about using the extra power, don't try. Mario's words were echoing somehow.

He had used a little of it. What about the rest? It couldn't matter. Sure, he could use it. Now was the time. Now if ever on this lap. Maybe the chance would be gone next time around. Try now.

He forced down the pedal and felt the Corsatti surge forward. The Mercedes grew larger until he could look at them in frightening detail. Relax, he thought, looking at them; just relax.

But there was no relaxing. Not for this moment. He was on them. He could smell their exhausts and almost hear their motors screaming above his own.

There was no strength for battle or wary sparring, no time for tricks. The chance to pass would be gone again, the road curving too much again. It had to be quick, without hesitation.

Heldmann tried to block him, swerving to the center. But there was no bluff. He could not bluff a man who was too tired, too tightly drawn. Heldmann's face whitened as the wheels of the Corsatti came too close and he pulled out of the way.

Mart kept the speed, sitting like a statue as Heldmann fell behind. Schiller now. Schiller was the last one.

But time had run out. They were at the pits and coming into the beginning of the south turn quickly. The pit had held up the blackboard, but he hadn't been able to read it. There had been a signal from the flagman, but he had not understood it. He could see only one thing, like a beacon. Schiller's white car ahead.

Martin held close to him, but there was no chance to pass. All he could do was hold on and wait.

Up again, through the mountain heights, the dizzy places that fell into the downward sweep again. The long laps, but somehow with the thing they did to time here, the long laps seemed short laps that would not let him breathe.

Hoff and Heldmann were still behind, but making no effort to come up. The pace was too hot. The pace! ... He wished he could close his eyes for a moment and let cool darkness rest them and wash the images away. The pace—it was straight from hell.

The bridges came again. Again the horrible soaring, the sickening skids, and once more the desperate fighting to stay on the road.

But then the chance was there again. The last bit of speed. Mart went to the limit, the Corsatti singing a new and frightening song up high where it hurt the ears. Schiller fought the acceleration with his own for a moment, but then was gone back there somewhere.

Mart did not see him go. It was sudden and unexpected. He did not know the German was out of it or why until he looked back and saw the blue smoke on the road and the white car spinning away from the edge of it, chewing up grass and dirt and jarring to a stand-still. It had remained upright and Schiller was climbing out.

You've done it, he thought. But there was no triumph in the knowledge. He was in first place. This was the German Grand Prix and he was leading, but he felt no different. He was too tired, and there was so far to go, and tension was building up in his body.

Take one hand off the wheel while you have the chance, he told himself. Wave it and move your legs. Flex every muscle you can. You shouldn't be this tight. To drive, you must relax!

He tried to turn loose of the wheel but couldn't. He tried to move his legs, to turn his head, but only his eyes would move, and only his arms would move with the wheel as a support. There was sweat running down under his goggles to sting, running under his shirt and pants, and the landscape flew past like an evil dream, with the car going faster and faster. Or was that just imagination upon entrance into a twilight world.... What's the matter with you? he demanded of himself. Goddamn it, what's the matter?

He tried to focus on the tach needle. How many rpm? He squinted but couldn't see for the sweat in his eyes.

The start and finish line ripped by. There was excitement there, a blurring of activity. He thought he saw Mario jumping up and down and the flagman acting like a frantic puppet, and the sounds of the crowd came from far away. Sure, the young American who only yesterday was a novice, now leading the favored Germans, beating them on their home grounds.

He found no pleasure in it. He felt as if he were watching the event from a space six feet beyond his car. It was not him providing the great upset, but someone else ... someone else.

The course again, the fourteen miles of hell to a lap. It was coming again—Quiddlebacher Höhe ... Adenauer Forst. It was tricky now. Watch those turns, the speed is higher. Got to give her a place to drift, got to hit the turns right. Do that and the car will take care of the rest. But he was not taking them right. He could see himself taking them through dead center, unable to change it somehow. He should have done it right. He knew how—the car would handle the rest—the beautiful car ....

Martin felt the left front wheel take the edge of the road, and for an instant it seemed all right, but then a wheel buckled and the rear end came up. Up and over.

The red car left the road, cartwheeling end over end, down an embankment and into a field.

He felt nothing, as if watching again from another place, seeing sky and ground smash into a turning blur, hearing metal rip and disintegrate, hearing ground and metal join and tear apart with explosive force and ... and then nothing.

Silence, the smell of smoke, sounds far away from this place under the trees and the deep blue of the air. A twilight, an immense twilight on the other side of the earth ....

Briefly, a dream, a hill in California. How tall the grass had grown, but the ranch had not changed, and the corn was ready for picking down where the truck road ran past it—the hill was the same—and how good to sweep down on two boards and baby carriage wheels, to feel the sick-sweet thrill of leveling off at the bottom and scooting up that truck road. Tomorrow, the new bike. That would be faster, much faster—and it had brakes ....

CHAPTER TWENTY-TWO

A T FIRST there was light. Just a smear of it way off somewhere. It was a feeling of standing at the end of a long dark room, with the thin, pale light down at the other end. There was a sensation of moving toward the light, but it never came closer. It seemed forever and far away. Sounds echoed strangely there, too. There were voices, hollow and metallic and strangely hushed. The voices moved and flowed, an echo of Babel in the darkness, and meaningless.

The light moved closer then, and there was a desire to run from it, to hide, to sink back into the dark, velvety warmth. But it did no good to try. It seemed as if he'd been running when the light surrounded him suddenly and flared into brilliance, and the voices took on meaning.

Lips brushed his cheek and warm tears fell there.

"Oh, Mart..."

The light became the light on the ceiling, the voice that of Charlotte.

Martin Janis opened his eyes all the way and stared incredulously around the room.

Charlotte moved away from the bed, weeping gratefully and trying to hide it.

"So, the great man moves," a familiar voice rumbled.

Mart turned his head and saw Mario sitting there. A nurse flitted from the room, carrying a small tray.

"What is this?" he mumbled. "What's going on?"

"You have caused us to sit here for hours, smelling the evil antiseptics, suffering at the hands of that female general in the stiff uniform. That is what is going on."

"Oh, Mario!" Charlotte reproached him. "He probably doesn't feel very well. Be nice to him."

It came to him then. The reason for these white walls, the smell of antiseptics, the nurse, the hundred and one sore and tender spots of which he was becoming increasingly aware. The race ... Nurburgring, and taking the lead from the Germans. The crash ....

"I remember now."

"He remembers," Mario grumbled in the direction of Charlotte. "I should think so. One should always remember almost killing one's self. None of this would have happened if you had stopped when we told you to stop .... Ah, but what does it matter? What is done, is done. How do you feel, my friend?"

"Like the jack slipped." He looked at Charlotte and smiled a little. "I guess I scared you pretty badly."

"I don't even want to think about it, darling. You're here, and you're alive, and that's all that matters to me."

The doctor, a tall, blond Germanic type with icy blue eyes, walked in and unceremoniously lifted the blankets and checked the bandages. Martin was suddenly aware of the number of them plastered and tied to his body. Particularly, his left leg.

"What all have I done to myself, doctor?" he asked.

The doctor checked his pulse without answering and then consulted a folder the nurse had left for him on the door.

"Damn, I wish I could speak German," Mart muttered at Mario.

"I speak English quite well," the doctor said with a trace of a smile. "How do you feel?"

"Not too good."

"It is understandable. You have three broken ribs, a good collection of lacerations and bruises, and a broken leg."

"Nothing incurable, then. How long do I have to stay here?"

The doctor frowned and shook his head. "You will be here a few weeks. I do not like that leg. I do not like that leg at all."

Martin felt a cold sensation pass through his stomach.

"I—I will be able to walk on it, won't I?"

"Oh yes. Yes, of course." The doctor took a deep breath. "But you must expect a certain amount of stiffness. You see, it broke in two places. In the middle, between the knee and the ankle—this much would have been all right. It will knit cleanly. But the other break involved the knee itself. I'm afraid you will not be able to bend it much."

"I see."

"The nurse will be here in a few moments with some light nourishment. She will give you sedatives to relieve the pain and help you sleep. I will have a look at you tomorrow."

The doctor bowed slightly to Charlotte and Mario and left.

"Well …" Mart tried for the old grin. "Just a stiff leg. That isn't so bad. I don't guess I'll be the first driver with a stiff leg, will I? I can learn to use it. Might have to alter the angle of the clutch pedal a little."

Mario frowned, and Charlotte wouldn't look his way.

"What did I say?" Mart looked at them.

"You know very well, my friend, that you will not race again."

"You heard the doctor. Just a stiff leg is all."

"The leg does not matter. You will not drive again, and you know why."

"What does Corsatti have to say about it?"

"The same thing I have to say about it. He knows. I know. And you know, my friend."

Yes … he did know. But he did not want to turn loose. It was hard to turn loose.

"It is not often that a man can step into a racing machine and drive like he was born in its seat. These things do not come to every man. And it was frightening how much you resembled

227

in skill a man you would not have dreamed of imitating. In a few years you might have equalled Nuvolari, except for one thing. I must confess the blindness of those who stand too close to see plainly. I can only put all the little pieces together, the fragments of knowing a man by watching him in practice, in races, in watching him get into a car and seeing him climb out, and what the other drivers are able to see and tell me—tell me too late because the race is over, and here you lie with broken bones and torn flesh. We might have prevented this. We tried—you began to drive like a maniac! All the smoothness was gone. But you could not see our signals!"

Martin sank back into the pillow and closed his eyes. "You called it buck fever once. Back in England, you remember?"

"I remember .... Christ, I remembered a thousand times when you came past the pits like a blind man—like a wooden man. Yes, I remember. I should have seen it. It's cruel ... yes, we good-naturedly smile and slap the poor fellow on the back and say, courage, my friend, it will be better next time! And then next time the same thing happens, and we watch it for a little while, thinking it will pass. But it does not pass, and when we try to stop it, it is too late. That is the evil of this thing. He is good. He is ready to drive. But inside is this thing."

Martin looked at the ceiling. "Maybe it was the bridges that set it off."

"They were nothing to your skill."

Mario paced the room for a moment. He seemed to be looking for something.

"In Italy, we have a saying about our greatest race, the Mille Miglia. He who leads at Rome never wins the race. This means that the man who takes the lead too soon instead of gradually, often burns up his motor or kills himself because he cannot hold the pace with so much of the road still before him."

"I don't think I understand," Charlotte said.

"Martin never drove the Mille Miglia. But perhaps it might be said that his career was in reality a Mille Miglia. Perhaps it is the thousand miles for all drivers. Only Martin was too good, too fast too soon. He led at the Rome of his years."

Charlotte shook her head.

"What he means," Martin told her, the truth coming cold and clear, "if I understand him right, is that I had the basic skill in the States, and what I was doing was not too much. I came over here and learned more. Learned and really developed this skill. Only…"

"Only when he developed it, he found out he could not use it," Mario helped him and then stood unhappily at the window to look at the rain. "He can drive with champions. He has the skill, all the wonderful skill. In my eyes he *is a* champion. But inside—how shall I say it? He is like a beautiful machine, the like of which we do not often see, but it is as if the gas tank were too small. The energy he needs, the steady power runs out too soon. This machine becomes helpless. He tenses up, his nerves tighten…"

"But I knew that!" Charlotte stopped him. "I've seen him that way! Even before we came to Europe. It's my fault, then. I should've tried to stop him. I should've known!"

"Please. Do not misunderstand. We all are tense after a race, even after only a few miles as relief. That much is harmless. Listen. It is the tiger and the lamb. All races are exciting and dangerous. American sports car races, a hundred miles and maybe speeds of a hundred and forty in short bursts. This is the lamb. Here, except for a few, three hundred, three hundred and fifty miles, and speeds up to two hundred miles an hour. This is the tiger. This is what stopped him. Here this thing had a chance to show its face. Don't blame yourself. No one is to blame. It began somewhere far back. Perhaps you are born with it. I do not know. But no one could know it was there until it was too late."

Martin watched their faces as the uncomfortable silence fell over them. They looked sad.

"Where's the funeral?" he asked.

"All you Americans are this way," Mario grumbled. "You do not have the decency to weep. You do not have any emotions."

Mart shrugged.

"All right, so I'm through with racing. I don't like it. I'm sorry as hell. But there's no use crying in my beer. Crying isn't going to change anything. Let's change the subject."

"That's a good idea." Charlotte smiled, made an attempt to perk up.

"But not too far," Martin cautioned. There was one thing he had to know. "Who won the race?"

"I don't know, my friend. Some relief driver probably. I can't recall the name. We were too busy with you."

Martin looked at him. Mario's face wasn't suitable for lying. It was too big and too open and the eyes too expressive.

"Of course you know! Now listen, I don't want to talk cars if that's what's worrying you. I just want to know who won and then we'll forget it."

"You won the race, Martin," Charlotte said softly, and when Mario threw his hands up in despair, she shook her head. "I can't help it, Mario. I couldn't keep it from him. He'd find out."

Mart stared at them, not believing.

"You're crazy!"

"She is telling you the truth. The last time you went across the finish line, before you crashed, you took the checkered flag."

Mart tried to sit up, but his ribs stopped him.

The German Grand Prix. He had won it. The big one. He had beaten the mighty Mercedes and the Germans on home ground. He wallowed in the glory of it for a moment, and then sobered.

"Why didn't you tell me?"

"Mario was—" Charlotte began.

"I was afraid," Mario interrupted her, "that you would think it made everything else all right. I thought you might refuse to quit driving instead of going home and taking up sensible work. I'm sorry if it seems dishonest."

"I could go home and race as I used to," he said defiantly.

"It wouldn't be the same, my friend, and you know it."

"You seem to have all the answers." Mart was close to anger. But anger would not come to help him fight it. He was remembering the last few months too well. He found himself nodding. "Yes, I know it."

"So what now, Martin? You will be sensible?"

He looked out the window for a long time. Evening was coming and a light rain fell. Winning had made everything else all right. For a moment he had thought it could go on. Like a man who had turned loose of something, and a little while later uncertainly took hold of it again, he had to smile foolishly and let go once and for all. And strangely, it was not so hard. Maybe it was because he had won a big race, driven a big race. Maybe that was enough to soothe most of the hunger .... His eyes turned to watch Charlotte now, and he relaxed, thinking how much he was in love with her. Maybe it was that too ... but it was as though the fire was gone and nothing more than the smoke and remembering remained.

"Sure. And it's all right," he smiled at them.

"I'm glad, my friend," Mario said quietly.

Charlotte smiled at him, her eyes watering.

"Damn it, you two! Charlotte, you remind me of a woman with muffled oars, and you, Mario! You remind me of someone's maiden father. Look at me! I've just won the German Grand Prix. Charlotte, you remember the little kid with the coaster on the grassy hillside? What more could that kid ask than to do what I've just done? And I can't go on driving forever. I have to stop sometime. It might as well be now, while I'm ahead."

Neither Mario nor Charlotte looked as if they believed him.

"I'm not saying there isn't any regret. Those wonderful cars— But look. I've been bumming around quite a while, and I think I've had enough. I ought to find a good steady job somewhere and I've got a wonderful girl I should spend more time with."

They were silent. They still didn't believe him.

He held out his hands to Charlotte and she took them.

"I love you, Charlotte Greyne. Do you believe that?"

"Yes."

"Will you marry me?"

Her eyes widened.

She stepped back quickly and spoke to Mario.

"He means it! Driving—it doesn't matter!"

Mario shrugged and made a face.

"He is merely trying to be brave about it. Pay no attention to what the idiot says!"

"No. He's telling the truth. He said a driver should never marry. He was afraid to marry me while he was driving."

Mario looked at Mart as if he were remembering, and uncertainly began to smile, but the nurse came then and told them they had to leave.

Charlotte kissed him quickly.

"Yes … yes, I will."

Mario came to shake his hand.

"I was a witness, don't forget. I will hold you to the promise you made her. We must go now, but we will come to visit and keep your spirits up in the face of this incredible woman in the stiff uniform."

Mart looked up at him and grinned.

"Where is Corsatti? And the others? Will they be in?"

Mario sobered, and shook his head.

"I have not seen him since last night. Then, he was walking in the rain, down at the track. He weeps for Benito Taglio. He is a man who lives with a bad dream. Give him time. He will come to visit you. And the others. They have vowed to send you home, stupendously drunk. *Buona notte,* Martin."

"Good night, Mario."

They were gone, and he was alone, and he remembered the race and it was like a dream now. Only fragments remained, faded, as if it had happened a long time ago.

He had done his racing, and he had done well. There was nothing more to ask of it. He was content.

For a while, he thought he had lied to Mario and Charlotte. But no, it was true. He was content, and he smiled with it.

Yes, there would be times when he would stop what he was doing—perhaps at the sound of a motor—and suddenly remember how it was, the days of racing, and there would be a little sadness. One cannot forget the wonderful cars, and the wonderful times that easily. They leave their mark somehow. But the sadness would last for only the moment, and it would be gone again.

Benito Taglio was gone. Taglio, and how many others? Taglio had reached contentment or peace or whatever it was that existed beyond the smoke, and perhaps in some way, he too could remember the days as they were.

EPILOGUE

When the crowds leave, the last car and mechanic, when the pits are empty and the course is clear, perhaps amidst the echoes of that day's racing the gods of yesterday come to play. Nuvolari, Seaman, Rosemeyer, Bonetto...how many? With them, the unknowns, the hopefuls, the lesser gods who had sought the dangerous dream. The hunger is with them still. To search for the higher speed, to feed the consuming and insatiable need to race. It is in their eyes, their faces, in the trembling of their hearts at the sound of a motor...they talk a while, laughing and arguing there in the darkness. Which was the greatest...Ferrari, Mercedes, Maserati, Auto Union, Bentley? Of where did they dream the most...Monza, Nurburgring, Silverstone, Mille Miglia? They know them all, and they know to weep, to laugh, to curse, to be crippled and wait for more, to sit frozen in the final spin while their tires scream of death.

When the pits are empty and the course is clear, they race again.